"SHOOT THE CROW ON THAT TREE TOP!"
Capra said.

Tom took steady aim and fired; the bird rose with a squawk, heavily flapping, but one or two feathers came floating down.

"The wind swayed that tree just as he fired," said the boy.

Capra yawned. "Men are bigger than crows. I haven't slept sound for years, but now I am going to lie down under that tree. Today I shall sleep; you'll watch over me."

The hours went softly by. The dusk came, and the woods grew chilly. Capra yawned and sat up, and the boy sat up beside him.

Capra gave Tom Gloster a five-dollar gold piece. "That's for you—not your family."

The boy laughed, "They'll never let you keep it!"

Later, when Tom's brother and father called him a halfwit and demanded the gold piece, Tom recalled the boy's taunt. He knew he would have to leave . . .

D0681159

Warner Books

By Max Brand

Man From Savage Creek
Trouble Trail
Rustlers of Beacon Creek
Flaming Irons
The Gambler
The Guns of Dorking Hollow
The Gentle Gunman
Dan Barry's Daughter
The Stranger
Mystery Ranch
Frontier Feud
The Garden of Eden
Cheyenne Gold
Golden Lightning
Lucky Larribee
Border Guns
Mighty Lobo
Torture Trail
Tamer of the Wild
The Long Chase
Devil Horse
The White Wolf
Drifter's Vengeance
Trailin'
Gunman's Gold
Timbal Gulch Trail
Seventh Man
Speedy

Galloping Broncos
Fire Brain
The Big Trail
The White Cheyenne
Trail Partners
Outlaw Breed
The Smiling Desperado
The Invisible Outlaw
Silvertip's Strike
Silvertip's Chase
Silvertip
The Sheriff Rides
Valley Vultures
Marbleface
The Return of the Rancher
Mountain Riders
Slow Joe
Happy Jack
Brothers on the Trail
The Happy Valley
The King Bird Rides
The Long Chance
Mistral
Smiling Charlie
The Rancher's Revenge
The Dude
Silvertip's Roundup

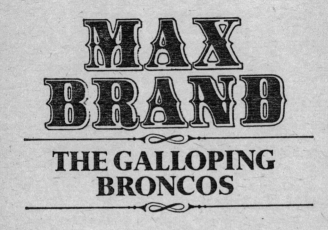

MAX BRAND

THE GALLOPING BRONCOS

WARNER BOOKS

A Warner Communications Company

WARNER BOOKS EDITION

Copyright © 1929 by Dorothy Faust
Copyright renewed 1957 by Dorothy Faust
All rights reserved

ISBN 0-446-94265-0

This Warner Books Edition is published
by arrangement with Dodd, Mead and Company, Inc.

Cover art by Roy Anderson

Warner Books, Inc., 75 Rockefeller Plaza, New York, N.Y. 10019

W A Warner Communications Company

Printed in the United States of America

First Printing: August, 1974

Reissued: August, 1979

10 9 8 7 6 5 4

CONTENTS

CHAPTER   PAGE

1   For The Family 7

2   A Way With Horses 12

3   Not For The Family 17

4   A Gold Piece 22

5   The Gray Mare Returns 27

6   David Parry, Jr. 32

7   "You Are My Luck!" 37

8   A Horse—And No Mistake 42

9   On The Wrong Side Of The Fence 47

10   One Might Need Two Guns 52

11   Birds Of Passage 58

12   A Sick Cat 63

13   Who Made The Cat Sick? 68

14   The Colonel Versus The Captain 73

15   He's Gone! 78

16   Facing The Music 84

17   An Unpleasant Story 88

18   Tom No Longer Doubts 93

19   Danger Won't Stop Them 98

20   The Good Guide, Ramon 103

21   Men Mean Trouble 109

22   It's Christopher Black 114

23   General Ducos 119

24   One Waits And Listens 124

25   Into The Tunnel 129

26   Hard Times Ahead 134

27   Ramon's Red Wrist 139

28   With Kind Wishes 144

29   Alicia, Jerry And The Moon 149

30   Tom Waits In Moonshine And Danger . . 154

31   A Precious Pair 159

32   Husband And Wife 164

33   A Cry Of Mortal Agony 169

34   Voices In The Night 174

35   Roger Runs 179

36   Where Men Know Men 184

37   The Answer Is— 189

38   A Young Fox 194

39   In The Attic 199

40   Beatrice Shows Her Skill 204

41   Before The Curtain Falls 209

42   When Dreams Vanish 217

43   A Whole Kingdom 222

1. For The Family

In the valley Tom Gloster plowed.

His older brothers had the pleasanter uplands to till, or, better still, they could ride herd, or bring in the cows to the market, or attend the fairs and the rodeo; but while these activities proceeded, Tom Gloster was kept at the hot and heavy work beside the river. Taking the ground on either side of the water, the stretch of it was not more than a furlong, all told, and it reached almost a mile, narrow here, wider there, but always rich, difficult ground. A few years ago, there had been nothing but a growth of brush here, until his father found, as by inspiration, this labor for Tom.

It was inspiration, for most things he did very badly. His mother said it was because he was tender-hearted; his father said the backwardness of Tom was that of a natural-born simpleton. He shrank from giving pain. He would not learn to use a rope, and he shuddered at the sight of a branding iron; and because of these shortcomings he never was worked in the saddle, the free, strenuous, exciting life of the range. A man who could not use a rope, indeed, was hardly a man!

Tom had other limitations. Above all, he had no genius for putting things together. He could not build a fence without having it stagger from side to side. He could not put together the simplest rack. He would stare at an item of repair work with a perfectly blank face for an hour at a time.

His mother said that he took a long time to get started because he was always thinking on both sides of the fence. His father, however, declared he was slow to start because he could not think at all. He was the fifth son and the seventh child. His birth was not a cheerful event. He was not wanted. From the first he was an extra mouth, and no more, except to his mother. So he grew up very close to her. His father was convinced that such a boy needed no education. "An educated fool is worse than a plain one," he used to say; but Tom Gloster learned from his mother. He learned to read, and write, and spell. He learned to speak like her, slowly, with a gentle voice, and without slang. Indeed, he was so little among other men that he had no chance to pick up either their good or their bad ways. He grew up along, tall and strong, with a beautiful face, and a rather blank eye. All the other six children were dark, like their father; he, alone, had his mother's fair hair and pale skin.

It was typical of his fate that he should be confined to that narrow valley where the wind hardly could blow, and where the strength of the sun, gathered in a focus by the converging slopes of the valley, made the ravine a baking oven from prime until six o'clock on a summer's day. But all the work, here, was done by Tom. It was, in a way, his glory; for the first time he had a purpose in his existence; for with his unaided hands he had cleared that land on either side of the creek; by the felling of two big trees which stood opposite one another on the banks, he had constructed the foundation of a bridge which linked the two narrow strips of plowland, and now he was laboring with the plow. He had an old mule, with a gray back and a roan belly, so that it looked sun-faded; and he had as number two before his plow a sturdy ox.

It made a strange team, and a very slow one. Every moment the plow was stopped as the share ripped into a tangled nest of roots, for it was the first plowing; therefore, it was the hardest one. Sometimes it took an hour to run a hundred yards of furrow, with the plow jogging back and forth, groaning, protesting. Now and again it broke down, and Tom Gloster would stand by and stare helplessly, for he never could make mechanical repairs. At last his father or one of his older brothers would descend to his help, contemptuous and silent. He had been known as a lost cause in the family for many years.

8

However, he had strong hands and infinite patience, and he was willing to put bit to bit to make a mass of effect. He began toiling early in the morning. He worked on until the sun went down, and then he would come up from the valley, with his weary team walking behind him, unled. For he had an odd power with animals. His father was apt to say that Tom knew the speech of the dumb beasts—and that was why he could not talk with men! But when he came up from the valley in the dusk of every evening, he never appeared tired, and he wore the same patient, faint smile with which he went down to his work in the morning. Some people were apt to think it a smile of mockery; but usually even a stranger could tell it was the outward expression of a vast, inward peace.

When he came to the house, as like as not the supper was over. And little would have been saved, for if the mother wanted to spare something for her youngest child, the others, strong, youth-famished men and women, were fairly sure to devour everything. If Tom did not arrive in time for meals, he could suffer for it. How else would he learn? But they knew that he never would learn. He was too absent of mind, too totally divorced from any sense of the passage of time. His eldest sister, who had passed in bitterness her thirtieth year, unwed, used to say that Tom learned two new things every day: That the sun rose and the sun set. Tom Gloster used to hear such things without apparent pain; therefore, everyone talked straight out before his face, if he were the subject of conversation; but usually he was not spoken of or to. He was like a face of stone set in the midst of that busy, chattering family. And they shrugged their shoulders if he came back while they sat around the table, their elbows resting upon it, not a scrap of food left on the platter or even in the vegetable dishes.

He would survey this scene placidly. His mother, rising to forage for her boy in the kitchen, would be ordered back to her chair by the father of the family.

"We've got to try to teach the boy sense! He won't always have us to look after him!"

So Tom would go out to the bread box and find some dried figs of that last autumn, perhaps, a little wooden, some, and a little moldy others. However, he did not seem to care. He ate whatever he found and never a ripple of disappointment or of pain disturbed the profound stillness of his eye.

But the most unregarded lake in the stillest wood will, at length, be troubled, and on this afternoon a voice came welling and falling down like a flung weapon into the quiet of the valley. Tom had paused to chop twenty pounds of roots from around the plowshare, and he lifted his hot face to the edge of the valley wall above him. There he saw his eldest brother standing, waving to him.

He mounted obediently, the mule and the steer being unhitched and following on like two dogs at the heel of the master.

"I been yelling at you for half an hour," said Jim Gloster. "Why'n heck don't you pull the cotton out of your ears, once in a while?"

Tom Gloster made no return to this comment. He merely waited; that was always his way in case of insult, and it worked very well indeed, with strangers. For the cheerful stillness of that eye of his began to appear significant during the pause. However, his family knew him too well.

"Why don't you say something, Tom? Why d'you stand there dumb? I had to shout myself hoarse. You got a chance to do something for us, today!"

He said this impressively, and Tom nodded his appreciation. He was always seriously interested in attempting to "do something" for the rest of the family, for it was a matter of standing comment that Tom was a great help. These words, uttered with much deep irony, if they had not eaten into his soul at least were printed upon his mind. Therefore, he worked with Herculean patience and might at the clearing of the river land. Already that work had doubled the value of the ranch; but no one thought of giving Tom Gloster any credit for that labor. And his eye, therefore, brightened when he heard that he had a chance this day, to do something for the family.

"You know Hank Riley's gray mare?"

"No," said Tom.

"You don't know the mare?"

"No."

"Danged if you know anything."

Tom waited. There was nothing for him to say.

"Anyway, Riley's gray mare is down at the village. He's found a fellow that bought her on her looks. Think of that!"

Tom's face registered no sense of news.

"Man," shouted his angered brother, "you know her! She's the mare that busted 'Pink' Lacey's shoulder, and savaged young Milton last fall. You remember now?"

"No," said Tom Gloster.

His brother regarded him with blank despair.

"Well, what difference does it make?" he said at last, to himself.

Bitterly sneering, he stared at Tom, and restrained the words which stormed up and swelled in his throat. Why flog a stone?

"Well," said he, "this is what's happened. This fellow comes along in a funny outfit, and he inquires has anybody got a hoss to sell, because his hoss is lame. And Jerry Peters says he should go to ask Hank Riley, because Hank had a pretty good mare to sell. Think of that! That Peters is a rum one, all right. That's his idea of a joke!

"Anyway, the fellow goes there; Hank sizes him up. He offers to trade the mare for the fellow's hoss, which wasn't bad lame and only needed a little rest. He'd take the fellow's nag and two hundred dollars boot. Well, the fellow flashed one look at the mare and he grabbed the top of the fence and steadied himself. Of course, he never seen no other hoss like her, hardly. He came to terms right off and he paid over his cash and takes the saddle off his own hoss. Then he takes his rope and goes after the mare. He got her, too; he saddled her, and then she busted him!"

Mr. Gloster laughed with savage content.

"I'd 'a liked to've seen that!" he said between his teeth. "He sailed clean over the fence. Got up and tried her again, and she slammed him so hard she made a print of him on the ground. He didn't get up so pronto, then. They had to pike her away with poles or she'd've eat him where he lay. When they had pulled him under the fence, he come to, inch by inch. And when he got his eyes open, he said he reckoned that he'd better get a regular horse tamer for the job. Now, kid, there's your chance. You got some kind of a knack with animals. I never thought about it before, but it come to me by inspiration when I heard that the fellow would pay a hundred bucks. There you are! You got a chance to do something for us, after all!"

2. *A Way With Horses*

THE MARE was in the corral behind the Riley barn. The "fellow" leaned on the fence and solemnly smoked cigarettes. He looked in part sad and in part fierce; his face was very thin, his upper lip spiked with a twisted mustache, and he had a way of rolling his eyes so that their yellowed whites showed largely. One would have said that he had a stiff neck, for he very seldom moved his head.

This fellow was dressed in a style which Tom Gloster never had seen before. He had on a short jacket with bright buttons on it, and he wore a sort of shawl fastened around his waist with a sash and reaching halfway between his knees and his feet. The sash and the jacket were gay, but a trifle soiled. He looked more than a bit both grim and grimy. To complete the distinction between him and Western Americans, he wore only one spur, and that was on the heel of his right boot, a spur with a great wheel at least two inches in diameter.

Hank Riley stood beside him, chatting cheerfully; in the near distance, beneath a tree, leaned a boy of eleven or twelve years, holding a saddled horse.

"Nobody in town wants the job, Hank," said Tom's brother, as they came up. "But here's Tom. He has a way with hosses. A hundred bucks is what you said, stranger?"

"He don't talk no English," said Riley.

That was no handicap, since everyone in that section of the range had learned to talk Spanish; even Tom Gloster could speak the tongue, and he noted that the stranger talked with an odd accent, quite different from the usual Mexican. The arrangement was made at once, with very few words on the part of the other, whose name was, he said, Capra. He would pay the hundred dollars, but only on condition that the horse tamer could complete the work by noon of the next day. On the other hand, he was extremely liberal in his interpretation of "completion." He did not mind a little bucking; it was only the display of such consummate wickedness as had thrown him out of the saddle that dismayed him.

Hank Riley, repenting him of his sharp practice in regard to the mare, now said: "Why don't you be sensible, stranger? There's a good horse that you got yonder. That's a good-bred one, too, I take it, that the boy is riding. Why don't you take that one, and put the boy up on a common mustang. You can pick up one of those for seventy-five or eighty dollars. That'll save you money, after all! And— I'll give you something back on the mare, here!"

To this Capra replied dryly: "When we travel, we travel together; we both go fast. No, I must have the mare."

So Tom Gloster prepared to work upon her. Riley, in the meantime, standing by in half contemptuous curiosity. And even Capra allowed some of the slumber to fall from his eyes, and the boy edged closer, out of the shadow beneath the tree. However, they had no startling things to watch from Gloster. The mare was quite docile except when she was mounted, and Tom Gloster easily caught her. He led her around the corral once or twice.

"When d'you get on?" asked Riley impatiently.

"Maybe tomorrow morning—maybe this evening," said Tom.

"Take a year and a day," growled Riley, "and anybody could do the job."

"You've had more than a year and a day to work on the gray mare," said Tom's brother sharply. And Riley muttered and returned no answer.

"I'd like to take her away," said Tom.

"What for?" asked Riley in suspicion.

"Take her, take her!" said Capra. "I don't care. But come back riding her before tomorrow morning."

So Tom Gloster led her away, past the curious, half-sneering eyes of the boy. He was dressed like his companion, dark-skinned like him, also, but with a degree of manly spirit and dignity about him. Tom's brother accompanied him home. He wanted an explanation of why Tom had to work in solitude with the mare.

To this simple question, Tom could not return an answer at once, but eventually he said: "Suppose you want to talk very hard about something important—to a stranger. You would want to be alone with him."

"You can't talk to a hoss," said his brother, amused.

"No. But you have to try," said Tom Gloster.

And this answer cut short the conversation. He took the mare straight down to the valley. There were two reasons for this. The first was that the place was secluded from all observation. The second was that there was a great deal of plowed ground, and if the time came to ride a bucking horse, the softness of the soil would take the snap out of the pitching.

In the valley he led her about slowly, pausing whenever she wished to pause, and that was often. She seemed to find every shadow behind every lump of plow-turned ground an object worthy of suspicious inquiry. The whirring wings of the water ouzel made her jump, as the little bird flirted into the spray of the small cataract in the creek. The shaking leaves of the poplars, struck suddenly to silver by the wind, made her start and tremble, also. And Tom Gloster led her up to each of these objects in turn until she had made the entire round of the little valley twice. By that time, she had quieted a great deal, but she was very nervous; the looming of a new cloud in the sky made her raise her head, even when she was grazing, and she could not eat in any comfort if Tom walked out of her range of vision. She had the manner of a tigress, rather than of a horse.

He remained with her for two hours, constantly beside her, speaking often, his voice always quiet. For every start and jump and quiver that went through her, he had a soothing word. Then he tied her to a tree and went up the slope for his lunch.

"You've got one day to tame her!" stormed his father. "Why are you wasting time like this? Can't you miss a meal once a year?"

"Only when he forgets," said his eldest sister.

"And he never does his forgetting on hundred-dollar days!" said the father of the family. "The first and the last day of that kind he'll ever have in his life."

To this, Tom did not return an answer. These remarks hurt him, but he did not know how to defend himself; his silence, even, was taken up against him.

"He's gunna make a mystery out of it," said one. "After this, we'll have to pay him to get him to talk to us, I guess! Don't be such a dolt, Tom."

"Why am I a dolt?" asked Tom.

"For wasting time when you've got your first good job!"

Tom laid down his knife and fork. He knew perfectly well why he had left the mare, and he knew it was not simply for the sake of his lunch.

He said: "It's a lonely valley. The sound of the creek is like the sound of a strong wind. There's a bird or two. But often nothing moves all day long except the water, and the shadows under the trees."

"That's sense!" said his sister. "That makes a lot of sense, don't it?"

The rest of the family shook their heads, except his mother; and even she looked at him with a puzzled and half-frightened eye.

"What do you mean, Tom?" she asked him.

"He don't know," said the father. "He's gunna think, but he don't know. It's something that he remembers out of a book, maybe!"

Said Tom Gloster: "It's a lonely valley. The mare will be lonely. Perhaps she'll be glad, then, when I come back to her."

"Glad of your company?"

"She always has had company," said Tom Gloster.

"What makes you think that?"

"She hates people; but she's not afraid of them."

"What d'you mean by that?"

"Well—" he paused, going back over his reasons.

15

"He's gunna think it out," sneered the nearest brother.

"Will you let him be?" cried his mother, her voice half stifled with indignation. "He has a reason—he always has a reason if you'll wait a little for him!"

"A man's only got one life," said her husband. "He'd have to have two to listen to Tom's ideas and do anything else!"

Tom flushed a little, disturbed by the friction of effort in attempting to trace his own fugitive thoughts, and in listening to the argument which went on about him.

At last he said: "You see—wild things are afraid of man. They've only had a taste of him. But when they get too used to us, then they may hate us."

"That's a fool idea!" said one of the brothers. "It's like the most of the rest of your ideas! Why should a hoss, now, wanta hate a man?"

Tom looked at him in bewilderment.

"Give him time," said the father cruelly. "After a while, he'll think up an answer to that, too."

"But I don't need time for that," said Tom. "Horses could hate us for the spurs we wear on them, I suppose. Then—we give them nothing but hay and oats for their work."

"And what should we give them? What could we give them?" sneered one.

"Why, five dollars a day," said another.

And the table laughed, and they looked at one another.

"They need kindness," said Tom Gloster, nodding his head with surety.

"You are a dolt," said his younger sister, who usually did not even notice him.

"Kindness?" echoed his father.

"Kindness has kept gray Barney tugging at the plow this last month," said Tom.

"The old mule? He's as stout as ever."

"I don't think he'll live another three weeks," said Tom Gloster.

"Hey, hey, quit it, will you?" shouted the eldest brother. "Don't let him open up on his dog-gone future-seeing and prophesying!"

"I don't see the future," said Tom, "except what any one can make out by looking at today."

16

"You've looked enough, now; go on back to the mare, will you?"

He went, and had his reward as he came down the slope to her. She did not flatten her ears, but pricked them cheerfully toward him.

3. *Not For The Family*

THEY WANTED Tom to stay up all night, working over the mare.

"You'll get her worn down. The safest way is to tire her out," they told him.

"What good would that be?" asked Tom. "She'd only buck again as soon as she'd been well rested, wouldn't she?"

"D'you care for that?" snarled his younger sister, clenching her hands into fists. "What d'you want out of the man more than his hundred dollars?"

Tom, in fact, stayed up all the night in order to stop the harsh talk, but he did not work over the mare. He simply remained close to her in the damp, chilly valley. He made a bed of evergreen boughs, and lying down on it he slept a cold, broken sleep. Once he thought a wolf sniffed at him, and waking, he found that the muzzle of the gray was close to his face. Again, he was wakened when she lay down, at the end of her tether, close to his side. He reached out his hand to her and saw her pretty head against the stars, lowering toward his hand, sniffing it like a dog. He was very pleased, and he went into a sound sleep for the first time, and remained asleep until the first coming of the dawn.

Then he wakened, stiff, tired, his head dizzy for lack of a better sleep; but he washed off his somnolence in the icy water of the creek. He took the mare to the creek, also for a drink, and with a few twists of dry grass, he rubbed her dry of the dew which had soaked her. All this time he had not attempted to ride her, but at the most he walked beside her, his right arm thrown across the saddle place on her back. Now he belted the saddle upon her, drawing up the cinches not too tight, for every horse hates a tightly gripping saddle early in the morning. After that, he mounted her. He had neither whip nor spur; he left the reins dangling loosely; and the mare turned her head far around and snuffed at his knee, and looked with bright eyes into his face. Then she walked away, rattling the bit in her mouth, and shaking her head at the taste of the iron. If there had been one touch of constraint or compulsion, she would have fought like a tiger, relentlessly, viciously, for the gentlest and the tenderest spirits are always the most terrible when they fight for the sake of the soul.

However, he did not bother her. He let her take her own way up the valley and down the valley. When she wished to pause, she could do so. When she wished to trot, she could trot, and walk when she preferred to walk. But by degrees he controlled her. She stamped impatiently when he drew against the bit, but presently she began to understand. It is not difficult to teach a horse to rein over the neck, and that is the way that all men ride in the West. In another half hour, the mare was beginning to understand. Then she allowed the cinches to be drawn up tightly, only grunting a little. The sun was hardly well up, when Tom rode the mare up to the house.

All the family came out to see the spectacle. They said very little to Tom, but they looked at him with secret respect. One of his brothers explained afterward: "You see how he can do it? He's like an animal himself!"

"Yes, and close to them. Therefore, he understands!"

They were very glad of the hundred dollars, too, and everyone in the family had immediate claims upon a part of it—everyone, that is to say, except Tom and his mother. They saw to it that he had a good breakfast, and his father promised that he should not have to work any more that day, so contented was he with the breaking of the mare. Then he took Tom and the mare to town, where they met the stranger, Capra.

José Capra looked at the gray with gleaming eyes. Hank Riley also had come to see the test, and there were fifty people in the plaza by the hotel.

Tom Gloster simply said: "No spur—no whip!"

At this, Capra looked fixedly at him and at length nodded his head, as one who hears something that has been heard before. Then he tried the mare up and down the street. Twice she stopped suddenly, on stiffened legs, ready for trouble, because he had used the reins with too much strength, and her mouth was sensitive; but at length he got the knack of managing her, and she went perfectly, but in the green manner of a horse whose paces have not been made by much labor.

"You sold her pretty cheap, after all," said someone to Hank Riley.

He turned a pale face of malice toward Tom Gloster.

"That mare's bred clean back to Methusaleh. I've lost about two thousand dollars, getting rid of her this way; because, of course, he wouldn't come and offer to work for me. He'd rather work for a stranger!"

Tom heard this, but did not answer. He had heard so many disagreeable things said to him that in time he had grown callous. His elder brother, however, took up the remark. All the Glosters except Tom showed a strong fighting strain. He said: "You wanted to beat the poor stranger out of his coin and his hoss. You got beat yourself, It serves you right, Riley."

The latter, seeing no friendly faces near by, went off down the street, his shoulders hunched as though he were unpleasantly cold. Capra came back and paid Tom Gloster without dismounting from the mare. The boy came suddenly up and joined his companion.

"What do you get, amigo?" said Capra to Gloster, from whose hand his father had hastily taken the money.

"I?" echoed Tom Gloster. "I had the pleasure of breaking her, of course."

"Humph," said Capra. Then, suddenly: "Can you work the rest of today for me!"

He looked at his father.

"What's up?" asked the elder Gloster sharply. "Ain't she broke and paid for? Of course she is!"

The stranger looked calmly on the father.

"A new job. I'll pay five dollars for his day's time," he explained.

"Take him!" said the father. "You go along and do what he wants with you—I dunno what!"

Tom Gloster went off up the street with Capra, he walking, and Capra on one side, the silent boy on the other. And as they went, Capra heard a man say: "Old Gloster would sell the hide of that kid for another five bucks."

At this, Capra looked at the still and smiling face of Tom. Then he looked at the youngster, and the boy turned his brilliant, biting glance upon the man who strode between them. They went straight out into a forest of lodgepole pines. It had been spruce, once, until the forest fire came that way like a dragon and left a black skeleton in place of the grandeur and the beauty. Among those monstrous stumps the lodgepoles immediately grew; they are the reserve and the advance guard of the forest; they make the way in new and difficult places, and also, they fill all gaps in the ranks. Capra led through this grim wilderness until he came to a small, secluded clearing. It had once held a hunter's cabin; the foundation was still visible, and the heap of stones which had made the fireplace. There Capra halted. He said to Tom Gloster: "Can you shoot?"

"I shoot a little."

Capra slid a long rifle out of the saddle holster beneath his knee. It was not a Winchester. Tom Gloster opened it and quietly examined the gun. "I can use this," he said.

"There's a crow on that tree top," said Capra.

At the hint, Tom looked fixedly at the bird. It was a fairly long shot. He took a steady aim and fired; the bird rose with a squawk, heavily flapping, but one or two feathers came floating down—black with a green glister on them.

"The wind swayed that tree just as he fired," said the boy.

Capra yawned. "Men are bigger than crows," said he. "Now, young man, I am going to lie down under that tree and wrap myself in my blanket. I haven't slept sound for—years, maybe. Today I shall sleep; you'll watch over me!"

A yearning appeared in his eyes! they were like two dead shadows with a light behind them. "I'll watch," agreed Tom Gloster.

"If a leaf stirs; if a shadow moves; if a twig crackles, wake me up!"

"I shall."

Capra lay down under the tree, with a twist of his blanket around him. Instantly he slept, and while he slept, he groaned with every outlet of his breath, so that it seemed his soul was departing from his body.

The boy, too, lay down beneath the same tree. For one moment he sat up, staring earnestly at Gloster; then he flattened himself against the ground and was instantly asleep.

It seemed very strange to Gloster, watching them, but he could understand, now, the agony which he had sensed in both their faces. It was the pain of infinite weariness, of infinite hunger for sleep.

The hours went softly by; the shadows of the trees shifted; and still Tom sat like a stone, and the sleepers had not stirred. All that while he was employed as though in the reading of a book. He had to note how a lightning scar was healing on the side of a young pine, and how expertly two squirrels leaped from the branches of one tree to the branches of the next until one of them fell from a height and was saved by the fluffiness of his spreading tail, like the spread of a parachute; he took heed of the brown lizard lying on the brown stone, moving as slowly as the hour hand of a clock, to keep within the focus of the moving spot of sunshine; he examined, too, the ghostly march of the shadows; he listened to the cries of birds, which came dimly and brokenly out of the distance, then with a sudden shout above his head. But he heard not a sign of human life about him.

The dusk came, and as the woods grew chilly, Capra yawned and sat up, and the boy sat up beside him. They looked on Gloster with the filmy eyes of sleep. Then they rose and mounted their horses. Five dollars in gold fell into the hand of Gloster. Never before had he touched such a sum.

"That's for you, not for your family," said Capra.

And the boy added, with a flash of wicked understanding in his eyes: "But you won't be able to keep it! They'll have it out of you!"

He laughed, with a little savage undernote of mockery in the sound.

"You've given me a good horse; you've given me a good sleep," said Capra. "Fortune repay you!"

Then he and the boy rode off through the woods.

4. A Gold Piece

THE SOLEMNITY with which this was spoken dwelt in the mind of Gloster. It was as though, in the midst of idle conversation, some man suddenly had burst out with a solemnly serious voice to speak of what lay nearest to his heart. It was as though, through the silence of the wilderness, the voice of a great church bell had boomed.

Into the quiet mind of Gloster questions stepped gravely. Who were these two? From what land had they come? To what land were they going? It seemed to Gloster that they had come almost from another planet, and he could not imagine a proper halting place. Then he went back to his home in the sunset and on the way passed his elder brother, galloping a mustang toward town. He pulled up with a shout when he saw Tom.

"You did your job?"

"Yes."

"You got the five dollars?"

"Yes. Here it is."

"Give it to me, kid. I can use that in town!"

Gloster extended his hand, and then he remembered

what the boy had said, in parting. He put the shining bit of gold back into his pocket.

"I think I'll keep it," said he.

"You young upstart!" cried his brother. "Hand that over, or I'll flog it out of you!"

He swung his horse toward Tom, but the latter took the animal by the bridle and, stepping closer, laid a hand on the knee of his brother. There was no larger man on that part of the range; there was no more rough-and-ready fighter; but Tom Gloster remembered what the boy had said to him and he looked deeply, with curious calm, into his brother's soul.

"Why do you want it?" he asked.

"Why? You loon! Who takes care of you? Who looks out for you? Who does your thinkin' for you? Who but me and the rest? Gratitude? You gotta lot of gratitude, you have! There ain't a speck of it in your miserable bones."

"You hate me, don't you?" said Tom.

"I wouldn't be bothered hating a thing like you. Leave go of the bridle, will you?"

He wrenched at the reins. As well have wrenched at a pillar of iron, for the grasp of Tom was still fixed upon the leather.

"You didn't work for this money," said Tom.

"Oh, dang you and your ideas!" said the other.

So Tom released him, and watched him spur down the road, curses trailing over his shoulder. And suddenly this big, rough man seemed no longer awful and formidable; but he seemed to have escaped as a bird flown from the hands of Tom.

This thought amused the boy and made him wonder, so that he stood for a long time in one place, looking vaguely around him, but seeing nothing except his own thoughts. And all that he remembered, afterward, about that spot, was the smell of tar weed from a field near by.

Then he went on to his home and it seemed to him that he looked upon it for the first time. Or rather, it was something he had seen before, but only in a dream; and this was reality, even seen in the dusk. The house was so small he wondered that nine people could live in it. He never had wondered that before. There was a vegetable garden on one side of it, and he could smell the old cabbages; on the other side was the alfalfa patch, irrigated from the clanking windmill. An elm tree stood by the front gate of the yard; a fig tree stood to the left of the house. Both the fig and the elm lofted great, shadowy arches of green against the sky. He considered their size and their shape carefully.

Then he walked around the house into the back yard where stood a vast pile—greater than the house, and the sheds behind it, and the two trees. This was the pile of brush which he had brought up from the valley.

A harsh voice said from the shadows of the rear porch: "You're late for your supper again. D'you get that five dollars?"

"Yes."

"You ought to've made him pay six, working you this late."

"I didn't work this late; I came home rather slowly."

"What for?"

"I was thinking."

"That means standing still, for you. Gimme that money."

"Jim met me down the road. He wanted it."

"Dang! You gave it to him? What right had he to it?"

"I didn't give it to him," said Tom Gloster.

"You didn't? Then what you talking about? What did he say?"

"He rode away out of my hand," said Tom.

"What you mean? Rode away out of your hand?"

"Like a bird let loose."

"You got one of your foolishest fits on you. But fork over that money."

"You were just saying, what right had Jim to that money?"

"Well?"

"What right have you to it?"

Silence; a deep-drawn breath; a profound oath.

"Are you raisin' up your head agin' me, you young—"

The father bounded from the porch and came to Tom. He was taller than his son. The dignity of his fatherhood, and of his height, and of his years, all dwelt within him. He laid a hand upon the shoulder of Tom, and the boy

24

flexed the muscles, and the hand of his father spread limply, and slipped away.

"By gosh," said Mr. Gloster, "who's been talkin' to you? Who's been puttin' ideas into your empty head?"

"The fig tree."

"What!"

"And the elm tree."

"This is the worst nonsense I ever heard even you talkin' before!"

"When you look at that pile of brushwood—" said Tom.

"That'll be something for you to work on next winter, turning it into cord wood. Now, there's a chance for you to do something for us, at last."

"Aye," said Tom.

He looked up to the brushwood pile, and found it loftier than the tallest of haystacks, and he wondered at it, remembering that every stick of it had been wrenched by his hands from the ground, or cut away, deep below the surface of the soil, by an axe in his grip. All of those roots were not tough. Some were shorn through like beets or carrots. But others, were like twisted rawhide. Yet in the year of many months, in the months of many days, and the days of many hours, his time, poured out as liberally as showers of rain from Heaven, had been able to accomplish this work, and now it stood against the sky, vast and substantial, larger in bulk than the house, and the great standing trees around it.

"How long ago d'you plant that fig and elm?" he asked.

"Dang the trees! I want that five dollars that you was paid."

"More'n thirty years back, wasn't it?" said the boy.

"A lot more. Are you holdin' yourself up agin' me, Tom Gloster? Are you holdin' out your pay on me, after the years of what I've put up with for you?"

"You have this. I give you this," said Tom Gloster.

"You give me what."

"This brush."

"You give it to me! Whose land growed it, I ask you? You give it to me!"

"I gave you the brush, and I cleared the land that it grew on."

"That swamp! You're takin' credit for that, are you? Because you didn't know enough to do a man's work—"

"Look!" said the boy.

"Look at what?"

"You see this pile of brush? Well, it's bigger than the house, and the shed, and the elm tree and the fig tree that have been growing for more than thirty years!"

"What d'you mean by this sort of stupid talk?"

"Is it stupid?"

"Well, ain't it, I ask you?"

Tom Gloster sighed.

"There is something in what I say," he declared patiently. "It came to me when I stood in front of the house, a while ago. Why should you want the money that I work for?"

"I ask you this? Are you my son?"

"Yes."

"Who feeds and clothes you?"

"You have."

"Why ain't I got a right to the money that you make, then?"

"Is Jim your son?"

"Yes."

"Don't you feed and clothe him?"

"He clothes himself. Besides, he's a man. He ain't a dang half-wit—"

"Am I a half-wit?" asked Tom thoughtfully.

"You've wrung it out of me, pesterin' me with your rot!"

Tom stepped past him. He went into the kitchen, and there he found his mother bent at the sink, finishing up the pans. The surface of the water in the dishpan was clotted with grease; and grease streaked her reddened hands and her arms.

"You need some more water," said Tom.

"Seemed like I couldn't go out to the well and bring in another bucketful, and you away from the house, Tom."

She smiled at him over her shoulder.

"I heard how wonderfully the mare acted, Tom. What a grand thing for you to have done! Everybody will talk about you now. What's the matter, Tom?"

This last she said with a gasp, and turned sharply to

him from the sink; he saw the front of her gingham apron, streaked across with the wet of the dishwater.

"Here," said Tom.

He held out his hand to her, and the gold piece sparkled in it; for the piece was newly minted; it was a rich circle of yellow light.

She only stared. She said then: "D'you mean that for me, Tommy?"

"Yes, that's for you."

"Gold!" said his mother. She did not speak again, and he saw that the reason was because her lips were trembling, and the tears ran rapidly down her face.

5. *The Gray Mare Returns*

AFTERWARD, Tom sat in the dark on the rear porch and pondered. He was beginning to see that there was misery around him, and that the pain inflicted upon his mother, and upon himself, was not justified. It seeemd to Tom that he saw this by the light which had been in the eyes of the boy who rode with Capra.

Then he went back into the kitchen just as his mother finished sweeping the floor, and straightened her back slowly after scooping up the sweepings in the dustpan. He said to her: "You'd better come out here with me."

She poured the sweepings into the stove, slid the lid back into place, and followed him out on the porch. Then he led her down the narrow board path which went to the windmill. They stood beneath it and listened to the soft clank of the pump rod, and the whir of the wheel, spinning rapidly in a fine breeze. Around them the water splashed in big drops.

"This is a better place for talking," said he.

"It's a cool place," said she. "I hope you won't catch your death of cold, out here in the wind and the damp, child."

"I wanted to ask you something," said he.

"Oh, boy," she cried to him, "tell me what's troubling you, that you should bring back home money to me? And to refuse it to those that have a right to it—to your brother Jim—to your own father!"

Grief and fear were in her voice, it was the fear of the unknown, which is the grimmest fear of all.

"Are you ashamed of me, Mother?"

"No, no! I never have been ashamed of you! No matter what—"

"Look!"

"Well, Tommy? What is it?"

"I mean the pile of brush."

"Well?"

"Who made that?"

"Why, you did, of course."

"I cleared it out of the valley and brought it there. How long would that last as firewood?"

"Gracious, child, of course one stove would never burn it in a lifetime! Most of that can be sold, I thank goodness! Your father promises me two new saucepans out of that money—when you've chopped up the pile. You won't be able to get at that till the winter, I suppose?"

"You can buy the new saucepans with the five dollars."

"Tommy! D'you think that I could spend that money on what I need? There's your brother Harry, his heart breaking for a new pair of boots. He's got the price made up, now, all but a few dollars!"

"Will you give him this?" asked Tom.

"And why not?"

"Because I want you not to."

"Tommy, I don't know what's got into your head, this talk about brush piles, and the rest. You know your father and brothers have a right to it."

"Why?"

"Don't they take care of you?"

"All of them together, and the ground raising trees for them, never built up a thing as big as that pile of brush."

"Gracious heavens! Is that what you mean? Is that what

28

you mean, after all? Poor simple Tommy, don't you see a difference between a pile of brush and—and a house, say?"

"Every one of those brushes, I pulled it, and dragged it, and cut it up. I hauled it up the hill; I piled it there. How much work to make that whole little house, Mother?"

"Little? No, it isn't so very big. I don't know. I don't know what you mean. My brain begins to spin, Tommy! I can't seem to think very well, tonight. But I feel that you're terribly wrong. I'm afraid, and my heart is cold, Tommy dear, so don't talk any more!"

"I've got to talk," said he. "I'm not afraid, and I've got to talk. You're the only one to hear me."

She took his arm, pressing it in trembling hands.

"You won't say anything harsh and rash, Tommy? That never is your way."

"What do you think, Mother, gets a man on?"

"Why work, Tommy!"

"More than that. Take the gray mare. Hank Riley had worked on her. So did the man, Capra. Work wouldn't tame her."

"But you worked on her and beat her!"

"I didn't beat her. Can you beat anything and make something out of it? I don't know. Somehow I can't see it."

"Then what do you mean? How is one to get on, Tommy?"

"No one but you makes me happy, Mother."

"My dear! And what are you driving at, Tommy dear?"

"Why, by loving you, I'm happy. Do the others love you?"

"What others?"

"Father, and my brothers, and my sisters."

"Tommy!"

She gasped, and held closer to him.

"You'd better take me back to the house, now. I feel pretty sick and dizzy."

"Do they care a rap about you?"

"My own husband? My babies? What's in you to talk like that tonight, Tom? You want to hurt me? You want to tear my heart?"

"You remember the gray mare?"

"You mean Riley's?"

"Yes."

"I wonder what's happened to you since you worked on her! What's in your mind, boy?"

"They showed me a picture of her mother. She looked like the gray, too. You can't get something for nothing, I suppose."

"I try to understand you, Tom. I can't make any headway against your words, though!"

"It's like this: Do the others look the least mite like you?"

She was silent, but her hands trembled more than ever, and she panted, so deeply was she breathing.

"If they love you, I won't know how! They never come to help, except about Christmas time."

"They have to make all their own clothes—the poor girls have to get out among young folks. It's the way with girls, Tommy. You'll understand when you get older!"

"They laugh at you; they laugh at me. What good are we to them? We're just slaves! We work. They take the money!"

"Who has told you this?"

"A boy in the woods," said Tom Gloster thoughtlessly.

"What boy?"

"There's no good trying to explain. The way my thoughts ran, they went through a terrible jumble—a boy that laughed at me, and the gray mare that wouldn't fight except you spurred her, and Jim cursing me, and the smell of tarweed, and a pile of brush, and you washing dishes in the kitchen. You see how extremely hard it would be to explain?"

She stopped trembling. She leaned back against one of the big wooden beams which held up the windmill.

"Is that the way that you've been thinking to such thoughts as these, Tommy?"

"Well, perhaps it doesn't mean anything. I had to tell you."

"How old are you, Tommy?"

"You know. I'm twenty-one."

"Oh, it's young, it's young! It's terribly young, and you're no more than a baby!"

"I think I am," said he.

"You think you are. Ah, Tommy, it's very young for what lies before you."

"What's that, Mother?"

"A way in the world with no home."

He was silent.

"You couldn't be staying here now?"

"I hadn't thought of leaving."

"Of course you hadn't but you couldn't stay here now, thinking that your father and brothers and sisters don't love you."

"I wasn't thinking of myself at all. I was thinking more of you, Mother."

"That they don't love me?"

"I can see well now that it's cruel to talk so. Only, when the thing came up in me, boiling and bubbling—"

"I know. You couldn't help talking. Let me tell you another thing. Truth is generally worth saying."

"You think it's true, then?"

"Haven't I seen it these years, begging and praying you would, or not till you grew up?" She added: "Come with me."

He went after her, his brain numbed with shock. It had been hardly depressing; it had almost been stimulating through the act of discovery to guess at what he had deduced. It was crushing to learn authoritatively that he had been correct.

He followed her to the rear of the house, she walking with a strangely quick, hurrying step. On the rear porch they saw a small smudge of red light. The light suddenly pulsed, and behind the pipe appeared the grim face of Gloster.

She stood before him, saying: "D'you know something?"

"Well?" he growled at her.

"We've lost our boy, it seems."

"What boy?"

"Tom."

"Is that Tom hulking there beside you?"

"Yes."

"What does the fellow want? He needs a cowhiding, and dang me if I ain't half a mind to give it to him, no matter how big he may be."

31

"He's going to leave us and go away."

There was an exclamation, and then a deep shout, like the booming voice of a bull.

"Leave us! Leave us? Before he's finished clearin' up the river land?"

Here they hard a loud whinnying from the corral gate, and then an exclamation, and next the voice of Tom's older sister as she ran toward the house:

"Dad! Tom! The gray mare's back with an empty saddle, pawing at the corral gates!"

6. David Parry, Jr.

THEY ALL hurried out to the corral gate, which Jim Gloster was unbarring, letting in the mare; but she ran across the road snorting.

"She's loco," said Jim Gloster. "You try your hand with her, Tom."

Stepping quietly, with a continually reassuring voice, Tom went up to her; she merely sniffed at him once or twice, more and more loudly, as a horse will do, and then permitted him to mount her. A pair of heavy Colt revolvers were in the saddle holsters; but the long rifle case that sloped down the right-hand side of the saddle was gone.

"She's thrown him," said the father. "I had an idea that she would."

"If she threw one man, wouldn't she throw another?" asked Tom Gloster.

"Tom's thinking again," said the sister.

But she lighted a match, and stepping closer to the horse, she showed the gleam of the silver knob which finished off that rich saddle.

"Hello!" said she. "This is somethin' worth seein'!"

She pointed out a stain which began on the withers of the mare and ran into the silver of her mane. It was a bright red, glistening even in the light of the match, and looking scarcely dry.

"The stranger's gone and got it," said the girl, without emotion. "Somebody must've got him through the heart. Look how the wound busted loose before he even had a chance to roll out of his stirrups!"

The match died in her hand, and her face, keen and hard with cruel interest, died back into the merciful dark of the evening.

"Get off the horse and put her in the barn," said Tom Gloster's father. "I've got her until her boss comes and claims her, and I reckon that's a thing that he ain't apt to do!"

Tom Gloster settled himself more comfortably into the saddle, and gathered the reins; the mare tipped her pretty head.

"Go on!" ordered his father. "Billy, open the gate wider for him. Looks like Tom is gunna bring me a little luck, after all!"

But Tom pressed the mare forward and leaned from the saddle above his mother.

"I'm going off with her, now."

"It's like fate—her coming back for you," agreed the mother. "But, ah, Tom, shall we ever see you again?"

"I'll come back," said he, "when I've something to offer to you. I'll come back to you when I can take you to a home."

"Hush, hush!" said she, trembling with fear. "And take this money, Tom. I won't need it. Then go quickly!"

He disregarded the golden coin, but he leaned and kissed her. Then he reined back the horse until its head was clear of the little group.

"What's all this mumbling about?" asked the father.

"I've said good-bye to my mother," answered Tom. "Good-bye to the rest of you, too."

"Look here! What? You young scoundrel, are you gunna try to steal my hoss right from under my nose?"

"Good-bye," said Tom, and he let the mare swing into a canter.

They shouted and ran after him.

"That mare is worth twenty-five hundred dollars. Hank Riley said so! Tom! You'll be jailed for this! Hey, Tom, stop, will you?"

That was their only farewell to him. If his heart ached, it was for the sake of the mother he left behind. She, at least, would think of something more than the money which he was taking away in the form of the mare. He let the gray out a bit, and the long stroke of her gallop soon sank the house and its light behind him. He held on the road until the lights of the town blinked suddenly through the trees; and then he remembered that he had no place in town. There was no goal and no home for him in it; for he had not a penny of money in his pocket.

He relaxed his hold on the reins, and the mare turned of her own accord into the first trail upon the left. It led through the woods, and the dark shapes drifted solemnly past Tom, like his own unhappy thoughts of the future.

Twice he stopped the gray short, tempted to go back to the house and face the ridicule that would wait for him there. And the little home where he had endured such slavery and such contempt now appeared to him a refuge. There seemed little in the world more beautiful than the familiar outline of the roof and the chimney against the sky, or the lofty, dark vault of the elm tree. The valley of his labors, too, was now like the waiting face of a friend, behind him, and the old mule and the patient ox which had tugged at the plow for him. He wondered who would finish the work in the valley? He could not imagine it done, but all would remain as he had left it, like an incompleted house, roofless, and open to the rain.

However, shame and grief made him endure these moments of temptation, and he went on through the woods, never troubling about direction, but letting the mare go as she wished. She traveled the trail as though she had been over it before, never hesitating at the crossways, but making a quick choice; perhaps it was a roundabout way to the place of Hank Riley? Tom Gloster hardly could guess; his mind was too befuddled to think out directions.

Now, through the trees, a mist of golden fire went up, turned white, and at the next clearing, he saw the full

34

moon standing low in the east. It seemed to be breaking its way through the uppermost tips of the trees, rushing swiftly toward the earth. Tom Gloster sighed as he looked at it—so calmly remote from man and his misery.

The forest grew thinner, except for dense spots of willows, in low, swampy ground, and the moon, with increasing strength, made the forest a study in black and vivid silver, the trail developed into a gently winding road, arching a little to go over a bridge, a furlong before him. The gray mare was stopped here by a sudden, thunderous outbreaking of gunshots; then came loud shouting; and a rider appeared over the bridge, which echoed hollowly for an instant to the beating of the horse.

The mare shied into a clump of saplings, and from this shelter Tom Gloster saw that the horseman was a fugitive, for, as he came closer, three more riders thundered on the bridge and then swept down the road in pursuit. They rode wildly guns flashing in their hands, and yet the fugitive seemed too small to be an enemy worthy of such fighting anger. It was the silhouette of a boy or a woman; and as the rider came closer, there was ample moon for Tom to see that this was the boy, the companion of Capra.

His heart leaped with fear; and then it burned with an angry compassion, for it did not take great powers of thought to link together the fear which had made Capra desire a guard before he could sleep, and the red stain and the empty saddle on the mare, and this pursuit of the boy. Here were at least three of those who had hunted the strange pair, and as the boy flew by, riding bravely and well, like a jockey in a race, Tom Gloster drew a revolver and fired straight at the three who rushed behind. He could not have missed such a broad target. The central horse went down with a crash and a grunt, spinning its rider far ahead; the other pair reined abruptly to one side, and the other into the woods, while Tom Gloster, wondering if he were mad to have interfered in such an affair, and troubled for the safety of his own skin, rode the mare back onto the roadway, and took after the boy.

At the next turn of the road, looking to the left through a thin veil of trees, he saw the glimmer of a form vanishing in the open country beyond; behind him there was no

35

sound of pursuit; and so he pushed through the edge of the wood and came into fuller view of the distant rider.

It was the boy, he judged by the manner of riding, and the size; so he let the gray run, and she went like a hawk on the wing. It was a well-ridden race, but there was no doubt about the winner; the mare came up on the other, hand over hand; and suddenly, on a hilltop, the fugitive halted and wheeled his horse about. The gray checked itself instinctively and halted beside the other.

Said the boy in perfect English: "I guessed it might be you that the mare had brought back!"

There were three things in this speech that surprised young Gloster. The first was the language in which it was spoken; the second was the quiet voice; the third was the implication that it was the mare which had brought him, rather than he the mare.

"There's a couple of fellows back there," said Tom, "who look to me pretty likely to take another try at you, tonight. Which way do you want to go, and what have they got against you?"

"My father's blood in me," the boy answered in the same quiet tone. "Did you pot one of them?"

"I shot one horse, and the rider got a pretty bad fall."

"I hope it broke his neck," said the youngster, "because that would partly pay for Capra."

"Is Capra hurt?"

"No, Capra's not hurt," said the other. "And what's more, Capra won't be hurt. No more than you could hurt that bald-headed rock, there."

"Do you mean that he's dead?" asked Tom Gloster.

"Dead? Of course he's dead! And likely they've gone back now just to make sure."

"Who are you?" asked Gloster, more and more amazed by the grown-up language and the somewhat more than grown-up thoughts of the child.

"I'm David Parry, Jr. Does that mean anything to you?"

"I have a pretty bad memory, I suppose. I can't remember it."

"If you lived in Uruguay, or Chile, or Argentina, Paraguay, or even Brazil, you'd know a lot about him—chiefly lies, of course!"

"What's he famous for?"

36

"Cattle. That's all you're apt to get famous for down there, unless you're a revolution artist."

"He's a rich cowman; is that what you mean?"

"No, it's not. He's not rich, because he spends coin like water; he's not a cowman, because he's a gentleman."

Tom wondered. He began to feel he had found a miracle of intelligence, at last.

7. "You Are My Luck!"

THEN TOM explained in his gentle way that he wanted to do what he could to help; and, speaking, he smiled to himself, with the thought of his own troubles.

"You can't help," said the boy. "You'd better go home. I don't know why you came here, anyway."

"I came here because the gray brought me here."

"Well, I could guess that."

"Suppose you tell me why I can't help?"

"I'm as good as dead," said the boy. "She never misses more than once, and with me, she's already missed half a dozen times. My good luck can't hold out any more. I'm as good as buzzard food, right now."

"She?" said Tom Gloster.

"Yes."

"A woman?"

"Yes."

"That wants to have you—dead?"

"There's no good talking about it."

"It seems a strange thing," said Tom.

"Oh, that's nothing down in Argentina. Everything is strange down there. I've got to ride on, now."

"Alone?"

"Well, you'll be dropping yourself right into boiling hot trouble, if you go along with me. So long!"

But Tom Gloster let the mare drift along beside the bay. The boy, in his crisp, heartless way, kept up the talk.

"I see. You want to know what happened tonight; well, you deserve to hear, I suppose; even Capra would agree to that. After we left you, we rode off through the woods. I think that Capra thought we were winning the race, this time."

"The race to what place?"

"My stepmother has a ranch somewhere north of this. We've been coming all the way from Argentina to get there. But this evening, about dusk, we rode right into a fire of rifles, and the first bullet knocked Capra off his horse. I happened to be on the far side of him, and so he was able to grab my pommel, leap to the bay's back and gallop on with me until we found a nest of rocks. We made the bay lie down inside; Capra told me to keep a lookout while he tended to his wounds.

"I kept the lookout. I saw some shadows move along the edge of the forest, and I took a couple of pot shots. But there wasn't much light, even of stars. Just then I hear, 'Amigo!' from José. I look around and ask what he wants; but he doesn't want anything. Then I go to him and I find that he never will want anything, no matter how long I wait! He's dead. He's plenty dead!"

"Dead?" said Tom Gloster. "Dead?"

And he thought back, with a shocked mind, to his picture of Capra; the man had seemed a savage; now he appeared a devoted servant, worn to exhaustion, nervous and helpless from the long strain of facing danger.

"He probably was a little glad," said the boy, in the same hatefully casual manner. "He was pretty tired, you see. He's been wanting to lie down for a good long time, what with all the riding that we've been doing."

"You've done it, too. But you manage to keep up; and he's gone smash?"

"A rifle bullet smashed him. But if he'd been himself, perhaps he would have seen the flash of the gun in time. I don't know."

"Did you see it?"

"Yes. I didn't have time to warn him, though. They

were afraid of José; they wanted me, of course; but they thought it better to start on him! You wonder why I wasn't tired out? Well, because I was fighting all the time for my own life. That's easier than working for some other man's."

"What is it?"

He jerked his horse to a halt and snatched up his rifle, which had been balanced across the bow of his saddle.

"Nothing—I hope! You dropped one of them?"

"Yes. He won't ride again tonight, I suppose."

"Then the rest won't come on," and the boy with decision. "Not two against two. Hired guns don't fight that way. They want a big edge."

Deliberately he pushed his rifle back into its holster and yawned.

"I waited in the rocks," he went on, "until the moon came up. As soon as it got high enough, they could climb the trees and get plenty of angle to their shots to cover every inch of the rocks. I got ready to bolt. I waited until I was sure that I heard a noise among the trees, like someone beginning to climb up; then I started the bay out from those rocks like a puff of wind. You bet he legged it! They peppered away at me; but they were surprised."

He laughed.

"Then I met you, and you slapped 'em in the face. That was a good, plucky thing to do," he added with casual afterthought.

"You'd better tell me where your stepmother's house is," said Tom.

"That's no good. While José Capra lay dead, one of the men sang out and tried to buy Capra out. He went up to three thousand dollars, and I began to thank Heaven that José was dead!"

"Wouldn't you trust him as a friend?"

"Not to three thousand dollars. That would have made him a rich gaucho, back in Argentina. But the point was that the man who talked named himself, and he was the foreman on my stepmother's ranch!"

Tom exclaimed in bewilderment: "Then you can send word to her?"

"Look here," said the boy with asperity, "how can I send word to her, when she's hired the men to kill me?"

"Your stepmother?"

"She's the one behind all the trouble. She's always been behind it, and she always will be!"

Tom Gloster was silent. The boy went on: "She has a son, too. That explains."

"I don't understand," said the bewildered Tom.

The boy jerked around in the saddle, irritated.

"Why don't you understand? It's as plain as the nose on your face, isn't it?"

"What is?"

"Why—"

The youngster paused.

"Well," he said, "I'll explain it to you, in small words. I'll try to make you understand. Suppose Dad dies, I'll get half the place, anyway."

"Of course."

"You say 'of course.' But she doesn't. She thinks of her own boy. She wants the whole thing for him."

"Isn't there enough for both of you?"

"No. There's about sixty square miles."

"That's a great deal, I should think."

"Not with Dad's way of spending and plastering on the mortgages. We just keep going, and that's about all."

"Did she drive you out?"

"She said that Dad being an American and I being an American, I ought to come up North, here, and spend some time on her place. She's got a little place from grandfather; there's a dash of American even in her, though you'd never guess it. I was to come up here and go to school. I saw what she was driving at and begged Dad not to send me. He did send me, but he gave me his best man for a guard. That was José Capra. Now José's gone. They'll not have much trouble about getting me."

Gloster drew in a great breath. This complication bewildered him, but he himself came from an unhappy household, and therefore he could understand in part.

"You ought to go to the sheriff," he advised.

"They'll be watching that trail. They'd tag me with a bullet just as I got to the front door."

Gloster shuddered.

"Could nobody protect you, then?"

"Dad might, for a while. But I can't get back to him."

"Why not?"

"Because they'll be watching the boats south. Besides, I haven't enough money."

"Sell your horse."

"It's spavined. It wouldn't bring fifty dollars."

"But this gray mare would bring a lot. You have this to sell."

"Why have I? That was Capra's horse."

"And since he's dead, it goes to you."

"To me? Why? What claim have I on it?"

He said it bitterly, tersely.

"Well," said Tom Gloster thoughtfully, "here it is. I don't see what's to keep you from selling it."

The boy returned no answer. He rode with his face turned toward his companion, never shifting his eyes from the face of Tom. They had entered a narrow canyon; the water of a little creek flashed and boiled in the moonlight beside them, and the trees stumbled this way and that among the rocks.

"You mean that?" asked the boy.

"Why, of course."

David Parry suddenly began to laugh, and it was a harsh sound, and most unboyish.

"It won't work," he said. "It never would work. They'd get me before I reached the place. But suppose I should land there?"

"Well, why not?"

"Oh, they'd have everything watched."

"They can't have people everywhere."

"She's like a vulture. She can see things that are out of sight. She'd soon know what I was up to! They'd have a knife in me when my back was turned and drop me off the boat some night."

"But listen to me," said Tom Gloster, his heart swelling suddenly high. "Suppose I go along and watch your back for you?"

"You go along?"

"I've nothing else to do."

To this suggestion the boy said nothing at all riding on

in utter silence for as much as a quarter of a mile. But all at once he threw up both his hands and cried out:

"Hai, what a fool I am! You are my luck, and I was trying to turn my back on you! Señor, amigo, through you I shall reach my home at last. Oh, what will she say when she sees me there? What will she be able to say to my father?"

8. *A Horse—And No Mistake*

So COMMENDED with dizzy suddenness to a most lofty and distant adventure, Tom Gloster found this strange youngster altered entirely, and turned into a sparkling brilliance. From being cynically hardened in despair the moment before, young David now glowed with enthusiasm. And it was he who made all the decisions upon which they acted, although he generally made the words of the idea seem to come from the lips of his older companion.

So, in the beginning, when they were deciding to what point they would first go: "What shall we do first?" asked the boy.

"We'll have to think it over," said Tom.

"We want to get to Argentina?"

"Of course. We have to do that."

"Shall we go by land, through Mexico, and Central America, and Colombia, and Ecuador, and Peru, and Bolivia, down into the south? Or shall we go by water?"

"Why, the land trip sounds rather long," agreed Tom.

"You decide on water, then? Then we ought to hit either New Orleans or San Francisco?"

"I suppose so."

"Which shall it be? If we go by New Orleans, every

boat is pretty sure to be watched. She'll expect us to come that way, of course."

"Then San Francisco, David, I suppose."

"Shall we sell the horses out here before they go lame, or should we ride twelve or thirteen hundred miles to Frisco, first?"

"We ought to sell them here, I should think."

"You seem to me to be right about everything," said David Parry. "I want you to lead on, Tom. It's my business just to follow you, if I can."

And simple Tom Gloster, though surprised by this pretended deference, was unable to see through it with any ease; yet he felt flattered and set on an elevation more than ever before in his life. He began to feel that conversation with this youngster always produced important decisions, but he could hardly tell that the decisions were always those of David Parry, and imposed with a Socratic skill upon the older man.

The traveling of Tom had been limited to a very short distance around his home town; and even in that town he had not been very often, but he did know the shortest way to the railroad line which ran on west to San Francisco, and to this trail they went immediately. Tom would have paused to sleep out for the rest of this night, but the boy would not hear of it. When he was definitely missed by the agents who were after him, surely, the first thing they would try to do would be to block their escape by any of the nearest railroads. But, if they hurried, perhaps they would beat the enemy.

All of this Tom was apparently made to decide, and they jogged on the horses during the whole night. They put seventy miles behind them when the cold night began and showed them close to the railroad town, to which they looked down from a slight eminence. And they saw the little silver streak which rose from the desert mists and went off toward the mountains, gently swaying through the higher lands. This sight of their avenue of deliverance braced their spirits.

The boy was utterly exhausted by the long ride, on top of the adventures of the evening before; but he locked his teeth, and in his sunken eyes there appeared no sign of surrender, as they trotted down into the town with the sun just dipping up into the sky.

It was a good, prosperous place of fifteen hundred people, but Tom had not the slightest idea of how he should go about finding a purchaser for the horses. At the boy's suggestion, they paused at a coffee-and-sausage wagon which, with its counter side arrayed for business, apparently expected to gather some harvest from very late or early patrons. But already the town was wakening, and tufts of smoke began to bloom, here and there, against the pale sky of the dawn.

From the sleepy proprietor of the cook wagon they ordered coffee, and bread, and a dozen sausages, and while these were cooking, and steam and smoke filled the wagon, they talked. Or rather, the boy talked for his party, and the proprietor answered.

"Railroad means a lot to a town," began David.

"It was just a crossroads hotel and store before. Hosses can't pull like steam. They ain't got the patience, and they ain't got the wind."

"Wasn't it old Wilkins that piled up all the money, getting town lots?"

"Wilkins? You mean old man Travers."

"Yes, that's the name that I heard. Travers!"

"Why, he's worth over a million, they say. Williams, his cousin, is the one that you must've heard of."

"Perhaps you're right. Is he rich, too?"

"He's pretty rich, all right."

"They've got everything in the family, then."

"Not much they ain't! There's a bigger distance between old skinflint Travers and Williams than you ever seen between two mountains."

"What keeps 'em from getting on?"

"Why, Travers, he's sort of a miser. Williams, he blows his money in on everything."

"That'd make bad blood, right enough. That must've been Williams' place that we passed coming in—the one with the line of poplars along the fence?"

"No. The Williams place is down on the other side of the tracks. You can tell it when you get past the station; it's got two wooden towers onto the front of it."

The boy talked of other things. And when they had

44

eaten their food and drunk their coffee, it was he who found the money in his pocket to pay for what they had taken. In the last words of the conversation he had learned that the first train through bound west was due in less than an hour.

"Now I wonder," said Tom, "how we'll go about selling the mare? Perhaps we'd better just put up a sign and stand by?"

"Why, you heard the way to Mr. Williams' house. Maybe we could try there?"

"Why not?"

They went down past the station and saw the morning sun blindingly bright above a pretentious house, with a stretch of garden before its face. They came up through an iron gate and a winding, gravel-covered driveway to the house; the Negro who opened the door said that Mr. Williams was not up, he wouldn't be up before seven.

"That's too bad," said the boy. "We have to go on by the next train. We wanted to give him a chance at the gray mare."

"What gray mare?"

"The one that Mr. Travers was going to buy."

The Negro squinted at the mare, and though she was tired, she had not failed to lift her head and look inquiringly around at the new surroundings. Her graceful carriage made the Negro open his eyes. He hurried off and came back presently to say that Mr. Williams, being awakened, had seen the mare from his bedroom window, and would like to know her price.

Tom Gloster scratched his head.

"Mr. Travers offered fourteen hundred dollars for her," said the boy. "Maybe Mr. Williams could give us something more!"

"Fourteen hundred!" The man retreated in awe, and went away, aghast.

"Did Mr. Travers ever offer so much money for her?" asked simple Tom. "Then why shouldn't we take her to him?"

The boy looked earnestly upon him. Then he sighed.

"We want to give a good horse to a good man, don't we?" said he.

"Of course," answered Tom Gloster, "but—"

A loud voice called down the stairs: "What the deuce d'you mean by that nonsense? Old Travers never spent that much for two hosses, let alone one."

"Come down and try her, sir, and you'll see why he wants to spend that much for her!"

"Him? Why, dang it—it's a fool idea, and a lie!"

Mr. Williams came down the stairs. He was big, blond, red of face. His neck was checked with many wrinkles that cut the fat in sharp lines; his mustaches were so red around the roots that it appeared they must be tormenting the skin.

"Fourteen hundred? Out of old Travers?"

Young David Parry tipped his hat to the rich man.

"He wanted to put you down, sir. That's why, of course."

"The old skinflint! What, put me down?"

And suddenly Williams put back his head and laughed.

"He's tired of having me throw the dust in his face every time I come up behind him on the road, eh? He's going to sail past me, is he?"

He was dressed in an overcoat, trousers, and slippers. In these he flapped down the front steps and stood at gaze.

"She stands well," said he.

"She's been working all night, sir."

"What?"

"She's done more than seventy miles since dark. We had to get here to make this train."

"A lucky thing if you haven't crippled her She's young for work like that. Too dashed young!" This, opening her mouth and looking at her teeth.

Said David Parry: "You bring out your best horse and try against her, sir!"

"Bah!" said Williams. "I can tell a horse by the look of it. My bay colt would eat her!"

"She's there to try, sir."

"Fourteen hundred? Nonsense! How's she bred?"

"Back to Methuselah," put in Tom Gloster readily.

"Humph!" said the rich man. "Where's the papers on her?"

They can be mailed later on, sir. We'd see to that," said David.

"I'll give you eight hundred cash for her," said Mr. Williams.

Tom Gloster blinked. He never had heard of such a price for a horse.

"Try her," suggested David Parry.

"I will, at that!"

He flung himself into the saddle, pulled her head around, and making a little detour, he sent her flying— at the hitching rack. It was more than a four-foot jump, but the tired mare rose at it and winged it like a bird.

"By George!" cried Mr. Williams. "This is a hoss and no mistake!"

9. On The Wrong Side Of The Fence

THE FIVE DOLLARS which the dead Capra had paid to him was the largest sum which Tom Gloster ever had held within his hand; but in ten minutes he had ten hundred-dollar bills of the United States Treasury, and five hundred in bulky gold. Mr. Williams said fiercely:

"This will salt down the old man for a year or two, may he be whipped for a crook and a cold fish. But I never thought he had a horse like this in him!"

They said good-bye to him, and Tom lingered for a moment to rub the forehead of the mare. Then they departed. They had thrown in the saddles and the bay which the boy rode, as well; they had a fine fortune in their hands now; to Tom it was a miracle; even the youngster was a little giddy. And when the payment of their railway fares to San Francisco had been completed, it hardly scratched the surface of their good fortune.

Fear rose in Tom Gloster. He felt the strongest conviction that the boy had robbed Williams—how, he did not quite understand; but he said to him gravely, as they waited on the station platform: "Did Travers really offer fourteen hundred dollars for the mare?"

The boy turned quickly on him and looked out at his big friend with a sharp focusing of his eyes, a characteristic expression.

"Well, what d'you think?"

"I really thought that you'd never been in this town before, and that you'd never heard of Travers until you talked to the man in the lunch wagon."

The boy covered his face with both hands and coughed.

"You thought that?"

"Yes, I did."

"Why," said David Parry, "the fact is that Travers has been trying for this horse for a long time."

"Has he?"

"Of course he has!"

"But how did you learn that? You didn't know the mare before you chanced on her at Riley's."

David laughed, with a superior air.

"You'd think that!" He scoffed. "Then how did it come that Capra was so willing to pay a big price for her? He'd heard how fast she was, of course; he didn't know that she was such a goer!"

It was difficult for Tom Gloster to doubt anyone, and particularly one with whom he had seen such adventure as had come to him and this boy. Therefore, he said no more; and if a good many details seemed not to fit the narrative of David, still he felt that it was best for him to make no absolute judgment; for he was keenly aware of his own mental limitations.

The train came down the track, leaning heavily from side to side as it rounded the curve; and the rails hummed and whined, and the light quivered until the steel seemed two living streams of water that poured West, like lightning.

The monster engine drew up past them, and paused, pulsing, breathing hard, while Tom Gloster, before he got aboard, looked wildly back to the dark forest of pines on the mountain slopes, and to the pale-blue sky above his head. There was one heart-thrust of homesickness;

then he climbed on board the train and followed the boy to a seat in the rear of the car.

A double row of heads and shoulders stretched before them, and Tom wondered at its length. He never had been in a train before; and now it seemed to him that the single car was as large as a big house. Awe made him quiet until his companion pointed out that they were very lucky to have a rear seat to themselves, because they could watch every one in the car without turning around.

"And why is that useful?" asked Tom.

"Why? Do you think that we're out of trouble yet? Of course we're not. We'll be followed."

"How can a train be followed?" asked Tom, bewildered, and he pointed out the window, where the landscape was streaming past them, and the more distant hills moving in a graceful line to the rear.

"Look at the telegraph poles that are jerking away behind us! The telegraph can outstep us, easy enough, and probably it will."

"I don't follow that at all," said Tom.

"Well, think it over. Suppose we're traced to the town, won't it be simple for my stepmother's men to telegraph ahead to other friends she has along the way to get on board the train?"

"But she can't have friends everywhere."

"Rich people have, though."

Tom was silent again. He felt helpless against the omniscient cleverness of this boy. Besides, he had other things to occupy his attention—the sweep of the train around the curves; the staggering and chattering of the wheels as they groaned up a grade; and the shooting, flumelike speed when they darted down a straightaway. Then they went awkwardly back to the diner, and sat at the most luxurious table that Tom had ever seen. He was almost afraid to touch the food, and the Negro waiter smiled in great amusement and good nature, and leaned over him, to give advice about the edibles.

Before their lunch ended, they had a special entertainment to observe; the whole trainload of passengers crowded to the windows to watch a desperate or foolish horseman riding down a twisting mountain trail.

The train, at this time, was steaming slowly up a long

and sharp grade, and in spite of the many twists and turns of this trail, the flying horseman managed to keep pace with it, constantly drawing closer and closer to the line of the tracks.

"He's showing off like a fool!" said someone.

But David murmured to Tom: "That fellow's trying to catch the train! You watch!"

This interpretation made the wild ride more interesting than before. And finally, they saw the puncher put his horse straight over a ledge, leaving the trail, and slide down in a shower of dust and of gravel, straight toward the railroad line. He came with an increasing speed. Plainly the horse was out of control, and halfway down the slope, its rear end began to swing around, until it was sliding broadside. It veered past a projecting rock on one side, a boulder on the other; and then slipped with increasing momentum at a stunted tree, near the foot of the slope.

"Will he hit? Will he miss?" said Tom, breathless.

The next moment the horse and rider struck, the horse was flung senseless, perhaps dead, to one side, and the man hurtled on, rolling over and over like a stone, until he catapulted into a thick bush just beside the tracks, and directly under the side of the train.

He hung helplessly for a moment; some one in the diner, as the passengers pressed to the windows and looked out, declared that the train should be stopped, but the wild rider was in motion before anything could be done. He disentangled himself from the brush, and it could be seen, then, that his head was cut, and that a streak of red ran down the side of his face. However, he paid no heed to the saddle and horse he left behind him. He merely staggered on toward the train; his expression one of the utmost determination. He had missed the forward part of the train, but as the diner went by, Tom saw the stranger crouch and prepare to spring, running as hard as he could in the direction the train was taking. In that manner, by his own speed he would diminish the shock of striking the train.

Then all view of him was snatched away. There was a general rush from the diner back, but David Parry plucked the sleeve of Tom Gloster.

"We'd better finish," he said. "We won't be able to see him at first, in this crowd."

Tom could not eat. Suppose the man had missed his grip and fallen under the wheels? Suppose in striking the train he had been badly crushed? For the train was steaming at a brisk rate, now, and gathering headway with every moment.

"What good can we do to him?" asked the boy, as calm as ever. "He gave us a good show. Well, I'm grateful for that. But we can't help him; we're not doctors!"

"Why should he want to catch the train?" pondered Tom. "As badly as that, I mean—to chuck away his horse and his saddle, and all his outfit."

"Suppose he wants to go faster than the law can follow him?"

"I hadn't thought of that," admitted Tom Gloster. "You see both chances in everything, David!"

"I've had to learn too, in Argentina, or else expect a knife slipped in between my ribs, some day."

They went back to their seats and found that the whole train was gossiping in excitement about the young range rider and his dash for the train. He was not badly hurt, it was said, and since there was a doctor aboard, the medical man was washing and bandaging the cut in his head, which was no serious matter. As for the purpose of his mad dash, he was rushing to San Francisco to meet the lady of his heart's choice, and there marry her.

"Now, isn't that a fool way of talking?" asked David of his companion. "To open up like that and to tell everything about himself in a flash?"

"What harm is there in that?" asked Tom. "Suppose he's done nothing wrong, what harm is there in talking about himself?"

"You start telling everything that you know," said the boy in his cold, sharp way, "and you'll be the death of us both!"

With this, they looked up and saw that the injured cowpuncher was passing through the car, the aisle being blocked by an officious group before him and another group behind, all laughing to one another and smiling at the other passengers, as though they had picked up a special prize, not to be shared.

51

For some time he was forward, but at length the daring puncher came back into their car, on his way through. He glanced from side to side as he came through the car until he reached the seat across the aisle from Tom and David. There he paused, and turning, he lounged into the chair and loudly yawned.

It seemed plain that he was physically tired, no matter how mentally alert, and of his mental alertness there was a sufficient proof in the continual brightness of his eyes which never for a moment became filmy.

He had become such a public character aboard the train that everyone who passed him nodded and smiled; most of them gladly would have stopped, it was clear, in the hope of another chat, but there was something courteous and yet self-controlled and distant in the manner of the wild rider that made each one drift by.

"I thought he was a talking fool," said the boy at last. "My, but I was wrong! I'd hate to have that fellow on the wrong side of the fence, eh?"

10. One Might Need Two Guns

THEY WERE so interested in the stranger that they could hardly keep their eyes off him, and he, as though to stop public observation from this point, curled up cleverly in his seat and went soundly to sleep.

"What's that bulge under the pit of his left arm, Tom?"

"That's a revolver."

"Do people wear them there?"

"Some people who want to make an extra quick draw are apt to wear them there. You keep a very loose coat on. Then you can jerk your hand up and down like lightning; and the best part of it is that you've brought your revolver out on a level with your shoulder, and a level with your eye."

"I never heard of that. Then why doesn't everyone do it?"

"Because the spring holsters are hard to keep in order, working easily, and because, too, it's not very comfortable, as you can imagine, to have a pair of big guns rubbing between your arms and your ribs, every step you take."

"What's comfort?" said the boy. "Being safe from your enemies—that is comfort!" He added: "Then that man is a fighter."

"You could tell that by the way he rode down the slope," said Tom Gloster.

"Of course. I mean, he's a great fighter."

"I don't know," said Tom, looking upward in thought. "Sometimes the best-prepared people don't make the best fighters!"

The boy glanced quickly at him, but he did not ask any questions. Usually, the remarks of Tom were so simple that a child could have laughed at them; but sometimes he said things which were quite beyond the understanding of David Parry. He was constantly between a sneer of contempt and a chill of awe.

The stranger of the great ride to the train now recovered himself and sat up suddenly, as though recovered from his fatigue. He was a type of the range rider, one of those lean men, lightly and yet strongly made, with capable arms and shoulders and a gaunt mid-section. He had a homely, seamed face, with big features, and a crooked smile which was very disarming.

"Such a man to be risking his neck for the sake of getting to the girl he loves!" whispered the boy to Tom. "And what sort of a girl would have him, anyway? Tell me—is he honest?"

"I cannot tell," answered Tom. "I never have spoken a word to him."

Although the stranger sat across the aisle from them, and sometimes looked across to stare at something outside the window on their side, yet he never met their eyes, and he never offered to talk.

That afternoon, as they rumbled through the mountains, Tom learned a great deal more about the affairs of the Parry family. David Parry the elder was a rough, overbearing, forceful man who could not be happy unless he were having his own way in everything.

He could not take advice; he could not wait for council; but on the spur of the moment, he must rush away to execute the first whim of his fancy. When he first came to Argentina, he had invested his little capital in farming lands, and the locusts ate every shred of his harvest during three or four years. The scar of that dreadful time remained in his mind, and he shunned farming, thereafter, like fire. At the end, he had nothing but debts. But he had learned something about the country and its ways, and he began in the cattle business, slowly. The very size of his debts as a farmer gave him credit now. When a man owes thousands, he always can borrow a few hundreds; and Parry was able to buy cows, and cheap but good land, and so the time came when his capital actually equalled his debts, and then surpassed them. But he made the vast mistake of not paying off his debts when he was able. Instead, he preferred to use his income for the purchase of new luxuries for himself or for his family, or for the buying of more land, more cattle. So the solid burden of his obligations became a permanent thing, like a national debt, say. And the interest he had to pay was ruinously high, for the very reason that though his creditors were reasonably sure of getting their interest, they all were in doubt about collecting their capital. Everyone expected that, before the end, he would make some foolish step, and thereby destroy his entire fortune.

His second wife, in fear of this catastrophe, constantly intrigued to have some of the land put directly into her hands; but her husband could not be wheedled into this. All was in a state of suspense. Yet it was constantly admitted by those who looked into the affairs of the estancia that the income of the place could be trebled if Parry chose to introduce more modern methods, plant alfalfa, and pump water onto it. This he would not do; ranching was all very well; farming he considered a curse.

"Heaven has hated every farmer since Cain," he was fond of saying.

Tom Gloster learned these things from the talk of the boy, who was perfectly capable of talking about theories of farming, mortgages, and interest charges. He had grown up surrounded by that talk, and much conversation about horses, which were the overmastering passion of his father.

They were glad when the supper hour came, and they could get into the dining car again; and here they had a stroke of extra good fortune, for there were two unoccupied places at their table, and the cow-puncher of the homely face sat down in one of them. He seemed perfectly indifferent to their presence; he was halfway through his meal before talk began; then he spoke freely enough. His name was Christopher Black; his work was preferably horse wrangling or broncho busting; every change of weather made his broken bones cry out in protest, so often had he been thrown and smashed.

But while he talked about himself and his work, he asked them no embarrassing questions about themselves, only saying as he eyed the strange outfit of the boy, that he supposed he came from a different country, which David Parry admitted with a nod, and immediately turned the talk back to the circumstances of the ride down the last slope to catch the train.

"That pinto should've took the slide with no trouble," said Chris Black. "He's done harder things, the brute. But the sight of the train snuffin' and puffin' was too much for him and it addled his head. They's a lot of hosses like that. They work fine in nacheral surroundings, but give 'em another start in a strange land, and they dunno what to do. I've seen a gent that was a card sharp in camp go all to pieces when he had to deal onto green felt!"

They had barely finished supper when the train drew up for a half-hour halt, and they climbed down for a walk in the town. It was the largest city that Tom ever had seen, and he went through it agape, staring at the long rows of lights and at what seemed to him the monstrous buildings, until his companion said to him in his quick, unpleasant way:

"If you don't keep your chin down, you'll have your head off."

"What do you mean by that?"

"That you'll have your pockets picked, or something worse will happen. I mean to keep on the watch for things around us, Tom! Everybody in the world is not the friend of everyone else."

At this, Tom glanced about him with wonder, but he could not by any means make out the meaning of this strange statement. They were, at that moment, passing through a fairly crowded and narrow street near the station. It was a block where there were few lights, and the pedestrians were hurrying on in both directions; so that perhaps it was the darkness and the crowd that caused Tom to be heavily shouldered by a fellow passing him hastily from behind. He gave ground willingly enough, and was at once bumped from the rear. This seemed a good deal, but the patience of Tom was infinite, when he heard the faintest of stifled cries beside him, barely audible through the outbreak of many loud voices in conversation about the spot.

When he turned, he saw that his companion had disappeared—or was that David Parry being bustled off between two fellows who were already melting into the crowd?

He sprang forward, and promptly he was tripped and thrown heavily on his face. It would have stunned an ordinary man; but Tom Gloster was made of whalebone and muscled with India rubber. He came lightly to his feet and ducked under a hard-driven fist; another man closed on him from the side. He was angered and not confused. Processes of thought troubled and dimmed his mind, but now it seemed to him a simple thing to take the first man by the throat, and as he turned limp, to drive his elbow against the head of the second.

He stepped over their bodies as they fell and hurried through the crowd. It had recoiled from this street fight; the spectators were barely beginning to enjoy it, when it ended as though by magic, and Gloster burst through their midst, splitting them apart as the prow of a boat cleaves through water.

Before him, he saw no sign of the two who had taken away David, as he imagined. He rushed straight forward, when from the corner of his eye, he saw a door opening in a darkened entrance, and a huddle of figures working through it. It would not take long to investigate this

56

cluster; to miss the truth here would be to miss it forever; so he sprang into the entrance, in turn.

"Here's the fellow now," said an angry voice, "bash his head in for him, Joe!"

Joe turned, with clubbed revolver raised, but the naked fist of Gloster was in his face that instant, hurling him back through the door and bringing down the other forms.

Out of that confusion, as Tom stood rather helplessly above the cursing, writhing tangle, emerged a smaller body, and a gasping voice:

"Get me away, Tom!"

And David Parry sprang past him into the street.

He hurried in pursuit, and instantly the youngster was beside him. Without a word spoken, they made their straightest way back to the station and stood on the platform where the lights shone the brightest and the crowd was most dense.

The boy was terribly shaken and very white. But he said: "They're after me already, you see? They've spotted you and me! Oh, Tom, I thought that I was done for! They got me by the throat. I could only choke out a word, and when I looked, I saw you come for me, and then go down! What did you do?"

"Two men jumped on me. I got rid of them and came after you."

"How did you get rid of them?"

"I throttled one of 'em, and gave the other my elbow."

The boy looked at Tom with a face into which the color was suddenly springing again, and a savage delight appeared in his eyes.

"That one you hit in the doorway won't walk again for a while. I heard the spat of that punch like the hitting of a club; and when he fell against me, his body was as limp as a rag! Where do you get that strength, Tom? You're a Hercules!"

"I?" said Tom, and he spread his hand and looked down at it blankly. "Oh, no!"

"And I saw you come through the crowd like a stone through grass! It was a fine thing to watch. But then, in a way, this is going to make things harder for both of us, hereafter."

57

"I don't understand why! We'll dodge trouble the next time, David, and we'll keep a closer watch. I'll have my chin down all the time, as you say."

David sighed.

"They've tried you out the easiest and the surest way. This isn't a country for murder, and they didn't want to do that if they could help it, but from this time on, they won't hesitate. Oh, Tom, the next time that they plan to get me, they'll begin on you with a knife, or else with a gun! They know what you're made of, now."

"You mean that they would stab me?"

"Yes. And in the back, by preference."

Tom frowned.

"Keep at my back, then, David, and I'll watch out in front, so that we may get through them."

"Yes, that's right."

The boy looked on Tom Gloster with new eyes. Suddenly he said: "What are you thinking of now, Tom? Of giving up the job?"

"Oh, no," said Tom simply, "But I've only one gun with me, and I'm thinking that one of these days perhaps I'll need two!"

11. Birds Of Passage

THE TRAIN grew cold from end to end as they crossed the Sierras that night. David was in the upper berth, and Tom Gloster in the berth beneath, with this odd arrangement between them—that a string was run down by the boy from the inside of his bed, and that was tied to the wrist of Tom. In that manner, silently, they could pass a signal from one to the other; but luckily there was no need of giving one, and when they got up in the morning, already the train was winding down to warmer levels, through great pine woods, and then the great central valley of the State lay broad and green and level as a lawn beneath them. They went across the valley; before noon they had slipped through the coast hills and the salt, fresh air of the Pacific was in their faces; and then at Oakland mole they boarded a ferryboat for San Francisco.

"Here's a better air," said Tom. "This is a better and a cleaner air and we'll be safe here, David!"

They were on the front of the upper deck. The sea gulls, with hoarse, dissonant calls, split away before the boat and joined in clouds behind it.

"Oh, we'll be as safe," said the boy, "as one of those gulls, with a hawk over its head!"

He was a pessimist, but he was not by any means a pessimist willing to surrender.

"They never can follow us out onto the sea?" queried Tom.

"Why not?" asked the boy bitterly. "They followed us with no lot of trouble all the way across on the train."

"They had the telegraph on shore. But how will they know what we'll do now?"

"It's as plain as the nose of your face to them. They'll simply be sure that we're going to ship for Valparaiso, and they'll have murder in their minds now, Tom. Oh, if they could make trouble for us when we were on the railroad train, with a crowd of people around us, what will they do when they've got nothing but the rail between us and the ocean?"

He clung to the arm of Tom for an instant. Then he stiffened himself.

"We've got to fall back on luck," he decided. "And as long as luck and a good Colt are with us—maybe we'll win through!"

Someone came up from behind them. It was the tall, lean form of Christopher Black, who was wearing the broadest of smiles, and whose eyes shone with expectancy.

"I'm a half hour away from a happy life," said Christopher Black. "But what are you two going to do in Frisco?"

"We've no real plans," said the boy in haste.

"It's a town for a general all round good time," said

Christopher Black. "Here's the end of this trip. Good luck to you both."

He turned and hastened down the stairs to the lower part of the boat. They followed, and soon they were pressed into the crowd which packed in the front of the ferryboat as it was bumped and slipped dexterously into the dock.

The ropes were tied, the chain whipped back, and the whole lot streamed up the incline into the ferry building, and still in a closely packed herd through the bending passages, all through which David clung firmly to the arm of his friend.

So they came from the shadow blinking into the sunlight which streamed down Market Street and blinding bright in the open square before the building. They saw the long processions of street cars turning in endless circles, with groaning wheels and with clattering bells. Tom looked on it as a sort of paradise, and a sort of madhouse, all in one. David, in the meantime, had bought a newspaper, and he was scanning it rapidly until he had found the advertisements of lines running south down the Pacific coast.

They found them at last. It was a long trip, through hot weather, so much the agency told them; but they made their reservations for a ship leaving that afternoon, and then they went uptown to buy clothes. A pair of suitcases were soon filled with ready-made clothes—more clothes than Tom Gloster had possessed in all his life.

They went to a gunsmith's shop and there they bought for the boy a light but long-barreled .32. It would not stop a man with its bullet; but if he struck a vital part, the bullet would drive through flesh and bone far more swiftly than even the big, powerful Colts. For Tom they got a Colt, range pattern, and a supply of ammunition for both weapons. Still, David was not satisfied until they had dropped into a cutlery shop and there he examined the knives for hunting, knives of all sorts, until he found a slender-hafted, long-bladed thing that looked like a gleam of silver moonlight dripping to a point.

"What do you want with it?" asked Tom curiously. "You couldn't skin anything larger than a jack rabbit with a knife like that!"

The boy looked earnestly at him.

"D'you think that I want it for skinning?" he asked. "But it's sometimes as good as a gun—and it never talks as much about what it does!"

He said this with a peculiar relish that seemed very horrible to Tom, and once again he felt that he must leave his final judgment of this youngster in abeyance.

They walked down to the wharf together, and through the lofty, cool, shadowy building beside which the ship was docked. At the gangway, they stepped back, and they saw a thin, upright, old gentleman with a bristling white mustache and a long linen duster approaching, with a porter behind him, carrying a pair of suit-cases. He stumped on in the lead, leaning on a stick, and going up the gangplank with the stiff dignity of age.

"Somebody for Chile," said the boy, "with a wad of money there at the other end of the line, waiting for him! But what about you, Tom?"

"What do you mean?"

"What's waiting for you at the other end of the line?"

Tom merely stared.

"I never thought of that," said he.

"I knew that you didn't," replied the youngster. "Suppose I tell you how things stand?"

"Well, you tell me, David."

"She never fails," said the youngster. "That's what stacks the cards against us. Whatever she wants, she gets. She always has and she always will, because she's a clever one. She's got everything in her favor, now. She has the game pretty much in her own hands."

"I don't see that."

"She'll know tonight by wire," said the boy, "that we've sailed on this ship, and some of her men will be aboard it."

He paused, and seeing that Tom was seriously considering this without making any answer, he went on:

"I'm ready to take a chance with my life. Because whether I try to get back to the house and see Dad, or whether I'm just drifting about somewhere, she'll still be reaching her hand out after me. But what about you, Tom? Turn around and walk off this ship, and you'll never be in any danger afterward. I think I'm sure of that.

They've had a taste of you, and they know what you can do. They know that you're poison, and they don't want to dish you up for a diet to anybody!"

He summed up his argument:

"I'm a hard one, Tom. I've had to be hard, the way that I've been raised. Capra was square and fair, but he was a hired hand. It's different with you. You've saved me twice, already. You've done more than your share for me. I've no right to expect any more from you, and I don't expect any more."

"Well," said Gloster, "if you're done talking, I suppose we might as well go on board the ship?"

The boy said not a word, but his lip twitched a little, and he had to frown to restore his usual expression of crisp, uninterested, impersonal alertness. So they gave up their tickets and went up the gangplank to their stateroom. The boy remained inside to arrange their luggage, but Gloster stepped out onto the deck, for he wanted to lean on the rail and inhale the strange, sharp odors of the dock, and watch the people coming up the gangplank, and the baggage and freight swinging into the main hatch forward.

A man stepped up beside him, a square-jawed, dark-skinned fellow.

In his hand he had a number of greenbacks, spread out like a hand of playing cards.

"Gloster," he said quietly, but speaking in a decidedly foreign accent, "I've got twenty-five hundred dollars here, if you'll walk down that gangplank and forget to come back on board the ship."

12. *A Sick Cat*

THERE WAS no word in the mind of big Tom Gloster to reply to this speech; he could only stare, and this seemed answer enough, for the swarthy gentleman suddenly folded the fan of money and slicked it straight in his finger tops, and then he nodded slowly at Tom.

"You're going to be the honest fool, I see," said he.

With this, he turned on his heel with a military briskness and went down the rail to the gangplank, down which he went with a quick, springing step, and disappeared in the crowd gathering to come aboard.

It was not a big ship, the *Santa Ines,* and it carried more freight than passengers, but altogether some forty were on her when she backed out from her pier and swung her head for the Golden Gate. Behind them, windows in Berkeley winked in the sun, and the hills of San Francisco flashed back light and color as the *Santa Ines* pushed through the choppy tide of the Gate and went out to sea. The Faralones, straight before them, were low, dim smudges of purple, and now the ship swung south and west and began to make full speed.

Before they were across the bar, Tom Gloster began to feel the qualms of seasickness; and for three days he lay prostrated with misery, unable to raise his head from his pillow. He had for company the howling of a wild storm, the constant attention of David, and the strange devotion of the ship's cat. It was a little Siamese, with a face that looked as though she had been sniffing in a coal bucket, pale-blue eyes, and a demeanor most affectionate. She had come in at the heels of the steward on the first day out, and she spent most of the rest of her time in the cabin, even taking her meals there from scraps from Tom's untouched plates.

On the fourth day, the wind fell, and the dreadful quartering roll of the vessel decreased so that Tom could sit up a little against his pillows. That same day he could drink a bowl of broth; and in the evening his appetite was strong, his eye was beginning to grow bright and clear.

David was delighted, for, as he said, he dared not leave the cabin without Tom Gloster to escort him. He knew of the bribe which had been offered to Tom, and the thought of it chilled him to the marrow. But now that Tom promised to be fully recovered, David gleefully ordered all the dainties from the cook's larder. Soup, and fish, and meat, and duck, were to follow in order. The soup came and was disposed of with a flourish. But when the steward came in carrying the fish, he was unsteadied by a heave of the vessel just as he passed through the door—the tray spilled its contents upon the floor with a great, general crashing.

The steward, pale and profane, scraped up some of the larger fragments and went off in search of a mop to clean up the rest from the floor; and in the meantime the Siamese investigated. Fish is nearest the heart of any cat, and soon she was busily at work; when the steward returned, her whiskers were bristling and loaded with cream sauce.

But she withdrew and watched wistfully while the remainder was cleared up. It was some time after that before the fish course was again brought in and duly laid out on the little table. Tom, now out of bed, a little weak but very cheerful, prepared to attack the food with a gigantic appetite when David Parry pointed suddenly at the cat, and laughed.

"Look at her! She's jealous of our luck, Tom."

She stood in the center of the floor, her hair bristling, her tail thrust straight up, and looking like a small clothes brush; they could hear the light scratching noises as her claws worked at the wood.

Tom Gloster, after a single glance, started up from the table.

"She's not jealous! She's in pain, David. She wouldn't take food from your hand right now. Look!"

The Siamese, with a screech of agony, rolled on the floor, and rose again to stand with stiff legs and arched back, close in a corner. There she *meowed* pitifully.

"Call the steward," said Tom. "She ought to be taken care of. She acts as though she had cramps in the stomach. And if—"

"Tom!" cried David. "Don't you see?"

"What, David?"

"It's the fish! It's the fish that was meant for us to eat. It's poisoned! It's poisoned! Oh, Heaven help us!"

Tom Gloster, quietly, but with a grim face, stared at the suffering cat. Then he stood up and pressed the bell which brought the steward. "Go bring the captain here," said Tom.

The steward blinked and grinned.

"The captain, sir? The captain?"

"I've got to see him," said Tom.

His manner was impressive. The steward looked, bewildered, at the cat, which was now seized with a fit and rolled in convulsions on the floor.

That fit ended and left it lying stretched upon its side, panting rapidly, with half-closed eyes and with froth rimming its mouth. In this condition it remained when the captain entered. He was a tall, blond Chilean, and his manner was decidedly crisp. He had been called from his dinner; he wanted to know for what·sufficient reason.

Tom Gloster pointed to the cat.

"That's dying," said he.

The captain stared as though at a madman.

"It ate the food that was brought for us into the cabin," broke in David Parry. "There's some more of it—the fish on that table. It was poisoned."

The captain started. He gaped at the dying cat, at the food on the table—

"It's the same fish that was served at every table to-night," he said.

"Is it the same sauce, too?" asked David.

Again the captain started.

"Who under heaven would put poison in your food?" he asked.

"There are some who would" said David earnestly.

"That's why we were suspicious the instant that the cat seemed ill. Will you call the cook, sir?"

"I'll call up the cook."

He was sent for, and came straightway, not the usual picture of a chef, but a pale, tired-looking little man, old and weary.

"Did you cook that fish?"

"I did, sir."

"Will you eat that?"

"I?"

"That fish on the table."

The cook, bewildered, stared at the frowning captain, and then at the silent, watchful faces of the others.

"I've had my dinner, sir," said he.

"You've had your dinner?"

"Yes, sir."

"Then start in and eat another dinner!"

The loud, stern voice of the captain seemed to stagger the little man.

"Do you mean that I should sit down here and eat, sir?"

"Yes."

Down sat the cook and took a forkful of the fish halfway to his lips when the hand of Tom Gloster stopped him.

"He hasn't done it," explained David. "He wouldn't dare to taste it, if he knew."

"What is wrong?" asked the poor chef, who was beginning to tremble.

"Why is this fish served in the cabins with a different sauce from that served into the dining room?" asked the captain.

"It is different," said the chef. Then, as though remembering, he explained: "We have some of this cream sauce left over from lunch. It was perfectly fresh. I thought I could save by dressing the fish with it tonight."

"Who made that sauce?"

"I did."

The captain tugged at his beard.

"You may go, chef. Boy, get the doctor in here!"

The doctor was brought and ordered to make a postmortem to the best of his ability to discover what had taken the life of the cat. So the poor Siamese was taken away and the captain sat down with his two passengers. He said nothing, for a time, but at length asked bluntly why their lives should be endangered. David replied that Tom Gloster was his protector; that it was he whom it was wished to brush out of the way, and Gloster would be murdered only because he made a stumblingblock.

The captain said with both surprise and doubt. "Do you expect me to believe that men would wish to murder a youngster like you, my lad?"

"Suppose you had a nephew," argued David, "that was heir to a million dollars, and you the next in line. Would you want him to have a long life?"

"You're heir to a million, are you?"

"More," answered David Parry calmly. "And to nearly a million in debts," he added, with a faint smile.

The captain was impressed, but before he could ask any further questions, there was a hasty, loud knock at the door, and the doctor returned, excited.

"This is a strange piece of malice," said the doctor. "The fact is that that cat has been poisoned, sir. There's enough arsenic in her stomach alone to have killed a mastiff—or a man."

"Arsenic!" exclaimed the captain.

"That's all," he snapped to the doctor, and that functionary withdrew, with a very surprised and curious look on his face. "The chef didn't do this business," said the skipper. "No other person in the ship—and many have had meals in their cabins—has been hurt by this sauce or the fish under it. Perhaps the steward had something to do with it. Or at least, someone who has had a chance to work at the food for your special cabin."

"It they've tried poison," said David Parry, who sat in a corner with a pale and desperate face, "they'll try anything. I'll never see Valparaiso. I know that."

The jaws of the captain clicked.

"Some scoundrel loaded that food with arsenic. Very well. Inside of an hour, I'll have the guilty man!"

13. Who Made The Cat Sick?

WHOEVER THE poisoner might be, it was hardly probable that he would make another attempt that same meal; so Tom Gloster and the boy finished their supper with other courses, as well as they could, young David very strained of face and manner, and Tom amazingly calm. Suddenly the boy broke out at him:

"How can you take it this way? Don't you see what it means?"

"I think it means that they'll do their best to get us, David, but they'll not succeed."

"What makes you think that?" asked the boy curiously, but still with an air of angry impatience. "There are hundreds she can hire; we're only two."

"We've come through odds before," said Tom.

"And now that they're willing to work with poison, too—why, how can we hope to live?"

"I don't know, but I do know that I'm not going to stop hoping that we'll win."

"Poison! Why, they can kill us with the air that we breathe at night!" He added: "Do you think we'll always have a cat around to taste the food for us? Why, Tom, wasn't there something miraculous in the dropping of that tray?"

"There was, maybe," said the big fellow, his chin on his fist, and his brow knotted with thought. "But there was a sort of a miracle in the way that I happened to meet you. Don't you think so? I'd never tamed a horse before I tamed the gray mare."

"Never?"

"And I'd never done any fighting, but still I was able

68

to turn back the three of them, so that you could get off, you remember?"

The boy groaned. "Of course I remember!"

"I got myself clear from two men, and you clear from another pair. That's a miracle, too, isn't it?"

The boy said nothing. He listened with an almost vindictive intentness.

"Then we come aboard, and the cat saves us from the poison, you see."

"Well, how do you tie all those things together, Tom?"

"I don't know, except that I don't feel that we could get this far without winning through——one of us, I mean."

"Which one, Tom?"

"I don't know. Both of us, perhaps, or one of us."

The boy began to dream. "Suppose I'm nicked on the way, what would you do?" he asked.

"Go on to your estancia, and there I'd see your father, if I could."

"What would you do when you saw him?"

"I'd tell him the truth."

"Do you think he'd believe you?"

"I have a great many things to tell him——about the way I found you and Capra, both afraid of falling asleep for fear of your enemies. And then the way Capra was killed and you were hunted, and the attack on you when we were making the railroad trip, and the poison used on the ship——don't you think your father would believe all that?"

"My stepmother would say," suggested the boy, his eyes half closed, as he strove to look far into the mind of the woman, "that all this is no proof at all. It sounds like a fairy story——a wild horse tamed in one day by a man who never had tamed a horse before; escapes in the forest, and escapes in the town from men who want to murder me; poison, and all that sort of thing. Well, it's too wild a tale! She'll tell my father that. Then she'll catch him by the hands and her voice will tremble, and she'll ask him to look her straight in the eyes and say that he doesn't believe in her. And he won't be able to look at her, and not believe."

"She can do everything with him?" asked Tom.

"Oh, everything. Look at her! She's beautiful, you see.

69

I never saw anyone more beautiful except her cousin. I'll tell you what. She's a champion in the way that she manages her face. You know how it is Tom. It isn't always the finest or the fastest or the strongest horse that can do the most work or make the best trip. It's apt to be the horse that's easiest handled and gives you the best ride."

"That's true. The way of doing a thing counts a good deal."

"And with her! You should see her, Tom. And when you do, I hope that she won't take your breath away. Sometimes even I almost love her. And then I change back, remembering how she hates me, and I try to look past her smiles and see the truth about her. But it's always hard to see! I can only guess at it. She can smile like a little child. She can seem to be simple and gentle. She's even talked to me as if I were a man and asked my advice about things. She's even cried, just to make me pity her! Oh, there's nobody in the world like her, you can bet!"

"I hope not!" said Tom fiercely. "I've never heard so many bad things about anyone. But I'll tell you. If I could come to your father, I think that I could make him believe what I said, in spite of her."

They never referred to her by name. But "She" or "Her" always meant the stepmother of the boy. Sometimes, Tom had seen her as a sort of wrinkled hag, out of a fairy book. And at other times, he thought of her as a fat, gross, fiercely whiskered creature, like a bad old woman he had known in the home village. But now another page of her infinite story was turned, and he learned that she was beautiful! It shocked him. And suddenly it made her seem more evil than ever before, to Tom. He began to hate her with a religious hatred.

The captain returned at this moment, and a very serious man he was. He said at once:

"I've narrowed the thing down as far as humanly possible, I think. It had to be one of the cooks, or one of the pantrymen, or the steward who brought you your tray. I dismissed the cooks, first of all. It doesn't seem probable that they could have managed it. The man who warmed and freshened that cream sauce had to prepare it for several dinners—not for yours only. And then you understand that he hardly would have a chance to corrupt the food without killing wholesale—and there has been no trouble about the other portions. That brings us down to the pantrymen. But there's trouble at that point, too. Two pantrymen were at work, serving the dishes. For the room stewards they passed out one window. For the dining room they passed out another. As soon as a course is sent in from the kitchen, the pantrymen begin to serve it, and pass the dishes rapidly out through the windows. There is very little conversation between them and the stewards. A little swearing, but practically nothing else. Now, if the pantryman has poisoned the fish, how would he have known that your room steward would take it, and not the other man? And even if your steward took that particular dish, how could he be sure that the man would take it to this particular cabin?"

The captain paused.

"I understand," said David. "Then it would have to be the steward, d'you think?"

"The steward's the man," said the captain.

Tom Gloster said quietly: "The steward didn't do it."

The captain scowled at him darkly. "What did you say?" he demanded.

"That the steward didn't do this."

"And what makes you think so, my friend?"

"I don't know."

David explained hastily: "You see, he gets ideas, sometimes, and can't explain just how they come to him."

The captain nodded slowly.

"That steward has been working on this ship for eighteen years, and he's never had a serious complaint registered against him."

"Might two thousand dollars buy him?" asked David Parry.

The captain bit his lip. "Do they pay that high for you?" he asked.

"There must be another man," said Tom Gloster.

"There isn't," said the captain. "I've talked it over with every man and I've questioned them, and been over every inch."

"Did the steward stop after he got the tray?"

This question was put by David.

71

"Why do you ask that?" said the captain.

"Because he would have had to stop in order to put the poison into the sauce, wouldn't he?"

"Yes. And he admits that he stopped."

"Why?" asked David.

"It was some trifling thing. Colonel Bridges was walking up and down the deck, and with the roll of the ship, he happened to upset the tray of Mrs. DeCabrez, who was having her supper in a deck chair. The steward saw, and he put down your tray on an empty chair and went to straighten out Mrs. De Cabrez."

"And while he was away, did anyone go near the tray?" asked David.

"Why, that he can't answer for," said the captain.

David snapped his fingers.

"I suppose the poison could have been put into the sauce very quickly. It would not have needed a great deal of time. It would have been hardly more than dropping it into the sauce dish and then giving the sauce a stir with the ladle to mix it, again. Who was near? Does the steward remember?"

The captain regarded the boy with a faint smile.

"You are going to grow up to be a detective, my lad," said he.

And David answered: "There's long odds against my growing up to be anything, sir?"

And, at this, the captain's smile broadened. He said: "On the deck there was Colonel Bridges, and Mrs. De Cabrez's daughter, and the two Peruvians were going about for their evening promenade, for they intended to come down late for dinner."

"Then," said David, "if you want the murderer; you'll find him among 'em. If you want to rule out the steward."

"Suppose we start with Colonel Bridges?" asked the captain. "Is it likely that he would have anything to do with it?"

"Why not?" asked David. "I'll go and ask him, and you come behind and watch his face."

14. The Colonel Versus The Captain

WHEN THEY walked out of the cabin, they found that the ship had traveled into a strange region, indeed. For the sea was filled with phosphorescence, so that it looked like shining milk, but it was so white and bright. The deck lights seemed dim; the stars were set back in a deep-black sky, so that they were no larger than pin points; and the ship itself was of unimagined blackness and hugeness. All about the ship, wherever a fish moved, it was presented to eyes as a dazzling thing of fire, and behind it streamed a comet tail of whiteness; and when the porpoises leaped, they made an arc of brilliance, suddenly appearing, and suddenly flying off into the deeps of the sea.

This wonderful appearance of the sea made all who left that cabin stand for an instant, hushed, and wondering until the captain said: "I never saw this before, in this quarter of the world!"

The cabins were emptied. All the passengers, and all the crew who dared leave their jobs for a moment, were on deck, devouring the beauty of that sight, and where they leaned at the rail, their faces were touched with a ghostly illumination.

However, David Parry had his mind fixed upon the work before him. He led the way up the deck, and presently he swung to the side, going slowly so that the captain and Tom Gloster could come up with him. He had spotted a solitary form leaning at the rail on the lee quarter. He tapped the man on the back, and upon them turned the tall, gaunt, impressive form of the man whom Gloster had watched go aboard in the linen duster the day of the sailing.

Said David Parry steadily, his voice not overloud:

"Why do you want to murder me, Colonel Bridges?"

The effect upon the dignified passenger was remarkable. The whiteness of the shining sea had been under his eyes so that he was blinded for an instant, and saw the boy only, and not the two grimly watchful forms behind him.

He muttered: "By the eternal!" and actually caught David Parry by the throat. That same instant, he saw Gloster and the captain step forward. He abandoned his grip upon David and cast the boy away.

"The intolerable little puppy," said the colonel, "has said a perfectly unconscionable thing to me, captain!"

And the blunt sea captain answered, in the sternest of voices, that he would be danged if he did not think that the boy had a right to say what he pleased.

"I want you back in yonder cabin with us," announced the captain.

"What under the sun do you mean?" asked Colonel Bridges.

"You'll learn."

They went back to the cabin, Bridges and the captain walking first, and Gloster and the boy behind. David, as often was the case with him, seemed to have gone to pieces and lost his nerve after the shock was past. He clung to the arm of Tom Gloster with a shaking hand.

They entered, the door was locked behind them and shut them in the hot, still cabin; it seemed breathless; the fish still lay untouched upon the table, the sauce now clotted and cold upon it.

The first place that Tom looked was upon the face of the colonel, and he was surprised to find that the gentleman had not changed color. Perhaps it was the long residence under southern skies that had given him a skin so thoroughly tanned, but now he looked the picture of athletic vigor for an old, white-haired man. A brittle vigor it was, to be sure, but the eyes, at least, were young and straightforward, and looked in the most fearless and commanding way from face to face of those before him. He was silent. It he had been inclined to bluster, at first, he now was perfectly still, as though he realized that this was a very serious matter.

"I want you to sit down and eat that fish," said the captain.

"What's wrong with it?" asked Bridges, his nose wrinkling a little at the sight of it.

"If there's anything wrong with it, you know what."

"I won't touch it," said the colonel with decision. "You talk like a madman, captain!"

"Do I talk like a madman?" said the other. "By heaven, I begin to feel like one! This is something that I've read of in wild books. I never expected to come into anything like it in the flesh! Why won't you touch that fish?"

"Long after I've finished an excellent dinner," said the colonel, his voice deliberately and coldly calm, "you appear to me in the strangest manner and ask me to come with you into the cabin. There I find a pair of portions of fish served out cold on a table, and you demand that I sit down and eat them. Would any normal, sensible man comply with such a request?"

"Colonel," said the skipper, "you know that you're at sea?"

"I do. What's the inference? That you have the power to command here?"

"It is! And I command you to sit down and eat one of those portions of fish."

"I'll see you hanged, first," said the colonel. "You talk like a fool, my friend. Is this the twentieth century?"

"Do I talk like a fool? A fool is better than a murderer, Colonel Bridges!"

This was rushing ahead rather fast, but Tom Gloster did not allow his glance to wander back and forth from one speaker to another, or to the table which had nearly furnished death to two men that night. He kept his staring eyes fixed steadily upon the face of Bridges, like a man who stares at an obviously important sign, written in a foreign language, and just beyond his understanding.

It seemed to him, as the skipper made the last statement, that a little glow came into the eyes of the colonel. He remained silent for an instant.

"Very well," he said deliberately. "You have irons to put me in, and Valparaiso has law courts. Or do you intend to hang me at the yardarm? You rather lack the yardarm, don't you? Or would the loading crane do as well?"

He was perfectly quiet, as he spoke in this ironic fashion, but still it appeared to Tom Gloster that the light in the eyes of the other was most unusual. He could not say exactly what it was. But those eyes almost frightened him; they seemed inhuman, and most unnatural.

"Colonel," said the skipper, with a raised forefinger, "when that boy spoke to you, you took him by the throat —an instinctive action before you saw the rest of us behind."

"And that proves?"

"That you would gladly have thrown him into the sea."

"Does it prove that much?"

"To my mind."

"I would like to cane every impertinent young scoundrel in the world," said the colonel. "And I would gladly have begun on that young rascal, today. In the meantime, suppose you tell me what was in my mind?"

"She is going to pay you a heap of money!" broke in David.

"She is? And who is she, my clever lad?"

He turned suddenly upon the skipper.

"What nonsense have you in your mind, captain?" he asked. "After all, no matter how foolish I think your idea is, you must imagine that you have some basis for it."

The captain answered gravely: "I charge you with having poisoned this fish, tonight, for the purpose of bringing about the death of these two."

The colonel looked for the first time at Tom Gloster; and with that meeting of the eyes, a shock ran through the latter. So that he cried out: "I've seen you before!"

"Very likely," said the colonel, "because we've been at sea for some days, I suppose?"

He turned again to the skipper.

"They have judges and juries in Chile," said he. "I don't know what testimony or proofs you think you have, but I'm cheerfully willing to undergo arrest if some dastardly thing actually has been done. Only, man, for Heaven's sake, don't remain content with my arrest. Search farther! Bring all your wits to bear on it. Don't

76

let the real scoundrel escape while you're having an excellent good time prosecuting the case against me!"

This the colonel said with real fire, and he added: "Poison? Faugh!"

This last was in an undertone, with an air and expression of the most profound disgust, which impressed Tom Gloster in spite of himself, and impressed the ship's captain, also.

Suddenly the latter said: "The case can be brought when we come to port. In the meantime, I'm going to indulge you in the freedom of the ship. I certainly don't —believe in unnecessary harshness."

"Thank you, sir," said Colonel Bridges, and a smile of mockery flashed onto his lips and disappeared again. He added more gravely and sternly: "I want you to understand, Captain, that I'm not without influence with the owners of this line, and by Heaven, I shall see to it that they make you pay for this night's work and asininity!"

"You are free to leave this cabin!" snapped the captain, and Bridges turned about and left the room; and as he disappeared, the pale glimmer of the sea appeared and disappeared around his erect, angry form.

"There you are!" said the captain, with an air of dejection. "I've stepped into the fire, and for no good. He's innocent, I would swear. But when he took you by the throat, boy, I could have sworn the opposite!"

"If you'd felt his grip," said David Parry, "you'd be a good deal more sure that he's guilty still!"

"I'm going to present the charge against him when we touch port," said the captain, "but I'm afraid that nothing will ever come of it, and that we have nothing stronger against him, actually, than the fact that he was walking the deck at the time when the steward was carrying a tray of poisoned food to this cabin."

David Parry exclaimed in answer: "But it has to be he! You've accounted for the cook, and the pantryman, and the steward; there's only this man left!"

"You can't hang a man by such a method of elimination. The law doesn't see it that way," said the captain. "This is a very ugly thing," he continued. "I'd give a great deal to be at the bottom of it! If I had a wireless aboard, I'd work up the past of this Colonel Bridges, as he calls himself. All I can do now is to promise you that I'm not sleeping on the bridge in regard to your case!"

15. He's Gone!

THE MILK sauce, and the attempted poisoning, and the death of the Siamese cat, provided the last hint of excitement during the voyage. Even the wind was still during every day after the first four; and the sea lay calm and unruffled before the prow. There was only the throb of the engines, driving them southward, and the transparent rise and curling of the bow wave, never ending. At night, since he knew the constellations, David Parry used to sit on deck, close to the side of Tom Gloster, and he would point out the new stars which were rising out of the smoky, southern, tropical horizon. Otherwise, there was no change, and half a dozen times a day, they could see the erect, brittle shoulders of the colonel passing them on the deck, for he was one of those grimly consistent pursuers of exercise while on board a ship. He never paid the slightest heed to Gloster and the boy, but, with an English talent for overlooking the undesirable, he stared before him and regarded them not.

Often, Gloster and the boy talked that eventful night over, and always David insisted that there was the malicious eagerness of a murderer in the grip which the colonel had fastened on his neck as he turned from the rail. And the one contribution of Tom Gloster was that he had seen the man before, which he repeated over and over, so many times that at last the boy said: "And what if you have seen him before?"

"It would clear everything up, I mean," said Gloster,

78

and he stuck to his guns on that point, in spite of a good deal of sarcasm from David.

Eventually they cut in close to the northern coast of South America. By night there was what appeared to be a cloud stretched with level head along the leeward horizon; by day that cloud was more apparently a steeply rising mist, and above the mist appeared now and again the white, enormous head of a mountain, startlingly high in the blue of the heavens.

They reached Valparaiso harbor with a growing excitement. The captain declared that he would take no chances whatever, and, since they were due inside the harbor in the early evening, by mid-afternoon he placed a guard at the door of the colonel's cabin, and vowed that he would see the latter safely into the arms of the law.

"What will happen?" said Tom Gloster, overawed. "What will happen in the court, David?"

"Nothing," said that cynic bitterly. "Nothing at all will happen."

They sailed in between Punta Guesa on the north and Punta Angeles on the south and saw before them the narrow beaches upon which Valparaiso stands in a semicircle, with its houses running back up the gorges and defiles of the steep hills to its rear. It made a pleasant picture, but all the foreground was dwarfed by the magnificent mountains to the east. For there, from north to south, were Aconagua, Jumeal, Plomo, and Tupangato, one after the other, and all their heads crested and sparkling with white; though around their knees the mist clung, a pale and impenetrable blue. It was almost as though that ponderous upper structure were based upon the air alone, and floating in the mist like ships in a sea.

All new things were, to Tom Gloster, to be taken by slow degrees, or else not at all. And when he saw this glorious and mysterious procession of mountains, he stood agape before it and forgot the colonel, and the captain, and the law courts, and all the strange events which had drawn him south from his homeland.

A tug put out to meet them as they floated softly through the smooth waters of the bay and began to help them maneuver toward the dock, while Tom Gloster, the boy ever at his side, watched the smaller vessel puffing and straining and laboring to bring the bigger ship into place.

"Look," said Tom at last.

"At what?"

"The fellow there who's wearing the red sweater and the wide straw hat."

"What about him?"

"There, as he pulls on the rope! Do you see his face?"

"What of it?"

"Look again."

"I don't seem to make anything of it at all!"

"Suppose," said Tom earnestly, "that instead of being smooth-shaven, that face wore a mustache, and suppose it were not quite so brown, and didn't have that smudge of soot across the cheek—Look hard, David! See that big nose, like an eagle's beak! Who would you take that to be?"

David studied the sailor earnestly.

"Don't look too close and steadily," warned Tom Gloster. "I don't want him to know we're looking."

Suddenly the boy exclaimed: "That's—No, no, it couldn't be he!"

"Who, David? Who does he make you think of?"

"Why, it makes me think of the man who made the crazy ride to catch the train—of Christopher Black!"

"And that's the man he is!" said Gloster with warmth.

At that moment, a cabin boy ran up to them and called them farther aft, to the captain, who greeted them with great excitement.

"There's the door of the colonel's cabin!" he cried. "We got no answer, and it was opened, by my orders, just now. He wasn't inside! He couldn't have been inside when we first set the watch there. And yet he isn't on board ship. We've searched everywhere!"

"He's overboard and swimming for shore!" cried David.

"No, no," broke in Gloster. "I'll tell you where he is. He's with the crew, forward. He's wearing a red sweater and a wide straw hat, and there's a big smudge of soot across his cheek. David, I knew that I'd seen the colonel before, somewhere, and now I understand. He's Christopher Black!"

"Who's followed me down here all this way?" asked

David, his cheeks wan and his eyes large. Then those eyes burned and danced. "We have him, then!"

"We have him," said the tight-lipped captain. "If this is the case, we have him properly! Show me that man!"

They hurried forward again, for the mate was taking charge of the docking of the big ship while the skipper attended to this grimmer matter. Standing at the rail above the waist of the ship, where the hatch had been uncovered and the sailors worked here and there, rigging the crane, and some paying heed to the handling of the ropes, under the boatswain's eye, the three peered down at the rapidly shifting groups of laborers.

"There!" said David.

He pointed, and at that moment the man of the red sweater looked up toward them and the face of Christopher Black, that most gallantly daring rider, was plainly recognizable.

He gave them no long glimpse of him, but stepping over the rail, he jumped down on the dock of the tug.

"Tug ahoy!" thundered the captain. "Tug ahoy! Stop that man in the red sweater and the straw hat! Stop him, do you hear?"

The boom of that voice, long practiced in roaring against the wind, now sounded above the puffing engines of the tug as that vessel worked the steamer into the wide jaws of the dock.

"We hear!" answered an apparent officer of the tug, in Spanish. "Which man?"

"There! There! The one who's running toward the other rail of your boat. Stop that man! We want him for murder!"

That word made the tugboat's officer whirl about. Then Christopher Black was seen at the farther rail, where he stood with a great coil of light line in his hand. A noosed end of this he swung in his hand and then flung straight and true through the air, so that it settled about the top of a pile on the farther wall of the dock.

The tugboat officer, in the meantime, had run up behind Christopher Black and laid a hand upon his shoulder. The other turned, unhurried, knocked the mate flat, and then leaped over the rail with the coil of rope.

The rage of the captain exploded.

"The scoundrel will get off!" he exclaimed. "Ahoy the tug! A hundred American dollars out of my own pocket to the man who will stop that fellow!"

The voice of David rose instantly, with a needlelike thrill:

"Five hundred!"

"Five hundred!" echoed the big captain. "Five hundred dollars' reward! Five hundred for that man!"

Dead or alive, he might have said, but did not.

In the meantime, Tom Gloster had roused himself as from a dream. He did not stand still at the rail and shout about rewards. His tongue was far slower than his hands in the case of an emergency, and now he went over the rail like a sailor—or a monkey—swung down to the waist, where the sailors stood amazed by the talk which was coming from their captain, and so, with a spring, over the side and onto the tug's deck.

Along the farther rail stood the tug's crew. There was the mate, with a bruised face, shouting the most terrible oaths, and brandishing a revolver in his hand. He was yelling instructions and promises, and rewards to three or four men who had gathered at the edge of the pier.

Now Christopher Black dragged himself out of the water, and with his feet against the side of the slippery pile and his hands playing powerfully upon the rope, he began to run up toward the top. The mate, without waiting for the men on the pier head to act, began to fire wildly from his gun; but pure fury kept his hand shaking. The *whiz* of a random bullet made the crowd of watchers on the pier leap back and scatter with yells of terror.

And Tom Gloster drew his Colt in turn.

It was an easy shot. He had against this fellow an undoubted attempt to take his life and the life of the boy by means of poison, for there could not be the slightest doubt in the dimmest mind that this fellow was the colonel, and that the work had been his.

Twice and again he drew down on the swaying, struggling form of Black, but there was something about that desperate struggle for life, and something in the activity, the keenness, the power of hand which the man was showing, that made it impossible for him to fire.

In another moment, Christopher Black gained the level

of the pier above. He turned his head and threw up his hand in exulting defiance of the row of excited faces along the rail of the tug, in defiance of the last wild shot from the gun of the mate and the steadily poised weapon that Tom Gloster held—then he turned and started for freedom on a run.

It was not to be his so easily, however.

Those idlers who had been driven back from the post of best advantage by the bullets of the foolish tugboat officer, had in their ears the promises of rewards which seemed like ample fortunes to them. They rushed like hunting dogs at the fugitive.

In every hand there was a knife; the sun glittered on them; and the heart of Tom Gloster swelled in his throat. No matter what scoundrel Christopher Black might be, now he only wished him well out of this terrible corner.

He need not have felt such grave concern.

Christopher Black snatched a revolver from beneath his armpit, and at the gleam of it, the others halted with frantic speed and turned back. Straight on ran Black, and in another moment he had disappeared around the farther corner of the big warehouse which filled most of the surface of the pier.

He was safely gone, unless the dock police, seeing him, should arrest the fugitive on suspicion.

And for that, Gloster did not hope.

He climbed back to the bigger ship and found David Parry grim and white, and the captain raging out a multiplicity of orders.

"He's safely gone," said Tom Gloster.

"You," said the boy with startling venom, "could have shot him off that rope!"

"I could—but it wasn't in my heart."

"His knife will be in your heart, then," said David. "Because as sure as that's Aconcagua, we'll see him again."

16. Facing The Music

AFTER ALL, Christopher Black, alias Colonel Briggs, was not captured. Tom and David knew this before they left the ship, thought the captain assured them that he had called upon the police and that it was most unlikely that a foreigner, probably a stranger to the town, should be able to escape. The police of Valparaiso did not sleep on their jobs, the captain declared. Tom heard this gratefully; David with the bitterest of sneers.

They went ashore and took a carriage straight for the railway station, for David would not pause, no matter how much Tom wanted to see the mysteries of this large city. It was sadly shaken and scarred by the great earthquakes; around even its best and largest buildings there were swinging platforms and extensive scaffoldings. But David called attention to the people.

"Look at those men, Tom," said he. "Do they look feeble or good-natured?"

"No," admitted Tom, "they look very strong and fierce."

"They are! They are!" cried David Parry. "When the Spaniards came south from Peru, conquering, they had their hardest fighting against the Chilean Indians. The hardiest Spaniards and the hardiest Indians mixed their bloods to make these people. Look at them, Tom!"

They were worthy of regard, being big, rangy men, on the whole, with a fair percentage of pale complexions. They had athletic shoulders and a touch of grimness in their expressions.

"They'd be at home on your own cattle ranges," suggested the boy, and Tom admitted that they would, David went on: "They're the sort that we'll have after us—they, and, Christopher Black, of course. They'll hound us like dogs. They'll tear us to pieces, with Christopher Black heading them."

He broke off in one of his furies, beating his knees rapidly with his fists.

"When you recollected seeing him before, why didn't you look closer and remember where? If only you'd done that, he'd be jailed now."

"And we'd be sitting still in Valparaiso," said Tom Gloster. "We'd be waiting there to speak against him. And that would give a chance for all the cats to gather around us."

The boy groaned and threw himself back in the seat. He was silent for some moments, and then he said, with a shudder in his voice: "You remember how he clambered up the rope out of the water, Tom? How like a cat he went?"

Tom remembered and nodded gravely. He was beginning to regret that he had not used that excellent opportunity for shooting the rascal on the spot. He reverted to another thing—the apparent omniscience of Señora Parry, who was able to pick up Christopher Black on the cattle range and send him madly dashing across the hills to intercept the train on which her stepson was traveling. What heroism Black had shown, what fiendish and almost successful ingenuity on board the ship! All this indicated that his price must have been high.

"High?" exclaimed the boy. "She'd pay a hundred thousand dollars in hard cash, and promises that couldn't be broken. I know what she'd pay. I've had her say so to my face. She'd give a hundred thousand to have me dead and out of her way. But see what we've done, Tom! We've smashed through their hands on the range, we've got clean to San Francisco. We've dodged poison on the way down, and here we are in Valparaiso! She started trying to trip us five thousand miles away, and she's failed every time. Think what she's feeling now, when she knows that we're down here in Chile, with only the Andes between us and home. Think how she's eating her heart out!"

He had interspersed these observations with quick

glances to either side and to the rear. For, as he told Tom, he never could pass the shadowy mouth of a doorway, now, without half expecting that an enemy would step from it, gun in hand, and open fire. Now he called Tom's attention to a carriage which was coming behind them. It was filled, even to an extra man on the driver's seat. Besides the driver, there were six men in the carriage.

"Are they going to the station—or are they following us?" asked the boy. And he told the driver to take them by a more roundabout way to the railroad station. So they swung sharply off at the next side street, and began to angle through a maze of twisting ways; but as soon as they came out on a straight avenue again, sure enough, the crowded carriage was straight behind them and making great speed. Their driver now seemed to notice what was happening. He turned in the seat and pointed his whip to the rear.

"Do those men want you, friends?"

"They do. Look! Five pesos more if you bring us first to the station out of these lonely streets!"

The followers, as though they knew that their game now was exposed, suddenly burst forward with a wild speed. The driver handled the reins, and his companion on the forward seat plied the whip; the horses galloped wildly forward, and the carriage bounced with frightful uncertainty over the rutted street.

"Quick! Quick!" cried David Parry to their own driver.

The latter had only one horse to match against two; he was, besides, an elderly fellow. But his face was like iron, and he turned a careful glance over his shoulder.

"Put your trust in me," he said. "A slow beginning makes a sure ending, my friends!"

With that, he began to make his roan gelding trot at high speed. A gallop would, of course, have been faster, but the trotter had the advantage of taking the corners more smoothly, and every square meant a turn to them now. Looking back at each of those turnings, they could see the enemy skid about on two wheels, see him rock back upon all four in sickening fashion, heel far over the other way, and then straighten out again in plunging pursuit.

Between every pair of corners, the galloping span

gained; but at every corner, it lost much ground, for the elderly coachman knew his business and took every turn with a wonderful precision and accuracy.

And presently he swung aside and brought his carriage up before the station front, in safety. The others did not attempt to follow here, under the eyes of the police, but shot on through the plaza, as though all the while their interest had been in some other goal.

Tom and the boy looked carefully after their pursuers, but as the carriage of the latter whirled past, all heads were turned in an opposite direction and no faces could be identified.

"Some of them we'll see closer up, later on," said David Parry, with his usual gloom. "Oh, Tom, we're in the finish of the race; and even if we've been leading from the start, it isn't any sign that we'll get home!"

In a scant half hour they were in their compartment on the train. David told the guard that they wanted to be left alone, if possible, and a five-peso note made that man grin and nod. But, two minutes before the train was to start, the guard returned, opened the door, and dropped the note back into David's hand. Then he stepped back, and into the compartment walked four men, one after the other. Three of them sat down opposite Tom and the boy. Another took his place next to David; and all the four, in a stark silence, stared fixedly at the two.

It seemed to Tom like the end. And it seemed, also, that they should have thought of this long before. By entering the train they had entered a trap; how could they issue from it? He looked askance at David, and saw that the youngster was pale with uneasiness. And he knew well that they were settling down to a long and miserable vigil.

In the meantime, the train was gathering speed; it drew rumbling out from Valparaiso, heading toward the mountains, and still not one of the four stirred, or spoke to one another; but in a deadly silence they continued to stare at Tom and the boy, like four dogs, ready to leap on their prey.

Then, openly, Tom transferred a Colt to either coat pocket, and sat with his hands in those pockets. One gun he trained upon the man opposite him, and one upon the central form of the trio, who looked more or less the leader of the set. He was a small, withered fellow, but with long-fingered hairy hands, which looked capable of swift and strong exertions. Next, at Tom's suggestion, the boy's own lighter weapon was brought into his right-hand coat pocket, and this, in turn, dragged forward, so that the gun in its shallow masking of cloth lay across the stomach of David and pointed straight at his near neighbor.

These maneuvers were not executed without some sign of protest. At the first shifting of Tom's hands, the small man between the opposite pair stiffened suddenly and slipped his hand with unmistakable significance into his coat; but, though he remained rigid for a moment, his teeth exposed and his lip stiffly curling, he did not attempt to stop Tom. And David was permitted, in turn, to prepare himself for defense.

Suddenly, David laughed.

"Friends," said he, "when does the dance begin? We're ready and waiting for the music."

17. *An Unpleasant Story*

ON THAT strange ride, there was little talk. The first childish and gallant remark of David brought no response whatever. With a sort of confirmed and sulky bitterness, the others watched the boy and scowled upon him. It seemed that they were in no hurry to execute whatever violent project was in their minds, but brooded upon it, and enjoyed it grimly in foretaste.

But the weight of suspense was all against David and his companion. The others could rest in pairs, as they chose. But he and Tom Gloster had to keep constant

88

watch. Only, from time to time, they could glance out the window and see big, sandy hills, with great cactus standing on them like the stubble of a gigantic Chinese beard. But in the bottoms of the valleys among these hills irrigation had been set at work, and by means of it the sand had been made to flower. All was green, streaked with crimson cactus bloom; and all the trees were apt to be touched by the red of an unknown parasite.

Out of this belt, they climbed to a differing region, the ground growing more broken, more rocky, and at last they entered into the truly Andean scenery.

Tom Gloster was shocked. He had an American's patriotic and foolish belief in the essential superiority of his country over all others, at least on the physical side; but here he looked upon monstrous rock effects such as one never would dream of finding in the greatest of the Rockies, or even in the bold Sierra Nevadas. They were truly grand mountains, lichened, rudely carved, gray-faced, and looking as though they had outwatched eternity, and would continue forever, unchanged.

Suddenly the apparent leader of the four spoke.

"Señor Gloster!"

"You know me?" asked Tom mildly.

"You guessed before that I know you," said the other.

"I did," admitted Tom.

"You thought," said the stranger, "as soon as you laid eyes upon us, that we had been sent down here by the Señora to do away with you both. Isn't that true?"

Now, this little man, in announcing such gruesome things, had a suave and yet a firm manner of speech, and he looked to Tom with a sort of polite expectation of acquiescence. Tom Gloster listened in deep surprise. The last thing that he expected from any Latin was frankness.

"Let us be open with one another," continued the other. "What we have come to do is exactly what you surmise."

"I thought so," said Tom.

"The cur!" broke in the boy. "Don't speak to him again, Tom. He has murder on those snarling lips of his. Look, and you'll see it there!"

Tom looked, but it seemed to him that the other was pleasant enough. He was nodding at the boy before speaking again.

"He understands," said the emissary of the señora.

"What?" asked Tom.

"He understands that it is as well that you should not listen. He knows that the truth would be a great blow to him."

"Truth? You lie!" cried David. "I'm not afraid of all of the truth in the world!"

"So you say, young man. So you say!"

"Why should he fear it?" asked Tom Gloster.

"You, Señor Gloster, are a brave and gentle and kind man. That we all know."

"Having tried to murder him enough times, eh?" asked David.

"We have tried to rub him out of the way," answered the other. "Of course, if we cannot get at you, young friend, except through him, then we must do what we can to dispose of him. We have tried before. We have failed. But we cannot always fail. Today I feel a reasonable certainty that we shall succeed."

He said it gravely, as one who speaks after consideration. And this open avowal of his plans made the flesh of Tom Gloster creep.

"But we wonder," said the little man, "if you know that your young friend, beside you there, is really a sneaking cheat and an impostor?"

"He?" cried Gloster.

"Don't listen to him, Tom," cried the boy, in a sudden agony, and he leaned forward and gripped the arm of Tom.

With a thrust of the elbow, Gloster pushed him far away, and sat alert, tinglingly intense and ready. It had seemed to him that, as the boy gripped his arm, the little man had leaned a trifle in his seat, and that the man next to him, with a sudden bulging of eyes with determination, was about to draw a weapon. But the powerful thrust of his elbow removed the encumbrance. He was free to fight, as before, and instantly he could not help noticing that the opposite trio relaxed a little, with a shadow of disappointment upon their faces.

"Ah," said the little man, "for one instant, there, I thought that there would be no need of persuasion, and that the boy would throw away his own chance, and

90

yours. But you are very quick, Señor Gloster. You are very quick, indeed. And, for my part, I have no desire to see those terrible guns of yours begin to spout fire."

"You hear?" said David. "He confesses what's in his mind. He'd murder us both without a moment's hesitation!"

"Watch your young friend," suggested the little man. "Watch him closely from the corner of your eye, Señor Gloster, and I think you will see that he is very worried. He expected to be attacked only with knives and with guns. He did not think that such a great lady would condescend to send out men to argue her case against this boy. However, that is exactly what she is doing. Will you hear the truth from me about David Parry?"

"I will listen to what you have to say," agreed Tom Gloster.

"It will be lies, lies!" cried David.

But he cried out in such an agony that the heart of Tom Gloster shrank.

"If it's such a great lie," said he, "isn't it possible that I'll be able to see the falsehood, even if I'm not clever?"

"You can hear and judge for yourself," said the other. "Now, in the first place, you know that Señor Parry is a pale, blond, big man."

"Why, I never have seen him," said Tom.

"Of course not. But perhaps the boy will admit that what I say is right."

"No, no!" cried David. "But suppose I admit it, then his grandmother was a very dark woman. I have seen her picture. My mother showed it to me, when this first talk began."

"What talk?" asked Tom Gloster.

"That I am really not the son of my father and of my mother."

Tom shifted uneasily in his seat.

"No one, could say such a thing, surely," said he.

"No one?" cried the little man. "Dear señor! You have a great heart of gold. You cannot believe the evil that is in the world. Even in the first wife of the señor. She was a lovely woman; she was a good woman; she was full of charity and kindness. Would I, to whom she has shown her special kindness, would I deny that in many ways she

91

was an angel, a saint? But, alas, there may be a shadow even in the face of a saint! I am going to prove to you what manner of creature this boy is."

"Oh, you lie!" cried David through his teeth. "If you speak another word, I'll fire straight at your heart!"

"You will die then," said the other, "and so our work will be accomplished and justice done, even though Señor Gloster should kill us all afterward."

"I think," said Tom, "that it is right that I should hear."

"Tom, Tom," pleaded the boy, "are you ready to believe men like these against me?"

"But why shouldn't I listen to them, David?"

David groaned and threw himself back into the seat.

"Listen, then! And Heaven forgive you if you will believe these murderers!"

Said the little man: "I can tell you the story in brief. Señor Parry, whom this boy claims as a father, is a very impulsive, hot-tempered, strong-minded man. He lived with his first wife for five years. There were no children. He grew impatient. In short, he declared that he no longer could live with her—and he left the country for England.

"The señora was very unhappy, and what did she do? declared that she was going to change her manner of life, so as to become more robust, and she went up into the mountains. And there she lived with only one man and one woman to serve her. Do you follow me, señor?"

"I follow every word," said Tom Gloster.

"Then suddenly a message flies to England to her husband that she expects that a child will be born, and she begs him to come back. But he is a careless, headstrong man. He delays. Finally he comes. He sends for her. She is not at home. She has preferred to remain in the mountains, it is said. Very strange, you will admit, señor, that a delicate woman, at a time so terribly important to her, should prefer to live in the mountains, with one old man and one woman for her servants? But that was the case, and finally Señor Parry makes the long journey into the mountains, and there he finds his wife, and at her side there is lying a baby.

"Now observe two odd things. When the child was born, the manservant was sent out of the way; and the señora was alone with the woman. Furthermore, the señora was unable to nurse her child, but a woman from not far away in the mountains was found who would do so.

"These are two things to be remembered, Señor Gloster, are they not?"

Tom Gloster blinked.

"I don't quite understand," he admitted.

An expression of contempt for a single instant darkened the brow of the other. Then he said cheerfully: "You'll understand presently. After some years, as the child grew up, it was noticed that though both his father and mother were very fair, he is dark, his skin swarthy. Ah, señor, was it not enough to make any man think?

"Do you yourself look on him. Tell me if he might not be my son, or the son of any other man in this group? He has the same color of skin, the same eyes, the same harsh ways and manners. He is a true Gaucho! How could he be the son of Señor Parry? Ask yourself that question, señor, and when you have the answer ready, I shall gladly listen to your reply!"

18. Tom No Longer Doubts

To the simple mind of Tom Gloster it had not for one moment occurred that his companion would have any other than a just cause to fight out; and now he was brought to a pause, partly by the great assurance with which the stranger spoke, and partly because of the extreme agitation of the boy, which hardly seemed the excitement of a man who is sure of the goodness of his cause. In this moment of pause, the other drew out from his pocket a little locket which he hung in the air from his extended hand. And as he turned it, first Tom saw a very beautiful, golden-haired lady, and on the reverse of the locket he saw a strongly featured, handsome man, as blond as the woman.

"That is Señor Parry. This is this first wife, who claimed that this boy is her son."

Tom Gloster drew in his breath, and as he did so, he heard the boy exclaim:

"They've brought in my mother's face to speak against me!"

"Now, señor," said the other, "you have heard. You have a chance to judge. How does your mind lean?"

"David is my friend," was all that simple Tom could say.

The eye of the other flashed.

"He is your friend! True! But if you will admit the justice of our cause against him—"

"Is it partly your cause, señor?"

"It is partly mine, it is true."

"Why is it partly yours?"

"My name is Felipe Guzman. I am the cousin of the second wife of Señor Parry."

"Ha!" cried David. "That is who you are!"

Don Felipe bowed slightly.

"I feel that the claim of this pretender is an insult to the true heir, the son of my cousin. We Spaniards, señor, do not sit quietly by when the affairs of their friends are hanging in the balance, but we arm ourselves and strive to act for them. Exactly as you, señor, have been acting on behalf of this boy; and for this noble and chivalrous behavior, we all honor you—I and the señora—as I am sure she will, when word of what you have done comes to her."

"Do you mean that she doesn't know? That she didn't send you here?" broke in David.

"She only knows that you are coming back, like a blight on the land."

"See what a shallow, wicked lie!" exclaimed David.

He was panting and trembling, but his fierce eyes clung to the face of Felipe Guzman.

"And," went on Felipe Guzman, "you need not think, señor, that if the claim of the boy had been good there would not have been many brave and strong and rich men in this country of Argentina who would have taken up his cause and fought for it with all their might. But here I am, knowing the truth of this cause, as I hold, and offering to answer, if you will ask me questions."

Said Tom Gloster: "I am not clever, and my brain is twisting and turning now. I cannot very well answer you —I cannot very well ask any questions."

"Tom, Tom!" pleaded David. "Do you doubt me?"

"Heaven forgive me if I am at fault, but I cannot help doubting you a little," said Tom Gloster.

How the eye of Guzman flashed at that! And the other three sat a little forward, like three dogs to spy the enemy.

"You are an honest man," said Guzman. "You cannot help feeling honesty, therefore, when you come to it."

"I don't know," said Tom wretchedly.

"Tom," said David, "when have I been dishonest to you?"

"Never to me. But do you remember how you sold the gray mare?"

"Ah, but what else could I do to get money?"

"I don't blame you, perhaps. Only, you see that it helps to shake me. Trust me, David. I want to be true to you."

This he said from the heart, and Felipe Guzman went on: "Let me state the case clearly and in short: We have shown you that Señora Parry had a reason for wishing to commit the crime; she had the express threat of her husband, a very determined and headlong man. In the second place, I have told you how she slipped away into the mountains and lived there for several months. Yet she was a tender, sensitive, nervous woman. Was it likely that she would withdraw herself into the mountains under the protection—if one can call it protection—of one old man, and a helpless old woman?"

"It is strange," said Tom, sighing, for he did not wish to admit any evidence against David.

"I'll tell you the truth as I see it," countered David. "The fact is that my father is a bully. Just as he bullied me, he bullied my poor mother, and when she had a chance to escape from the big house, where she was spied upon and tormented—"

"Why should she be tormented?" asked Tom.

"Because my father is extremely jealous. He had her watched constantly. And at last, when he went to England, she wanted to draw herself far from the place. She wanted to go to the mountains, and, above all, she wanted to go there so that she could be alone. Don't you understand that?"

"I can think of that," said Tom. "I can imagine that, yes."

"Of course, there's one chance in three that this was the case," argued Felipe Guzman. "I don't want to poison or to corrupt your mind in this matter, señor, as I think I shall prove later on. Let us look at all sides of every question, by all means. She wished to be alone, and, therefore, she moved up into the hills, and specially chose a section which was infested with brigands and cutthroats."

"I can not tell," said the boy. "I—I don't know that the mountains were so dangerous as all that."

"Ask, ask!" said the other. "You will have plenty of opportunities, Señor Gloster. Ask when you come into Argentina about the neighborhood where she went for refuge. Well, it was not explained by the fact that she wanted to have around her people who would not readily be brought into a court of law? She paid a great brigand chief for protection. She paid high, and after that she was perfectly safe. That is their manner of working? Having done that, everything was arranged. She could buy game, she could wander freely when she pleased, her house and her servants were never troubled at all."

"I deny it all," said the boy, "but even if it were true, I tell you, she might have gone to such a place for a good, honest reason—to be alone!"

Felipe Guzman smiled, and David clenched his fist.

"I wish that my knife were in your throat!" said David, snarling like a young tiger.

"Do you mark that?" said the other. "There speaks the son of a brigand of the first water! Listen to him my friend! Listen to him, honest Señor Gloster. Let your own heart and your good sense interpret that! Is it not clear that this is not what you could expect from the son of that lovely lady whose picture I have just shown to you? As a matter of fact, is it not clear that you have a convincing

96

proof here? She wanted a child. She remained several months. In the mountains, she found a young woman about to give birth to a child. Literally, she bought that child, and the mother came to her as a nurse! Ah, well, such things have happened before! But unfortunately, she could not find among those wild people a child that was apt to have her own delicate features. Look at him! A young, wild creature, worthy of his father and his mother —bandits and ruffians that they were!"

Tom Gloster, as this crushing speech drew to a close, fell into thought, and stared entreatingly at Felipe Guzman, as though he begged that nothing but the purest truth should shine forth from the face of the other, and cast the right light upon this confusing problem.

Then David said: "Will you believe him against me?"

And Tom could not speak!

"Furthermore," said Guzman heavily, with a serious conviction, "you must know that we have the actual testimony of the old woman who was with the señora in the mountains and was supposed to act as a midwife to her, and we know from her sworn testimony—and she was an honest woman—that Señora Parry never had a child at any time!"

To this crushing blow, David Parry replied, in a sort of groan: "You know in your heart that you paid her to make such a statement in case of need!"

"That is what you say and what you cannot prove," said Felipe Guzman. "You see, señor, that this bold and clever young boy—bold and clever as his brigand father and reckless mother have been before him—is forced against the wall, and he is made to say that our proofs are sworn to by liars. Though he has not equal proofs to offer against them!"

"Tom," exclaimed the boy, in a vital agony, "you know what these people are by what they have tried to do. If their case is so good against me, why have they hounded me away from the country? Why not wait and prove their case in a court of law?"

"Because the boy's father is a hot-tempered, willful man. He is apt to swing over to this false son by a mere passing whim and hold him against his true son."

"They try to dodge the truth, Tom. But you know—you

know! What have her men tried to do? They have tried to murder me in that dark street—you remember, when you saved me from four men?"

"I remember," said Tom slowly.

"And poison, then, on the boat?"

"What foolish emissaries would do"—went on Felipe Guzman— "of course no man can be prepared to answer for!"

"Do you hear?" said the boy. "And what are these four here for? Murder, Tom, murder! And at the worst what have I done that's worth murder?"

"He tries to becloud the issue," said Felipe Guzman calmly. "I have tried to offer you good proofs. What can you offer against them, young boy?"

"Only this, Tom, you saw the face of the woman I think is my mother?"

"I did."

"Would she lie?"

"Ah, I think not!"

"It was she who swore that I was her son! Who will you believe, Tom? Her and me or this—murderer?"

And suddenly Tom felt that he saw the light. He said in his simple way: "Now I know that I could never leave you, David, or stop trying to save you. I am sorry that I ever began to doubt you."

19. Danger Won't Stop Them

THE ASSUMED good feeling and easy nature which Felipe Guzman had been displaying up to this moment, now suddenly disappeared, and all in a trice. He sat back with a sneer.

"One cannot drive an ox with words," he said insolently.

In that instant, he had given up his hope of ever persuading Tom Gloster, and, therefore, he did not care how he spoke or acted. Only he added now, at once: "You know what follows, Señor Ox? Señor Dullwit?"

"I know that you are trying to make me angry," said Tom Gloster. "But that isn't what you need to do if you want me to fight. I won't fight you because of your words, Señor Guzman."

"You'll wait for me to give you a formal challenge, then?" asked Guzman in a very ugly manner.

"Look at me, Señor Guzman. You have three to help you. I cannot take any chances. Now, you know that I have a gun in each pocket of this coat. I have those guns pointed. And when I feel that there is need to shoot, I shall begin. That is all. Words will not make me start shooting. But if you wish me to begin, just slip your hand into your own coat pocket."

This he said without bravado, but simply as a child, and Felipe Guzman made no reply. He merely hunched his shoulders, folded his arms, and dropping his head upon his chest, he muttered to his companions to waken him before the train reached Caracolles.

After that, he went to sleep, or appeared to do so, and at least he did not stir until one of the men with him touched his shoulder and murmured in his ear. At that he roused himself, stretched, yawned widely, and then sat up straight. He grinned at Tom Gloster.

"You could have used a few minutes of rest yourself, amigo?"

He waved out the car window.

"We are almost in Caracolles," said he. "Did you ever hear that name before?"

"On the railroad ticket," said Tom. "I saw it printed."

Guzman sneered broadly.

"It is the last city you ever will see," said he. "Use your eyes well in it!"

Tom said nothing to this. The train slowed; houses shot past; they halted, and as the door opened, Guzman was the first outside. His adherents followed him, and young David Parry fairly groaned with relief. "They didn't dare,

Tom," said he. "They didn't dare tackle you, otherwise our two dead bodies would have been pitched out of the compartment long before we got to Caracolles. But he just lacked the right amount of nerve. Thank Heaven that you had a reputation that traveled before you, Tom!"

They walked out under the heads of the topmost peaks of the Andes. The air was thin and clear. Yonder on a hillside the ice flashed, but the surface was broken and mottled by figures that looked like shrouded statues. It was the ice, thus worn down by the dry air and the sun and making these rugged forms which the boy called *penitentes*. To Tom Gloster, it seemed a mournful introduction to this naked and formidable upland that the first thing his eye lighted upon should be a white series of *penitentes*.

He had no time to worry about such fanciful ideas, however. They had their hands full in preparing to depart from Caracolles. It would be useless to attempt to continue the trip by the railroad, for the trap which had been set for them would surely be set again, and the next time with sufficient force to ensure their destruction. Even now it seemed wonderful that Felipe Guzman had allowed them to escape.

But if they did not continue by train, they would have to trust to mules.

Luckily, there were several outfitters in Caracolles. At one of these places they bought four mules. They were strong, capable animals, guaranteed sure-footed and fast, and cost well over a hundred dollars apiece. For the mules Tom and the boy were willing to spend money with a free hand. For the rest of the outfit they effected some economies. For instance, they got a pair of pack saddles at second-hand—much battered, but thoroughly strong in the frame. For these they paid hardly a fifth of the cost of new saddles. The riding saddles were second-hand also. And they then could turn to such matters as clothes.

The outfitters warned them that the cold would be intense, climbing to the summit, Cumbre. They had to get heavy sheepskin sleeping bags, and extra woolen clothing of all sorts. Their food supplies were plentiful but very simple. They had to have necessaries, but they wanted to keep down all the weight possible, for a light mule meant a swift trip. They bought, finally, a pair of good rifles, a Winchester of the regulation Western range model for Tom Gloster, and for the boy a 28-caliber, light, handy rifle with which he was delighted.

Greatest necessity of all, they had to find a guide. The selection troubled them.

"Suppose the man we hire is really one of the men of the señora?" murmured Tom Gloster to the boy.

But David shrugged his shoulders.

"Even she can't have her men everywhere. See that fellow there with a face like a goat. I think he couldn't lose his way, and he doesn't look smart enough to be a crooked bandit. Suppose we take him?"

The man the boy suggested was at least fifty-five, made long and lean, and dressed like an Argentine Gaucho. In fact, he came from the eastern side of the mountains. He was glad to be employed; his rate was most reasonable; and he swore that he knew the very hearts of the mountains, as well as every trail across their rocky breasts. Satisfied with what he said, and a hearty recommendation which the storekeeper willingly gave the man, they hired him on the spot. He looked over the luggage and suggested several alterations. He looked over the guns and nodded at them, approvingly. As for the immediate start, he was ready, and so was his mule.

They went out and set to work strapping on the pack saddles and building the packs, which was done with a great deal of expedition. And, while the sun still hung in the west, on the blue rim of the distant ocean, they started out from Caracolles, the guide at the rear, and they were taking the lead, feeling out the paces of their mules. These were no common beasts, but big fellows descended from the fine and ancient line of the Andalusian jackass. They went on with their long, velvety ears pricked and their heads high. Their steps were small and dainty, as befitted animals used to going up and down mountain slopes.

Climbing out from Caracolles, David and Tom waited for the guide to come up beside them. They told him then that they proposed not merely to go on to the Argentine end of the railway, but to continue their voyage straight on through the mountains, until they came out upon the plain of Argentina far away and below them. The guide heard this without excitement. But he pulled slowly at his goat-like beard, which was set a little back from the point of his chin.

Then he said: "Friends, you are both in a great hurry. You both look over your shoulders more often than you look ahead. And you are not going where most trails lead. I have told you that I would be your guide, and I will. But one is not a guide to death and back again without some reason given for it."

"Tush!" said David Parry. "What makes you think that there is going to be any death about it?"

"I cannot tell," said the guide, whose name was Ramon. "But few have luck, and all have death, as the proverb says."

"You have smelled out something, however, or think that you have," insisted David Parry.

"When a boy plays the part of a man," said the old mountaineer, "it is because there is a spur sticking into his ribs. What is the spur with you, friend?"

David looked at Tom Gloster, and Tom said: "He must be told the truth."

"Good," said the other. "I like the way in which you say that. I am to hear the truth, and that pleases me a great deal. Truth is good light by which even a blind man may see, as they say."

"Well," said Tom Gloster, "this is the truth: We are trying to get into Argentina, where the father of this boy owns a great estancia. There are other people who don't want him to arrive. They are spending great sums of money to prevent him. Already they have tried to take his life four times since I have known him, and that is not very long."

The guide considered again, rubbing his beard in his usual manner when in thought, and asked if the enemy knew the boy had taken this direction—or at least had gone as far as Caracolles?

"They know," said Tom Gloster. "They had men riding with us on the train. They know where we went to buy our things. I hope that you are not one of their men."

Ramon smiled a little. It was like the smile of a monkey, without much meaning. He said at last: "Well, this is a dangerous business."

"It is," said Tom Gloster. "And I'm glad that you know about its danger. Because I wouldn't have dragged you into it with your eyes shut. If you are afraid, don't go on with us."

The guide combed his beard and thought a little.

"How am I to be persuaded?" he asked at length.

"Name your price."

"Five hundred pesos."

Tom sighed.

"It's hardly a hundred dollars in American money," suggested David. "Let him have it."

"Half in advance," said the guide. "Because, suppose you die before you get to the other side of the mountains?"

"That's true. Pay him, Tom."

So he was paid in golden coin, and he chinked this lovingly in his hand before he dropped it into a lank-sided purse.

"It is the best meal," said he, "that this belly of chamois has eaten for a year! Now, then, let us go on."

"And the danger won't stop you?"

"Stop me? Tush! I hope that I've lived well enough to know how to die. And he that dies troubles his parents but once, as they say. March on, my friends, and turn right at the next forking."

He gripped his rifle, and chuckled in a voice as goatlike as his beard.

"This will kill more than sheep," said he.

20. The Good Guide, Ramon

THEY TRAVELED on by the clear starlight until midnight, and then camped; but there was little sleep for the boy or for Tom Gloster that night. The cold was dry and deadly sharp; a stiff wind drove it through their heavy sleeping bags as through paper and numbed them to the bone, and they had to keep twisting from side to side, looking grimly up to the bright, big stars above them.

In the morning, with dizzy heads and aching bodies, they marched again, and pushed on with great fatigue all the day. Thrice they found patches of rank, sparse grass, and there Ramon insisted each time on stopping in order to graze the mules; for he pointed out that grass was a luxury in the Andes, and that to pass it by is to turn one's back upon the evident providence of nature.

It was such a country as Tom Gloster never had seen before and never had dreamed of. It was as cold and hard as iron, and almost the same color. There were no trees; there was little grass; now and then they would find the spoor of *guanacos,* but otherwise those iron mountains seemed to harbor no life. In the day it was not so bad. The sun was a fierce glare, but it was not at all hot, owing to the great altitude, and to the dryness of the air. In the shadow, it was instantly chilly.

They were climbing all that day, persistently, winding through one naked, rockstrewn ravine after another, with the big hard mountains lifting up to snow on either side of them. When the sun set, a wave of coldness pushed upon them from the horizons and literally took their breath; and, in the afterglow, Ramon pointed out to them a great shadowy bird which slid on moveless wings over the nearest summit. It was a condor, he said; it looked to Tom Gloster big enough to carry off a man—or even a horse! But Ramon said these things were quite beyond its powers, though it often snatched a lamb from the flock, or even a sheep.

These mountains of gray iron they saw patched and glimmering with fields of ice above them, and the cold of the night before was more than duplicated when the sun fell on the day. Then they camped in such a place as they had found before, but more sheltered, in a way, from the pouring ice of the night wind. They munched a dry dinner; and instantly they were asleep, for all were exhausted.

The sleep of the boy, however, was short, for his bones were covered with only a thin padding of flesh, and he wakened after a while, with all one side aching. He turned upon the other side, but this was only a short respite, and he sat up with a gasp of vexation.

He looked toward Tom Gloster's bunk, and saw the starlight faintly gleam upon the face of his friend. He settled back upon his elbows; and as he did so, he saw the guide rise softly from his blankets and disappear down the slope, only pausing to cast one glance behind him.

There was something in the manner of Ramon that made the boy curious, and since he was already out of love with his uncomfortable bed, he was up instantly and after the guide. He could see the form of Ramon glimmering uncertainly before him in the darkness, and he slipped in stealthy pursuit.

He saw Ramon turn into a shallow draw and strike into a shambling run, which taxed the boy to keep up. At length, the guide disappeared as though he had dropped into the bowels of the earth.

Yet when the boy went cautiously on, he heard voices to his left; he crawled upon his knees, and made out Ramon in talk with another man, and both so overshadowed by rocks that it was impossible to distinguish faces.

The stranger was saying: "I thought you would leave me here until I was frozen. This is good friendship, Ramon, to treat me in such a manner!"

"You think that I am guiding a flock of sheep, do you?" said Ramon. "I have two wolves back there, friend, and I dared not come sooner. Or rather, I have one wolf, and one fox, and the fox has eyes and ears that see in the dark."

In spite of the fear that had risen in him, the boy smiled to himself in the darkness, to hear this description.

"Very well," replied the other. "But at last you are here. What a wind and what a night! It has been thrusting knives of ice through my brain. But you are here. Well, then, the master wants to know your plan for tomorrow."

The boy turned sick at heart. It was enough to hear this to know that their guide had betrayed them; he thought of turning back at once for the camp, but he hesitated. Greater than his fear was his interest, and besides, he was restrained by a wretched curiosity. For, without a guide, how could they possibly make their way through the mountains?

"My plan is simple enough," said the false Ramon. "I shall take them through the great ravine on the right side of the Doloroso."

"Which side?"

"The right side, as it faces us."

"I know that ravine very well.".

"Could there be a better place?"

"No, I think not. We can hide twenty men in any place and put an end to them."

"As for the boy," said Ramon, "he is a fox, as I said before. And I hardly care what happens to him. But the man is very simple and kind. Why could he not be spared?"

"Because he would fight like a wolf and never leave us until he had covered the ground with dead. The master told me that with his own lips."

"Ah," sighed Ramon, "let it be as you say, then! I shall bring them on to the trap before noon. We can see the blue of the Doloroso as soon as the sun rises."

"Did you leave them sleeping soundly?"

"Yes."

"Listen to me, Ramon. There are only two of them. Let you and me steal back to the place where they sleep. You take the boy, and I'll take the man. What could be simpler than that?"

Ramon snarled like a dog over a bone.

"I thought you were a sensible man," said he. "Do you think that it would be safe for us to attack such a fellow as this one? I tell you, he is covered with guns. And the young fox is sure to hear me when I come back to the camp."

"Wait!" said the other. "Still you don't understand. What do you get for bringing them into danger?"

"A thousand pesos."

"The master will give us five thousand for the death of the boy and as much more for the death of the man. Do you hear? We have fortunes laid waiting for our hands!"

"There is also death laid waiting at our hands," said Ramon, unmoved. "You have heard of this man; but I have seen him. Besides, it is well known that Felipe Guzman and three others rode from Valparaiso on the train with them. And yet they dared not attack them during the entire day."

"I have heard that, but I did not believe."

"It is true. I saw them all come out of one door on the train. I was put there to watch for Don Felipe."

The other sighed. "Then we had better let the matter go."

"We had, indeed. Now, tell me, will you be ready and willing in the work tomorrow?"

"Yes, of course. There are to be ten men placed on the selected spot."

"For Heaven's sake," said Ramon, "let them all shoot together, and let them shoot to kill, ten rifles for the man, and two for the boy. Otherwise they will surely murder me for having guided them to their death. If they escape the first fire, I am no better than a dead man!"

"There is absolutely no danger. We have the picked shots of the mountains. There is not one of the set who does not boast of at least one dead man."

"True, true," said Ramon, "but this gringo does not boast; and yet he has his dead men, too, I have no doubt! If that is all, farewell, friend!"

"Farewell, honest Ramon!"

Without waiting to hear any more, the boy turned and fled back toward the camp. His legs were falling beneath him, and he went on with a gasping breath.

When he reached the camp, he sank into his bunk and lay shuddering until he saw a shadow lean above him, and then he saw the head of Ramon, silhouetted against the stars. He had not heard a sound! And yet here was the murderous guide bending above them. In that instant, the boy set his teeth, remembering how he had first recommended and believed in that ugly face.

For a long moment, Ramon remained there, without moving; and in his hand there was the faint, pale gleam of a knife to emphasize his watchfulness. Then his head disappeared; and the stars shone down, unblotted.

The boy closed his eyes, his brain whirled; and presently he slept, though he himself would have said that sleep was impossible at such a time, before he had managed to convey his warning to his companion.

But, the first that he knew, the dawn was in the sky, and the loud voice of Ramon was rousing the camp. They breakfasted, washed at a stream of well-iced mountain water, and then started on the day's march.

Not until they had gone some distance was the boy able to find an opportunity to speak aside to his companion. Then he said:

"Tom, Ramon belongs to her."

"To your stepmother?"

"Yes."

Tom Gloster sighed. "Are you sure?"

"Last night he left the camp, and I heard him promise to take us into a valley on the right-hand side of a mountain called the Doloroso. There, a dozen men will be waiting to murder us."

To this Tom Gloster observed at last: "I suppose then, that we should not ride in on the right side of the Doloroso, David?"

"Great heavens!" said David Parry, "don't you understand? He's sold. And once we're rid of him, what can we do? We'd simply ride on and die in such mountains as these. We never could get through!"

And Tom answered with his usual quiet way: "I don't know, David. I'm never sure about things, but it seems to me that it's better not to be guided at all than to be guided by such a man."

"Then what shall we do?"

"I shall kill him," said Tom, "and leave him for the condors to eat."

And he straightway turned his mule back toward the guide, who, as usual, rode in the rear.

21. Men Mean Trouble

NEVER BEFORE had there been such an emotion in the heart of Tom Gloster. With the serenity of a judge, he went to the rear to execute justice upon this traitor, and he saw Ramon come whistling and singing around the corner of the trail, the tune upon his lips a strange, harsh sound. It was like the distant screaming of an eagle, thought Tom.

While this was in his mind, he advanced upon the guide, who halted his mule.

"You have dropped something on the trail, señor?"

"I wanted a word with you," said Tom.

"Ten thousand, señor."

Then, looking up, though Tom had noticed nothing, Ramon cried out: "Quickly, quickly! The rocks are falling!"

That instant Tom Gloster heard, and he saw above him a rattling fall of boulders leaping down the sheer slope of the mountain; the mule knew the flying danger as well as he, and whirled about to flee, but rapid as was its motion, the mule of Ramon had darted past him.

They were too late to save themselves with speed. Behind them, twenty tons of rocks crashed thunderously upon the trail, blocking it with a high pile of boulders. And though this was the main stream of the landslide, in front of them a few big stones also fell, and a half-ton monster, smashing into the solid rock of the trail just beneath the horse of Ramon, seemed to explode like a shell. The force of that impact cast man and mule over the edge and into the void beyond.

It seemed to Tom like the hand of Providence striking.

He leaned from the saddle of his frightened mule and saw the riderless animal of Ramon hurtling through empty air far beneath; but just below the lip of the trail was Ramon himself, his ugly face now contorted with agony, and his hands fixed in the branches of a shrub.

His hold on life was the hold which the roots of the shrub had in the crevices of the rock, but that hold was not great. A whole section tore out, as Tom looked. There was no cry from Ramon, but he cast a wild glance toward the man above him, and that glance was more than Tom Gloster could resist. He was out of the saddle in a trice, and gripping hard on the ledge which bounded the trail, he let his feet hang down to the other.

"Heaven have mercy!" he heard the voice of Ramon cry.

And then his legs were violently grappled, and Ramon climbed eagerly up over his body to the safety of the trail. That would have torn loose the hands of another man, but Tom Gloster endured the added weight with ease, and then drew himself up in time to see the white face of David Parry, who was riding furiously up to them.

As for Ramon, he sank down upon a fragment of the great rock which had cast him and the mule from the trail. His face was yellow-green with the shock; his eyes were closed; and his tongue stammered forth choked words:

"So the hand of Heaven upon sinners! St. Christopher alone has saved me! May my miserable life be consecrated to him! Oh, sin! Oh, strange mercy!"

So stammered Ramon. And the boy and Gloster looked again over the edge of the cliff and down to where the mule lay, a small form lost on the bosom of a great gray rock, with a streak of dim red beside it.

They turned back shuddering to Ramon and found him getting unsteadily to his feet; he held out his hand to Gloster and Gloster readily gave him a firm grip.

"We have lost a mule," said Ramon. "We must readjust the baggage of the others so as to make a place for me. That can be tomorrow. Today, we shall go forward, and I shall go on foot. You will find that I shall go fast enough to lead you. Because now," said Ramon, "there is a need that I should go in front. We have come into a region of tangled trails."

And he marched off before them with long strides. They followed, speaking quietly together.

"Why didn't you let him fall?" asked David. "Now you'll have to settle him with a bullet; the landslide would have taken the job out of your hands. Why not let Providence work for you, Tom?"

"When I looked over the edge of the trail and saw his face," said Tom, "I was pretty badly shaken. Even then, I would have let him go, I think, except that he was silent. Well, that was a man's way, I thought, and so I did my best for him, and there he is ahead of us again."

"And leading us into the trap!" said David bitterly. "Tom, Tom, what were you thinking of?"

"At least," said Tom, "we have until nearly noon. According to what you say of their talk, it would be nearly midday before we get to Doloroso."

So they went on until the sun was high overhead; and then they came up with their guide, who had halted at the top of a long ascent to get his wind.

He pointed before him to a great black mountain.

"There is the Doloroso," said he.

"That's a fine mountain," suggested Tom.

"It is. A famous and sad mountain," said the guide. "It is nothing now, but men have lost their lives, there, in the snows of the winter."

"Tell me, Ramon—"

"Señor?"

"There is a pass on each side of it, it seems from here."

"There is a pass on each side of it. Yes, you have good eyes."

"Which one do we take?"

"We, señor, will hold to the left-hand pass," said Ramon.

David Parry looked suddenly down to the ground. But Tom Gloster argued gently; "It seems to me that right-hand pass is lower and more open. It is easier to come at from here, likewise."

"Yes, that is true, in a way. But I am too good a guide, I thank Heaven, to take you into the evil way of the other pass. To the left hand we shall stick, friends."

"As you wish," said Tom gravely. "You are the guide and know this country."

"Do you think so? Now, Heaven forgive me for the many mistakes which I have made in my life; and yet afterthought will help forethought many a time, for which I thank the saints, and above all St. Christopher! To him I commend my heart, and all your lives, and may he be merciful to us! Now keep well forward, friends, because we must travel fast."

And like a limber-legged goat, he went down before them, showing the way down the ragged and broken trail.

The other two fell in side by side.

"I understand now," said the boy to Tom Gloster. "They bought Ramon, and you bought him back—and not with money! Oh, Tom, if I ever think cheaply of you again, beat me! We have our guide back, and now let them try to buy him again if they can. Why, now he's committed to us body and soul, and our battle is his battle. The others will feel that he's betrayed them for us, and they'll thirst for his blood. Why, we're impregnable now, and they can't come at us!"

"It's all chance, every bit," said Tom. "I hadn't a thought in my mind, and it just worked out for us. Luck, David, just luck! Look how that man goes forward, like a mountain goat!"

They entered the broken defile on the left side of the Doloroso, and through this they came shortly after noon, and headed down the slope, then crossed a valley and turned to the left, sharply, on the farther side.

"But this seems to change our direction," said Tom.

"It does, of course," said the other, "but we have to change, now and then, where there seems to be no reason for it. Trust me, that I am taking you to the easiest way across the mountains."

He went on, trotting unwearyingly before them.

"I'll tell you what," said David to Tom. "The easiest way across, for him, may be the toughest for the mules and us, but we want a sure trip, now, and not a fast one. See how he's changed, Tom! He's like a hunting cat, eyes on every side."

That was exactly how the guide went forward through the mountains, not only on that day, but thereafter. It was a season of bitter hard marches for every one. The baggage was readjusted; some of it was cast away, and a place was made for the guide on one of the mules. And so they pressed on.

Those grim days of marching brought them slowly through the mountains, over the summit, and so they came down on the Argentine side into a new region, where the mountains were no longer so gigantic, so ancient in appearance, but darker, newer, and more clean-swept by the wind, so that they seemed to be disintegrating under the eyes of the travelers.

But now the way was easier. There were still many ups, but on the whole the way was down, and a day came when they could see, far-stretching to the eastward, the plains of the Argentine.

It was like a promised land to them. No matter what great dangers lay before them, they knew that the greater part of the long journey was ended, and whenever some high point on the trail gave them a view of the soft blue sea of distance beneath them, they could not help glancing at one another with a smile of hope. Perhaps they would have smiled less and shrugged their shoulders instead, had they known all that lay before them, but every day brought them down, first out of the nakedness of the upper Andes, and into the belt of dwarfed trees, and then into the region of the big conifers, and down to the place of the hardwoods, and down farther into the vast, almost treeless plains of Argentina.

They halted, one evening, in sight of smoke.

The Gaucho, Ramon, pointed toward it.

"Yonder," said he, "is a town of men. Do you wish to go there?"

"Our mules are thin and we are tired," said David. "Let us go on and find a *fonda*."

"Wherever there are men in this world, there will be trouble," said Ramon gloomily. "However, let us go on. The cards are already shuffled and who are we to prevent them from being dealt? Let us ride on, friends, and may St. Christopher ride with us."

They looked at him in wonder, hearing him speak with such solemnity, and so they headed on toward the rising smoke.

22. *It's Christopher Black*

THAT SMOKE which they saw was not actually the smoke from many chimneys, alone, and though there was the smoke of cookery mixed with it, when they came closer Tom Gloster saw that three or four great factories, all pouring forth from big flues, could not have given such an overwhelming canopy above the town. It was discovered to be chiefly the blowing sand. Where the pampas are chiefly of a sandy soil, they break the surface of the grass-bound land and destroy the tangle of roots, large and small, which holds it together, and at once it begins to blow. Such flags of dust are put forth as may be seen a dozen miles away. And when Tom saw that it was not chimney smoke alone which made this smudge upon the landscape, he was filled with wonder.

Already the country was strange to him, but now it seemed doubly strange; for in the mountains of his home, it had always been the hand of a man which disfigured nature, but here it was nature herself which seemed to be breathing the volleyed sand at the little town, striving to blast it off the face of the earth.

Now the town opened before them, and they rode into a place laid out by rule, with wide streets, and regular. But with that regularity ended its claim to grace. There were no trees, and there were no bushes, there was no grass, there were no gardens. There were no houses of stone. All was blow-sand, dust, barrenness, brick, and corrugated iron.

All the houses had false fronts along the street, but since those houses were nearly always detached, with a considerable space between one and the other, there was no more sense in the false front than in black hair on a man with a red mustache. These false fronts, moreover, made everything seem flimsy, and cheap, and pretentious. The gutters of the streets, too, were clogged with rubbish, which the dust had pooled around, and partly heaped over; and yet the chief atrocity was always the quantities of corrugated iron. Cheap, durable, easily put up, the men of the camp towns used it constantly, disregarding any sense of human comfort which taught them that the iron made a house an oven in summer and a refrigerator in the winter. It was used by itself, or to make roofs, and, most incongruously, sheds and outbuildings around brick structures were composed of this cheaper and swifter material.

Tom felt a sense of infinite laziness about the place. The laziness of men, let us say, who work willingly and very hard, but only at one thing. The field of their labors was upon the unending plains, from which they gathered a constant inflow of dollars. When they came to town, it was for the sake of wine and brandy, or to buy supplies for the estancias. This town was a combination of store and saloon for the vast district around it.

They went on to the first *fonda,* as the Argentine inn is called, and entering through a sort of bar, where a number of low-class peons were drinking, or eating at the tables, they went through a better class dining room and beyond that passed into the patio. Around this were ranged the bedrooms. And never in the course of their tour of the town did Tom see a two-storied building. It was as though the builders feared that the wind would snatch away the top.

They could be accommodated here, they learned, so the mules were brought around to the stable, and the three were shown to rooms; that into which Tom and the boy went had been tightly shut, the window battened down, and the door locked; but the dust which smoked above the town was also throughout all the air inside it, like the smell of soot, which penetrates into every crevice of a train or a steamship. The sheets were rough with dust; the table tops and the floor were faintly grayed by it; and the acrid taste of it was never out of the mouth.

David sat down on the edge of his bed and smiled at Tom.

"You're wondering, now," said he.

"At what, David?"

"Why, at me, for one thing!"

"And why at you, David?"

"At me or at any man who should want to come down here to Argentina. Isn't that right?"

Tom smiled a little; he was growing accustomed to the manner in which this shrewd youngster penetrated his mind.

"It is all a new face," said he, "and I never have seen it before."

"Well, would you judge your own range from a cow town?"

"No," admitted Tom Gloster.

"No more can you here. But once you get to know the pampas, you can't live and breathe in any other place."

"There's plenty of them, I suppose," said Tom, "and they look flat enough to make good riding."

The boy shrugged.

"Look at your own West. Well, that's pretty big, isn't it? But it's not nearly big enough for an Argentinean! Look at the map of your land—all chopped across with mountain ranges and broken up with rivers, slicing here and there! Why, it's no place at all! But out here it's different. One can get a *tropilla* of horses and ride a hundred miles a day for the rest of one's life, and never come to the end of things, if one winds around a little. This is a country, Tom. You can stretch out your arms here."

"I suppose you can," said simple Tom. "But you don't have to defend your country to me, David. I'll believe what you have to say about it. The next thing to do is find out how we can turn in our mules and get some horses for them. Mules never could take us away from danger in country like this, where a horse can run as long as it has legs to gallop with."

There was a heavy hand at their door; they opened it upon the Gaucho, Ramon, and he came in with a wild eye and a haggard face.

David did not wait to hear a word. He leaped from the bed to his feet and burst into tremendous curses. He raged across the floor and back again, beating his fists

116

against his head and then shaking them in the face of Ramon.

"You are like a crow! You bring bad luck wherever you go; you never have taken good tidings in your life! Tell me! Is it true?"

"What?" asked Ramon sullenly.

"That you have seen some of them again?"

"Some of them? I have seen him!"

"Who is it?"

"Señor Negro."

"Señor Negro? Who the deuce is he?"

Ramon opened his eyes.

"From whom else have you been running away across the mountains except that man, who misses you in the hill, only to pounce upon you in the plain?"

"Negro?"

"Yes, yes! But you are from Argentina. Have you lived here, and still you don't know his name?"

"Negro? Christophoro Negro? Oh, now I remember!" cried the boy. "And—Tom, Tom, don't you see? It's only another way of saying Christopher Black! It's Christopher Black that you've seen, Ramon? A man with a lean face and a big nose—"

"Like an eagle. Yes. That is Señor Negro."

"But Negro is a great man," said the boy. "He's been a great bandit with thousands of men under his thumb; he's been in revolutions, and made revolutions, people have told me. He's been famous everywhere!"

"Well," said Ramon, with a shrug of his shoulders, "now it seems that he wants to end your life. Is there no one who would pay enough for that job to suit even Negro's purse?"

"Christopher Black!" sighed Tom Gloster. "How completely he fooled me, David! I thought that he was an American, as much as I!"

"American? Some say that he is," said Ramon. "He is whatever he wants to be—American, English, French, Argentinean—but always, whatever else he is, he is first and last a monster!"

He groaned and closed his eyes. He had the sad look of a monkey in the zoo as he pressed a hand against the

117

wall and steadied himself in the shock of his fear and of his grief. Then he said:

"He was standing by the front entrance to the stables. He was filling a pipe and lighting it; his face was down. But I knew by the chill in my blood that he was watching me all the time. Oh, what a mouse-catcher that man is! And every other man is a mouse compared with him!"

David went through one of his sudden transformations of spirit. He began to dance and clap his hands together. He beat Tom's heavily muscled shoulder.

"Now do you see what we have done? We have made a fool of the great Negro! There's not a man in Argentina that wouldn't shake in his boots, not a man from Patagonia to Buenos Aires who wouldn't turn green if he knew that Negro was after him. But see what we've done! Listen to me, Ramon! We've dodged him and his men in the train down. Do you hear, Ramon? We have dodged him and his four bloodhounds there. We've made his poison miss on the ship, and we've crossed the mountains in spite of him!"

Said Tom Gloster slowly: "That was only because Ramon was with us, showing us the best way."

He looked at Ramon, and Ramon looked back at him. A little silence fell upon the group, and then the Gaucho's face turned a dull, dark red. He straightened himself beneath the glance of Tom Gloster, and then he relaxed.

"Perhaps," said he, "you can tell me more about myself than I can tell you about Negro."

"Perhaps we have had a glance and heard a word or two," said David.

Then Tom Gloster put in: "It was that great man, that Negro, that you were defying, when you brought us safely across the mountains, Ramon. You knew it then?"

"Yes. I knew it then. He put me to watch you! I thank Heaven that I could do nothing against you after you had saved me!"

Then he made a slow and wide gesture with both his hands.

"Oh, my friends, it is one thing to wish you well. For that I do, with all my heart. My cause is now your cause, and my life is in your hands. But Señor Negro is here—

and how shall we escape from him? Every blade of grass on the pampas obeys him here!"

23. General Ducos

EVEN SUCH FEAR as had fallen upon the three could not destroy an appetite built up by the long ride of that day, and the accumulated hunger of their many days of journeying.

It was the Gaucho who said cheerfully: "If we have to die, friends, it is better to die full than empty."

They went into the dining room, where only three or four tables were occupied by parties from neighboring estancias, and here they sat down at a corner table, for, as Ramon pointed out, here they had two friends—the two walls beside them.

When they came in, every one turned and stared at them for an instant; after that, not an eye was allowed to fall upon them, and Ramon interpreted with an odd nonchalance: "People stare at men who are about to die, but they really don't care. But these dogs of waiters should be a little more attentive!"

He stopped one, reaching out from the table and grasping his arm, as the fellow went hurrying by.

"Meat! Meat!" said Ramon. "And, mind you, we can eat a calf whole!"

The waiter acted as though he would have broken away and passed on; his face changed color; and Ramon added: "If you feed a starved dog, it does not mean that you are his friend or his master."

Then he let the man go, explaining to the other two: "He is afraid that if he pays any attention to us, he'll have his neck stretched with a rawhide rope! I told you that even the grass of the pampas obeys Señor Negro. Look around you! No one has a glance for us, as though they would catch the fever by looking at us, even!"

Ramon began to laugh. It was like the cackling voice of a goat, blatting and harsh. Yet, he really seemed amused by their situation. David said sourly to him:

"You are happy now for the first time. I've never seen you laugh before."

"I've never been happy in my life," said Ramon. "I've been more hunted than hunter. Therefore, why should I not laugh now? In that way, I defeat Negro. If I die happy, I have done more than another who lives sad."

"Why have you been more hunted than hunter?" asked Gloster.

"I'll tell you why," said the guide. "If you let a dog play with wolves, after a while he begins to think that he's a wolf, too. But he isn't. He never will have as strong a bite, and he can't run as far, and hunger will kill him more quickly.

"But I played with the wolves and I thought that I was one of them.

"I was as ready to cut a throat as the next man. However, after the throat was cut, my heart weakened. I ran off to the mountains and began to live there. I have lived there ever since, miserably. You see that when the pinch came and I had a chance to become rich and strong, and accepted by all the real wolves, I threw that chance away. I preferred to throw in with a pair of house dogs—pardon me, friends!—because they were more my own kind. That is another reason why I am happy tonight. I shall not die as a thief but as an honest man, and a good death is a great deal better than a good life. At least, so a wise man once told me. Though I have always thought it a strange thing that fifty years of crime could be washed out in ten seconds of good repentance."

Once more the ugly laugh of Ramon jarred upon their ears. Then food was brought to them, and a stale-tasting red wine. David hesitated before trying it.

"Once before we were almost poisoned," he said.

Ramon shook his head.

"Not even Negro would dare that—here among his own people. He would lose all his power in one moment, if he did that. Off there on the ship, with the ocean ready to bury you—why, that was a different matter, you see! But here, he has the pride of a good Gaucho, and a fighting man. He is as proud a man as there is in the world. He is as proud as the general, there!"

At this moment, as though to give point to the remarks of Ramon, through the door came a tall young man, flashing with colors, handsome, armed to the teeth. In fact, he leaned upon a long rifle as he paused in the doorway, and looked carefully about the room. He looked with care, but his eye was bright and disdainful. Then he crossed to a table in a far corner and sat down at it, with half a dozen companions near by. The waiters rushed to serve them.

"As if he were Negro himself!" said David grimly. "Who is the general?"

"He was a general in the last revolution. I forget on what side he fought. But sides make little difference in a revolution. The chief thing is to have the fun of fighting. I have been in three myself."

"But you say that you never have been happy?" grinned David.

"That was only a manner of talking," said the Gaucho, grinning back. "If I get some more of this bad wine inside my skin, I shall have more cheerful thoughts."

"Was he a good general?" asked David.

"He was no general at all. But I'll tell you how he got the title. One day his party was beaten. They ran away. That night, this Carlos Ducos turned back and went inside the lines of the enemy, and found the general of that army, and shot him through the head. Then he took the general's horse and came back to his own people. After that, he took the title of general. No one dared to deny that he had a right to the name. He is as proud as a peacock. Imagine a man who calls himself a general because he has murdered a man who had a real right to the name! One is born with such a soul! This Carlos Ducos is a rascal, but he is amusing. There are a thousand Gauchos who love him because he will attempt impossible things. I could tell you stories about him. There was the town of San Castellar. Some people there hated Carlos Ducos. They set a trap for him, but he broke through the trap and

121

came back with a hundred fellows as young and as fierce as himself. They burned San Castellar to the ground.

" 'I cannot breathe peacefully until there is a little taint of smoke in the air," said Carlos Ducos.

"I tell you this so that you can judge that man for himself. Look at him now! Those are fierce men he is with, but he never looks at them. He is like an eagle sitting among hawks."

"Is he a friend of Negro?"

So asked David, and the Gaucho, his mouth filled with food, shook his head. Then he explained: "He's no man's friend. He's too free for friendship."

"What thing is that?" asked David sharply.

"A man with a friend is a man with the gallows rope around his neck, grasped by another pair of hands. That is what Señor Ducos says!"

One of the men stood up from the table of the general and crossed to them. He stood close up to Tom Gloster and said slowly, in English: "Why do you look at us? Are we fish in a stream? Do you think that you can angle for us?"

Tom gazed at the man in horrified silence.

Then the Gaucho broke in: "Name of Heaven, señor, in what manner have his eyes done you a wrong?"

The other stared insolently and contemptuously at Ramon: "Since when," said he, "has dirt like this been allowed to sit at the table with men?"

Tom Gloster saw the knife wink in the hand of Ramon. His own hand leaped, and his grip paralyzed the arm of the Gaucho.

"This is not the way," said he. "The message was sent to me. If there is trouble, it is my trouble."

He rose quietly from the table; the emissary from General Ducos remained confronting him; but Tom was more aware of the white, strained face of David, watching them.

"If you have anything to say," said the messenger, "there are my ears to speak into, and outside, there is plenty of space for us two."

At that, a red haze glowed before the eyes of Tom Gloster and obscured his vision. He took the gay youth by either arm and gently lifted him and set him down again at one side. There the man remained, his face pale with pain, for the iron fingers of Gloster had bitten through flesh to the bone. Tom Gloster walked on; the Gaucho slipped suddenly to his side. The room was silent. Grim faces watched their coming from the table of Ducos. Only "the general" retained his smile.

Up to that table went Tom Gloster and halted.

He said: "Señor, I am a simple man. I have not meant to offend you, but it appears that I have. However, if there is trouble, it should be between us, and not between me and another of your men."

The extraordinary straightforwardness and gentleness of Tom's manner made the dark, thin-penciled brows of the general draw together in wonder; and here, before he could answer, the Gaucho broke in in anger, real or simulated.

He said: "Señor general, has not Negro enough men already to do his work with us? Has the time come when General Ducos himself is let out for hire to cut throats?"

The general sprang from his chair. He was shaking with fury.

His men rose beside him, and Ramon, falling back a half step, exclaimed to Gloster: "Guard yourself, señor! We are about to die, but it is better to die at the hand of a man who was once great than to be killed by a monster like Negro!"

This cunning mixture of flattery with defiance at the last moment made the general hesitate.

"Dog," he said to Ramon, "before your end, you have time to explain how it comes about that you have said such a thing to me! I a hired man? I hired by the ruffian, Negro?"

It happened that at this moment David, greatly frightened, had come up between his two friends; Ramon, making a gesture, laid his arm about the shoulders of the lad.

"What else can I think, señor?" said Ramon. "We, who have defied Negro for the sake of this poor boy, know that Negro himself has surrounded the *fonda*. Inside the place, we are attacked by your men. What are we to think, except that you have been hired by him?" He added sadly, "Alas, that such a lion should take a price from such a wolf! Such a carrion-eater!"

123

24. One Waits And Listens

THE RAGE of Carlos Ducos was greatly abated. He replied to the cunning Ramon: "I have heard more from your lips than ever was said to me before. However, a dying man does not care where his bullets strike. As for hire, there is not enough gold in Buenos Aires to buy me. Except for fools, every man knows this."

"Señor," said Ramon, bowing, "if I had been in my right mind, I should not have thought such a thing. I never should have said it. But here we stand with knives at our throats. We begin to suspect everyone."

Ducos rubbed his lean knuckles across his chin.

"Negro?" said he. "Here in this place?"

"Yes."

"For you?"

"For the boy, señor."

"The boy!"

"He has gone to the United States to murder him; he has followed him south again by sea; he has hounded him across the mountains; at last he runs him to the ground."

"And you two?"

"We have done our best to save him; now, at least, we can die for him!"

To this melodramatic speech the general replied with a shrug of his shoulders.

"Go back to your table," said he. "Afterward—"

They returned to their table. The room settled back again, with every man in his place. Only a subdued murmuring ran here and there, as the others commented on what they had seen and the battle which so nearly had been fought.

The eyes of Ramon glistened like fire—or like the eyes of a cat in the dark.

"Look friends," he murmured. "Now we have a chance. We have the fading ghost of a chance to escape!"

David shook his head.

"I have heard of General Ducos," said he. "I know that he is a brave man. But what is he here? Negro rules. You have said so yourself. If Ducos interferes the least bit, his throat will be cut as well, and nothing more made of it!"

"You talk like a silly child," said Ramon. "Let Ramon now think for you."

He drew in a breath like a man drinking.

"Life! Life!" exclaimed Ramon. "I take it in my finger tips, like a beautiful burning coal. I hold it now! I have snatched it out of the fire of danger! Did you hear me, friends? When Ducos turned on us like the monster that he is, then I spoke the right word. The hired man of Negro! The general will wake in the night and turn cold when he thinks of what I have said to him. A hired man! a cut throat! Do you hear, now? He will have to try his best to save us, or otherwise it will be said that he also, was bought and paid for the slaughter of us!"

"Ramon!" breathed the boy.

"I don't understand," said poor Tom Gloster, struggling terribly to follow through these intricacies.

"Hush, hush!" said David. "I begin to understand. Ramon—friend—your wits are worth more than the richest estancia in Argentina."

"See what an honest and modest man I am!" exclaimed Ramon. "I would sell them for half of that price."

"He will save us?" murmured Tom Gloster, who had just failed to notice the words and the changed attitude of the general.

"Because," said the Gaucho, "he saw that you are a man, friend, and because Ramon knew how to turn a new side to the fire. And so, we'll be nicely browned, perhaps, and not burned at all."

The grin of the Gaucho made David laugh with a world of relief and good nature.

"Do you think that he'll come to us again?" asked Tom.

"I know he will," said Ramon, with a nod. "Or else he will call us to him."

It was the former that happened. They had barely finished their meal and gone, all three, to the room of Tom and the boy, when the general opened the door without knocking and stepped in with a long and silent stride.

He said briskly: "You, señor!"

Tom Gloster stepped forward.

"Let us be quick," said the general. "I have learned that Negro is actually in the town. What should Christophoro Negro be doing in this town?"

"You have been told, señor."

"Is it likely," said the general, "that this boy, this slip of a boy, should be worth a chase through twelve thousand miles of sea and land?"

"My father is not a general," said David, "but you may have heard of Señor David Parry?"

The eyes of the general lighted.

"So, so, so!" said he. "And you put down one mystery and put up another. Why is the son of David Parry running?"

"Because he saw hawks in the sky, Señor General."

"Hawks cannot stoop through the roof or the glass of the window, my lad."

"What if someone wishes to leave a window open, Señor General?"

Ducos looked fixedly at David for another moment, and then he slowly nodded.

"That is not a very old brain," said he, "but it has learned something before this."

The Gaucho commented: "A knife is easily sharpened by friction, señor, is it not?"

"There you are again," smiled the general. "Where was your tongue sharpened?"

The Gaucho answered with his usual readiness: "It was sharpened in the service of my friends, señor."

"Keeping them amused?" smiled the general.

"A good lie often will outrun a horse, señor."

"Well," said Carlos Ducos, "I see that for such a keen Gaucho, and such a bright boy, and such—"

He turned and paused as he looked into the open, gentle, curious eyes of Tom Gloster, which seemed to dwell upon him with the kindly and vacant interest of an ox.

"And such an honest, honest man," said Ducos, "I must do something. But what can I do, I don't know, and how I shall go about trying to do it is a mystery, also. This scoundrel Christophoro Negro is followed by every man in the town. For all I know, the walls and the floors of the room will tell him what I have said to you!"

"All that he says is entirely true," said Tom Gloster. "There would be a great deal of danger, and he has only a few men with him. Now, señor, suppose I should ask you to stay here to help us, I should be ashamed. And if you wish to be free of any regret, ride on out of town, and we will do the best we can with the luck that remains behind."

At this the general opened his eyes in turn.

"Do you invite me to leave you alone?" he asked.

"He talks carelessly," said the Gaucho, with much anxiety. "His heart is not in what he says, this simple man! Señor General, we throw our lives into your hand!"

The general nodded. "But do you think, friend, that your request has half the weight with me that the señor's refusal has had? I can say now that I have known a man modest enough to die rather than ask for his life. And not of an enemy, at that! No, no! The more I talk with you, the deeper I walk into the danger. Negro has now become my enemy. You are my friends! Listen to me! I was Gaucho before I was general, and Heaven forget me, if ever a true Gaucho forgets his friends. Only— what shall we do? Let us think quickly, without pausing to sit down. I may be followed here. Who can tell? The seconds count. But here are several sets of brains which are not quite asleep!"

They stared, one upon the other.

"What shall it be?"

"What can it be," asked the Gaucho, at last, "except to fling ourselves upon fast horses and rush out of the town?"

Don Carlos half closed his eyes and then shrugged.

"Yes," he said, "we all can die, in the end; and it is better to be shot on the back of a horse than standing in the dust, I have no doubt."

He waited for another moment.

"In a half-hour, then," said the general, and turned with his long, light, sudden step to the door. This he cast noiselessly open. It struck some obstacle. There was a muttered exclamation. And the general leaped into the dark like a tiger; like a tiger, too, he came back, bearing with him a frightened man who shrank and turned pale before them.

It was the waiter whose services had been compelled by Ramon for the supper.

"He was crouched beside the door, listening," said the general. "Oh, what a great mule I was not to have this door watched! Search him, amigos!"

They searched the waiter. They brought from his clothes three knives no less!—and a good, short-barreled revolver.

"We should cut his throat three times with his own knives," said Ramon. "Oh, dog!"

The waiter winced before him. Then he found his breath as he cringed away, saying:

"Gentlemen, I am very poor; I am very weak; I cannot stand against you; I have a wife, and I have four small children! For the love of Heaven, think of that!"

"Who hired you, man, to kneel there beside the door?"

"Hired me? Señor, I beg you to forgive! It is a child's curiosity that drove me. My heart bleeds, when I think what a fool I am. I could not help pressing my ear to the keyhole when I passed but now."

"Liar!" said Ramon. "Who paid you to come here? Who told you to do it, since they pay such dogs with scraps of food and kicks, and with nothing better."

"No one!" protested the trembling man. "No one, gentlemen, for who is there that would have told me to do such a thing?"

"You!" said the general tersely to Ramon. "Stab the traitor to the heart!"

The knife flashed in the hand of Ramon before Tom Gloster in his horror could protest; and the waiter slumped helplessly to his knees.

"Mercy!" he groaned. "It is true that Señor Negro sent me, and now he will cut me to pieces because I have told."

25. Into The Tunnel

THE POOR MAN was in a frenzy of fear. They sat him in a chair and stood about him. He swung his hands and groaned in his abject misery.

It was Ramon who said: "Has the clever Negro surrounded the entire place?"

"He? Oh, noble gentlemen, how could such a man as he forget anything?"

"But there are many ways out from a place like this. Think of them! If you are found with us, friend—"

The waiter groaned again. He was panting with desperate anguish. But he said: "Everything is watched, even the passage beneath the stable."

"What passage is that?"

"It is the old passage through the foundation, where they started to dig the cellar. He has two good men, even there!"

The general demanded how one could get at this place, and the other replied that it could easily be done—if they wished to put their heads into a trap.

"But there is a passage clear through?"

"Aye, señor."

"If the passage was blocked, we might blow out the cork, friends?" suggested Ducos.

They agreed eagerly enough. And their plans were laid suddenly.

Word was sent to the general's men that they were to make a complaint as to the food and the accommodations in the *fonda*, and make the complaint in the bitterest language, saying that the general wished to leave at once. Then they should go to the stable and there take

129

out the horses of the general's *tropilla*. That done, they must bring the horses out of the patio and set all in readiness. At the sound of a pair of shots in rapid succession, they were to gallop the whole troop around the rear of the big *fonda*, and sweeping down the street behind it, they would, it was hoped, find Ducos and the others in waiting, if they had succeeded in forcing their way through the underground passage.

They started immediately on the execution of the scheme. The way to the opening of the passage was fairly public, lying off a corner of the patio, but, moving in a loose group, they swiftly made for it. The general himself, on second thought, determined to take charge of his own troop. Whatever Negro and his men might suspect, there was little to make them actually attack Ducos except that he had been seen to exchange a few words with the party of fugitives, and such a presumption would have been too general to lead them to action unless they actually saw the general and his men assisting in an escape.

According to the waiter, every one in the town now knew that the three were persons wanted by Negro, and that a price was upon their heads—a price larger for Tom Gloster than for the other two combined.

"He is the thorn," said the Gaucho, grinning, "and after he is trimmed off Negro is pretty sure of picking the flower!"

And he nodded significantly at the boy.

Ducos was gone. The waiter and the boy, Ramon and Tom Gloster, started for the passage, and soon found their way into it. It led down as into a cellar, a wide and roomy space, damp and cool. The waiter fumbled for a door and found it; when it was opened, they saw a long passage before them, and at the farther end of it, a gleam of light which flared a little, and then died slowly away—the light of a burning and dying match.

They whispered for a moment together. If a brighter light were cast down the tunnel, it would fall upon them and make them easy targets. However, they had hope, and they moved forward. And if they had no hope, despair would have driven them onward; for this was their only escape.

They gave the waiter into the charge of the boy, who

marched him ahead with a bare knife held to his back. That left Ramon and Tom Gloster to handle the guards at the other end of the tunnel.

So they slipped on. It was not hard to progress in silence, for the footing was damp soil, without gravel in it. They passed on close to the point where they had seen the light, and here Tom and Ramon went forward together.

They moved very slowly, now. It had been agreed that they would use revolvers on the stop-gaps, but, if possible, they were to strike to avoid noise, by beating the watchers on the head with the butts of the guns.

Presently they turned a slight bend, and then they heard the murmur of voices.

Said one: "Will you sing, Pedro?"

"Ha, señor! Is that a thing to do in such a place and such a time as this?"

"You dog," said the other, "are you to tell me my duty and what is fitting here?"

"It is true that that does not seem wise," agreed the other in a subdued tone. "However, señor, the man who makes noise unwisely, is often lighting a lamp by which another can shoot him."

"Do you think that they ever can get into this place?"

"How should we tell? Señor Negro feared that they might or he would never have put us here."

"How could they learn? From the general?"

"No, he could hardly know about it."

"From the people of the hotel?"

"No one would be fool enough to help the three after Señor Negro warned us against them."

"How does Negro have such power in this place?"

"He owns the *fonda*, señor, and his men are often about the town."

"Is he well liked here?"

There was a brief silence.

"I have no doubt that he is, Señor Guzman."

At this, Tom Gloster started.

Guzman again! Very strange it was that his trail was crossing and recrossing so often the men who had endangered him at the beginning of the work.

"Sing, sing!" said Guzman.

"In fact, señor, I do not find a song in my throat."

"You're afraid, then?"

"You are no coward, man!"

"A little fear, perhaps, will keep a man's eyes open."

"I have a knife for anyone who says so. However, one can be excused for feeling just a trace of fear at such a time."

"How? When we sit here in perfect safety with guns in our hands?"

"But this man for whom we are hunting has done terrible things, they say."

"He's like any other man—made of flesh and blood and bone!"

"But Señor Negro could do nothing with him. Is it true that he has crossed the ocean and then the mountains in spite of Negro and all of Negro's men?"

"That? That's a lie, of course. Or if Negro has let him come, it's only to bag him more safely."

"But to come here and to bring the boy with him! That is something foolish, señor."

"Of course."

"Could it be that he does not know that this is the special town of Negro?"

"Perhaps. That must be it."

Being ignorant, then, it would be a vast thing, would it not, if he were to get away again—and even take the boy with him?"

"You talk like a fool!" said Guzman with severity. "Light a match for me; I have none!"

The match scratched, and as the flare spurted, blue and trembling, Tom and Ramon rushed upon the pair. It was Guzman who appeared before Tom, and the barrel of the Colt rang hollow and loud upon the skull of the rascal. Ramon, however, missed his first stroke, and the man fled with a cry. After him poured the others. They heard the steps of the fugitive clatter upstairs. They bounded up them in turn. A door was dashed open and a light gleamed beyond. Then the door was hurled shut, and a bolt clanked. In the distance, they heard the guard shouting wildly for help.

So neatly were they trapped. Ramon, groaning out a

prayer to his favorite St. Christopher, hurled himself against the door. It flung him back.

"Dio, Dio!" cried the Gaucho. "The door is built all of iron, and I have broken my shoulder on it for nothing!"

"Room, room!" panted Tom Gloster.

He laid hold upon the inner ledge; he wrenched. Nothing gave. He leaned and slowly exerted all his enormous strength, and, behold, the frame of the door was rent suddenly away! Tom staggered to one side, dizzy with his own effort, and through the doorway pushed the other three.

Yonder was the guard, still shouting for help. And down the street came answering voices. So Tom raised his revolver and fired twice. Then they moved forward and found the outer door of the building into which they had climbed from the tunnel. However, this was a simple matter of smashing the lock with a bullet, and with the discharge, the door could be jerked open.

They stood on the slightly recessed threshold of the abandoned house. A block away the guard was still running, still shouting for help, and the answer was coming. For half a dozen men appeared low down in the lane, swarming rapidly forward toward them.

In the *fonda* behind them, bedlam seemed to have broken loose. Voices yelled; twice a gun exploded.

But now from the left there was a swift volleying of hoofs, and horsemen darted into view. The men of Negro, or the men of the general?

Suddenly they could see the general himself riding well to the front. He shouted. They ran out into the street, and in another instant they had tumbled into the saddles.

They bore straight on. The line of shadowy men with guns split to either side, afraid of such a charge. One or two guns were fired at random after them, doing no harm, and so they bolted into the main street and out upon the open pampas. Behind them, riding furiously, came the pursuit. But the general did not seem worried.

"Hai!" he cried like a boy. "This is better than winning a battle! I have made all Argentina laugh at Negro. That is enough to let one die happy."

26. Hard Times Ahead

THEY MAINTAINED a stiff pace; the night was pressing down from the sky; and now they no longer could see the pursuit; only when their own horses went through a soft spot in the sandy soil, they could hear the beating of hoofs behind them. General Ducos, in the greatest of spirits, drew his horse alongside that of Tom Gloster. He declared that it was the pleasantest evening he ever had spent, and that he would remember it to the end of his days. To assist Tom Gloster and his companions to such a memory, he wished them, with the most cordial good will, to retain the horses upon which they rode. And, when Tom resisted, the general became all the more firm. The horses they must take, to replace the mules which they had lost in the town, and which the villain Negro would doubtless appropriate and sell at auction! And when Tom insisted that this loss was no fault of the general's, Ducos laughed, and assured him that he had to vindicate the good name of Argentina, contrasted with the scoundrelism of such a fellow as Negro.

They rode on at a fine rate for nearly an hour, and still the significant, soft thunder followed them across the pampas, though drawn somewhat away toward the rear. Then Carlos Ducos suggested to Tom that the best plan, would be for the three fugitives to draw off to the right, following their natural course, while he and the main body of his men drove straight ahead for if they went softly on and made little noise, Tom and his two would hardly be noticed. This suggested maneuver appeared to Tom to smack of desertion, but at the thought, Ducos laughed loudly. He was not riding on into a strange land, he assured Tom Gloster, and if Negro and his followers persisted in the hunt very long, they would find themselves riding directly into a hornet's nest.

At full gallop, they shook hands; the thanks of Tom and his friends were hardly listened to; and the party split in two, Tom and David and Ramon turning off to the right in a depression which had once been a laguna, while the others pushed straight ahead through the night.

In the hollow of the laguna, the three heard the hoof-beats of the gallant general and his companions diminishing; and the crashing sound of Negro and his followers pouring after presently swelled, shook the earth, and rushed on in turn, while a puff of wind blew to the listeners a taste of the acrid dust they raised. Then they drew out of the hollow and went leisurely on their way.

Tom was so filled with emotion that he knew not what to do, and he knew not what to say. It was his first taste of great generosity on the part of any man, and the sense of it was new and wonderfully sweet to him. But Ramon declared that this was as nothing, and that every Gaucho was, in a manner, a true knight, ready to help the distressed.

"Yes," said the cynical David, "either help the distressed, or else help them out of the world with a cut throat."

"Ha?" said Ramon. "This comes of living in the houses of the rich men; here every master is envied and here every servant is suspected. For my part, give me a big estancia, where my horse and I can lose ourselves and where the poor wretch of an owner has more debts than hard cash. There is always better feeding and better fun on a place of that sort; and there you learn how to become a good-hearted man."

"Thank Heaven that we met a man from such a good estancia when we met you, Ramon!"

"If I were your father, I would have whipped you for talking with a double tongue," said Ramon calmly. "But since I am only Ramon, I cannot do that!"

"Hush, hush!" pleaded Tom Gloster. "Let us all be friends. There will be trouble enough for us from others, without making trouble of our own!"

"That may be true," said Ramon, "but let us sharpen

our tongues a little, now and then; otherwise, life becomes like plenty of good meat, with no salt whatever!"

This singular man was so full of contrasts and opposites that Tom never knew how to take him; but now they were fairly embarked upon the broad pampas, and they voyaged on day after day with little worth report. For two days, they made it a point to avoid the houses of ranchers which they saw. After that, feeling that they must have passed beyond the immediate sphere of Negro, they made free at every estancia that lay in their path.

No questions ever were asked of them. They would dismount at a low, stumbling, wretched-looking building of mud and corrugated iron, and putting their horses into the sheds, they would give them a hearty feed. Then passing into the kitchen they would chat for a time with the people they found there. There was always more or less of a crowd. For on every estancia it seemed necessary that the owner give shelter to a number of worthless, idle relatives who were good for nothing except to draw a knife in a time of fighting. Besides the relatives and their friends, there were idlers of another sort, men who attached themselves to the estancia as a sort of voluntary guard. There men rode out and worked the cattle when they felt like it. Otherwise, they remained lolling about the house, or else they would go off on wild rides and hunts. In addition to these rascals, there were corps of hardworking peons, or Gauchos, usually smaller in number than either of the other two divisions.

The coming and going of strangers was hardly noticed in these swirling pools of changing life, and Tom lived well enough for food on the trip across the plains. In other respects, life was not so pleasant, especially at night. Never had he known such hosts of fleas, or such mighty biters, and worst of all was the terrible *vinchuca* which steals a man's blood without pain, and only after departure makes the wound burn with poison. The nights, therefore, were unpleasant at first, but afterward he grew accustomed to such troubles.

They passed far away from the mountains. They were lost in a vast plain which made even the big stretches of the Western American cattle range seem small. For, through this green sea, they plowed their way endlessly, day after day, and always there was the same horizon, north, and south, and east, and west, unless they sighted an estancia. And once they went for three long days of journeying without sighting a human habitation of any kind. It would have been monotonous past words to tell of such an expedition, but Tom felt that it was by no means monotonous to actually ride in it. In this vastness of the prairie, he felt the curve of the earth pressing him up into the sky; and he felt, moreover, the immense strength of Nature, which dressed this hugeness in grass, and fed millions of cattle upon it. And the old humor of humiliation and self-contempt grew in Tom every day.

His companions spent most of their time talking together. They were usually busy sharpening their already deadly tongues. They rode side by side, paying little attention to Tom. Sometimes they forged on before him, and sometimes they dropped behind. Sometimes he could hear their voices subdued, mocking, and he was sure that they were talking about him. At such times, his face would burn.

And again they were talking of far other things, forgetting him as completely as they would have forgotten a distant planet in the sky, and the heart of Tom Gloster was wounded. He had never been able to press behind the veil that hung before the mind of young David Parry; he still could not pass it. He could not tell whether the youngster looked upon him simply as a tool of some value in getting back to his home, or whether there was in addition a feeling of actual devotion and friendship. Often he asked himself these questions, and almost regretted, in his bitterness, that he had ever taken this wild attempt upon his shoulders.

Then came a day when the Gaucho turned his horse a little to the side and announced that he had made out the outlines of an estancia in the distance, but the boy refused to go on to it.

"We've come into the land where people know my father," said he. "I've been at that estancia myself. I know half of the men on it, and they know me."

"Why shouldn't we go there, then, and have a good cup of maté to begin the day right?"

"To the mischief with you and your maté," cried

137

David. "You can't breathe and you can't think without it. Isn't that true?"

"But where's the harm?"

"You'll die one of these days for the sake of it. I tell you this: if we show ourselves at one of these estancias, now, surely within five minutes of our coming, a man on a fast horse will leave and ride like mad to get to my father's house."

"Why should he do that, unless he's your enemy?"

"Not that he is my enemy. But everyone knows that my stepmother hates me and that she sent me away. If I came back, especially like this, ragged and tattered, what would they say? Why, they would say little, but they would rush off at once and tell her everything and get the reward from her which they know they can expect. Oh, she has an open hand for those people who please her! And her soul is no bigger than the point of a knife, if you happen to make her angry!"

To Tom, these remarks, and others which he had heard before, had built up the picture of a demon in female form.

"How could your father have married such a woman?" he asked in amazement.

At this, without waiting for the boy to speak, the Gaucho broke out bitterly: "Because there's a streak of fool in him! To marry once is duty, twice is folly, and three times is madness, they say! He has married a second time—he has married a pretty face! Now do you hear me? I also married twice. The first time I married a fool; the second time I married a pretty face. Why should men marry a face? There are not more than five years of beauty in it, at the most. But still men follow the leader down the same trail of fools. Ha! If I had the making of marriages, I would have men draw wives by lot. Then afterward they could blame their luck and not themselves. Women? The witches!"

He added:

"Not that I mean this about your stepmother, señor, who is a great lady, of course, and much above my criticism. Still, a man knows what he knows about life! I would bet ten dollars to one that it was for her face he married her!"

"There's no doubt of that," said the boy. "But let's forget her. The one thing for us to be thinking about is in what manner we can come close to the house and see my father. And now my stepmother is sure to have heard word from Negro that I have slipped through his hands. Perhaps Negro himself will be there to try to trap us at the last! Of course there is nothing really sure, except that our hardest time is the time that's just in front of us, friends."

27. Ramon's Red Wrist

WHEN THEY came in view of the Parry place, far off, it looked to them like a cloud on the horizon. When they came closer, they could make out a host of great trees which completely hid the house; but they could see an extensive garden spreading out beyond the trees which furnished the shade and coolness for the house itself. And these gardens, in turn, were furnished with hedges, and with lines of brush, and with patches of big shrubbery. On two sides of the house artificial lakes, fed by norias, made pleasant streaks of silver in the green landscape.

Young David showed great emotion.

He left the Gaucho and turned to Tom Gloster, in this time.

"Look, look!" cried he. "There it is at last! I thought that I'd never see it again, but you've brought me back to it. You and Ramon, Heaven bless you! I think that there's luck in it. I think that we're all going to be rich —all the three of us! And there it is!"

He added, fiercely: "Think of what's going on inside of her heart now, Tom! Think of what's inside her! She knows that we're voyaging closer and closer. She doesn't know when we'll arrive. She doesn't dare let my father know a word. But all the while, she's straining every nerve to get me! Oh, what torment it must be for her! She hates me more than ever, if that's possible!"

"Is there nothing good about her?" asked Tom, curious.

"Isn't it good for a woman to be beautiful and brave?" asked the boy.

"Yes, of course."

"Then she has that much good about her. Oh, she can be kind, too! There's Alicia."

"Who is she?"

"That's a cousin of my stepmother's. She is pretty young. You see how that could be, that my stepmother would be kind to her? Alicia's helpless. There's nothing for her except what she's given by her cousin. So my stepmother is mighty fond of her."

"Is she an orphan?" asked Tom, touched by this suggestion.

"Alicia? No—I mean to say, yes, of course she is! But she's not the kind that you'd call an orphan. I mean, there's nothing pitiful about Alicia, any more than there is in a bull terrier. She's a terror, all right."

"Alicia?"

"Yes."

"She's like your stepmother, then?"

"You bet she is, when it comes to temper and smartness. No, she's not the same, either. Alicia's straight, and sporting. You should've heard her stand up for me against her cousin."

"Did that make your stepmother want to turn her out of the house?"

"Of course it did, and she said she would turn her out of the house; and Alicia said that she wouldn't wait to be asked twice. She walked right out and started across the fields. Think of that! With the fields full of cattle that would kill any man that they found off a horse! But Alicia is like that. She's all fire and does her thinking before she goes to bed, you might say.

"My stepmother had to run out after her and beg her to come back. And I'll wager that she didn't insult Alicia

140

again for a few weeks. Yes, sir, they're like a pair of tigresses, when they go after each other!"

It gave Tom a most extraordinarily clear picture of a disturbed household, when he heard the boy talk like this.

"Why did she stand up for you?"

"Because she's so square and sporting. She doesn't like to see the under dog downed, you might say."

"Well, that's a fine thing," said Tom.

"Fine? She's full of fineness. But—Heaven help the man who tries to marry her! She'd run an emperor like a lap dog. She'd have to have a couple of kingdoms to keep her busy, I suppose. You never could imagine such a girl!"

"Ha?" said Ramon. "You have described the wife for a Gaucho!"

"Have I?"

The boy laughed.

But they had serious thoughts on their hands, now. For they had to plan how they should approach the house. Evening was gathering, and that would permit them to come up fairly near; but it was almost certain that a close guard would have been posted around the place by the woman. It would take the cleverest of maneuvering to pass the posted men.

Ramon offered to attempt to scout the house, as soon as the darkness grew a little more complete, and when that time came he went forward on foot, having first shaken hands with his companions, silently.

Now they sat down to wait in the dark, easing the cinches of their saddles, full of suspense. They had come up to the den of the lion, and the bearding of the beast had begun.

They waited in this gloomy manner for well over an hour, when they began to be troubled.

"By this time," said the boy, "he's had time enough to sneak all around the house and come back again. He could have counted the wine bottles in the cellar, by this time! And still he doesn't show up. Confound him, what's he doing?"

He hardly had finished this, when Ramon came hurrying back to them. Even Ramon was excited. Trusting to the shelter of bushes behind which they crouched, he ventured to light a cigarette, as he said:

"I have seen everything. I can lead you on the way as easily as to walk down a safe road!"

"What?"

"I mean what I say. I have seen your father sitting in the library. The windows were open. I saw him clearly."

"At last!" breathed David. "Tell me—what was he like?"

"A big man, very big. Bigger than our friend here, perhaps. He wears a clipped mustache that sticks out like a horsebrush in front, except that the bristles are kept short—"

"That's he!" said David. "You saw him—and he didn't see you?"

"How could he see me? He was in a lighted room, and I was like a cat, looking in through the window."

Ramon laughed in his triumph; he had talked so hard and fast that he forgot the cigarette, and now he lighted another match.

"Don't do that! You make as much light as a bonfire!" warned David.

The match flared, nevertheless, and Tom Gloster saw a streak of fresh red on the wrist of the Gaucho's coat.

Ramon began to smoke with noisy inhalations, so deep was his content.

"It is a great house!" said Ramon. "It is worth riding across the mountains and the plains to bring a man to such a house. You won't forget me, when all the place is yours, friend?"

"Of course not," said David. "But now tell us how we can come closer."

"Why, it's an easy way. You come up to a place where there are three hedges running in toward—"

"Of course I remember that!"

"Well, there are plenty of men watching the gap between the hedges, but the second and third hedges are really very big."

"Yes."

"Like trees."

"Yes, they are."

"Very well, I tell you that the brush comes down almost

142

to the ground on each side of those great hedges, but under the branches there is plenty of room to crawl along. That is something that I learned when I was a boy! I crawled almost straight up to the house. Then I came out, and I was under the window of the library, exactly as I told you."

"That is exactly where you would be, of course!" exclaimed David.

"Very well. I looked in at your father, and then I turned around and went back under the hedge and came back."

"And that took you two hours?"

"It isn't that long."

"Very near!"

"Of course, I didn't come straight back. I stopped under the hedge when I came close to where the men were. I wanted to find out what I could about them from their talk."

"You overheard them, Ramon?"

"I? Of course! They were not five feet away, at one time."

"Who were they?"

"One was Felipe Guzman."

"What? I smashed his skull, surely," said Tom Gloster, in amazement. "How could he be here?"

"That I don't know, except that his skull was not smashed at all. And there he is taking charge of the watch, at that point where I went into the garden."

"What did he and the others have to say?"

"A great deal about Señor Gloster, whom they say is a demon!"

"Ha? He is, for them," said David.

"Of course he is! He shall be more demon to them all, before the night is over! You will help, Ramon. You can swear that they tried to hire you to murder us, or lead us into the murder trap!"

"Yes, I can swear that. That is one thing that they are afraid of?"

"How do you know?"

"I heard them talk about it, and say that if they could get me away from you, you would have very little proof against her."

"But we have you with us?"

"Aye, Heaven be praised!"

"You have been very brave, and you have had great luck, Ramon," said Tom Gloster in admiration. "You had no trouble at all getting in or out?"

"No."

"Not a bit?"

"Oh, they're keeping a good sharp watch, but this Ramon is not a fool, even if your grandfather tells you so! I slipped through them and had not the slightest trouble in the world."

"I am surprised," said Tom Gloster.

"Thank you," said the Gaucho. "But I have done harder things than that!"

"But how," said Gloster, "did you get the blood on your wrist?"

28. With Kind Wishes

THERE WAS not much pause, after this question. There was hardly a half second's delay on the part of the Gaucho; but at some times the least delay is like the gap of an hour.

"Oh, as for that—Why, which wrist do you mean?"

"The left wrist," said Tom.

Ramon started to his feet.

"That? Oh, well, that is nothing. I scratched it on a thorn, going in."

Young David said, in a voice like the clang of a steel trap; "Why did you ask which wrist? What's wrong with the other wrist, Ramon?"

"And why do you ask?"

Ramon drew back a little.

Said Tom Gloster quietly: "Will you let us see your wrists, Ramon?"

"I? I?" said the Gaucho. "And why should I?"

"Because," said Tom, "I have this gun looking at you, and at this distance it could not fail to kill you, my friend."

From the throat of Ramon came a sort of strangled noise. After that, they could hear him panting, as though he had been running with the most violent effort.

He delayed when Tom told him to come nearer; but by this time, young David was behind his back, muttering: "Heaven forgive him! He's betrayed us a second time!"

"I?" said Ramon. "I have betrayed you? May I fall dead this instant if that is true! I betrayed you? *Dio!* Am I not here? Am I not ready to lead you safely to the house?"

"Safely into some sort of trap," said the boy.

"What do you want? You drive me mad with such talk!" said Ramon.

"Hold out your hands!" ordered Tom.

Slowly the Gaucho obeyed.

"Put your gun against his back and shoot if he stirs," directed Tom.

Then he lighted a match and examined the wrists; around each there was a chafed circle, such as a strongly bound rope would leave; the skin had even been worn away on the left wrist, and a small flow of blood had followed.

Tom raised the match and let its light flicker into the eyes of Ramon. Then he dropped the match hastily, to put out that miserable picture of ugly guilt.

"Very well," said Tom, "and you've done this again, Ramon? Ah, man, did you forget what we have done together, the three of us?"

Ramon did not answer.

"They caught you in the garden," said Tom. "They offered you money. And you sold us again, as you sold us before!"

Ramon did not speak.

Then David broke into a whispering fury.

"It's your right to send your knife into him, Tom. But let me do it! Let me have the finishing of him! Oh, the cowardly cur!"

"Hold on!" said Tom. "I don't know. I don't think that's the way."

"What is the way?" asked the boy.

"You're forgetting, David, that Ramon brought us safely through the mountains."

"You're forgetting, Tom, that you pulled the traitor up out of the danger of death!"

"Doesn't that pay him back?"

"Well—"

"You can't pay for services like that," protested Tom. "You have to understand how it is. You can pay money for food; and you can pay friendship with friendship; but you can't pay life for life. There's something left over, I think."

"That's a funny way to talk!" declared the boy.

"I suppose it is, and that you don't understand me."

"I do, sort of. But what's left over on his side?"

"Not much! I suppose, not much! I thought he was a good man," confessed Tom sadly.

"But what shall we do with him?"

"There is his horse. Let him ride away on it."

"Let him ride away!"

"Yes."

"To go and tell them everything?"

"He's told them everything, already."

"Tom, you don't mean to let the dog go?"

"I have to. I remember too many things—too many nights he's camped with us, too many times when he's been true to us. How could we have got out of the town through the tunnel, if Ramon had not been working for us and with us? Do you think that I could kill him, after that? I'd rather cut off my own arm than do such a thing!"

"But what can you mean by letting him go free to turn over to the other side?"

"That's what I'll have to do."

"I won't have it—it's plain craziness!" declared David.

"I'm sorry for that. Ramon, you are free to go."

"Am I free?" said the hoarse voice of Ramon.

"Not yet!" said David savagely.

"No, not yet," said Tom, "until I've paid you for the work."

"Paid him!" cried David.

146

"Light a match, Ramon," said Tom Gloster, "and I'll count out your money."

"Tom!"

"Well, David, what else can I do? He's done all that we asked him to do, and he's done a great deal more, as well!"

Ramon fumbled at a match. Then he groaned aloud.

"What is it?" asked Tom.

"Señor Gloster, good and noble señor!" said Ramon, and one great sob burst from his throat.

Then they heard sounds as of stifling, as the Gaucho choked back the emotion.

In the east appeared a pale patch of light; the moon was about to rise.

Then Gloster said: "I think that I understand, Ramon. After all, you work very hard; there is not much money in your life. Oh, I've seen other people do bad things for the sake of a few dollars!"

For he thought, with a sudden sadness, of his father, and his brothers, and his sisters, and the bitterness and the cruelty that reigned inside the walls of his father's house because they were all poor.

"I, who hung to the bush, sliding to death as the mule had died before me—I—I—Ah, even in Heaven there is no more mercy than in you, señor! Let me speak and tell you!"

And he told the story, brokenly, stammering, and then composing himself to a greater steadiness so that the whole wretched narrative was made complete.

He had, in fact, attempted to get to the house in exactly the manner that he had described to his companions, stealing along underneath the hedge; there had been treason in his thoughts; he was content to die, as he had thought, rather than to have betrayed his friends for a single moment. Instead, his heart was filled with devotion to them and to the cause of young David.

But suddenly he had been trapped by many hands. He was dragged out, stifled, and carried to a little distance, where a light was flashed in his face, and he saw Christophoro Negro himself standing before him, he whom Tom and the boy had known as Christopher Black.

"I thought that it was not Gloster," said Negro, in the

bitterest disappointment. "There would have been no holding him with mere hands. However, we have the fox of the lot. We perhaps can get the lion and the cub afterward through him."

Then he had offered the Gaucho his choice between life and treachery, on the one hand, together with a pocket full of gold; and on the other hand, death immediate and horrible. And the Gaucho had asked for death.

But Negro was not content with mere words. He counted out a little pyramid of gold and held it in both hands before the poor fellow. And Ramon said that his eyes were dizzied and that his heart turned sick with hunger after that golden glittering. So he was seduced from his honor and from his duty and agreed that he would do his best to bring the other two into the trap. Even then, however, he stipulated that the lives of the pair should not be in any danger, and Negro, very willingly, had sworn solemnly that he would not injure a hair of the heads of the others.

"And did you believe what he swore?" asked David coldly.

"Alas," said Ramon, "I believed what I wished to believe, I fear! I saw the gold. Heaven forgive me, as you have forgiven me, señor. But how shall I forgive myself?"

Said David, as cold as ever: "What were you to do?"

"I am to bring you straight back to the house, just as I went myself; I am to go first, as if to show the way. The boy is to come next, and Señor Gloster is to come last, if I can arrange it so."

"And they?"

"They are bringing in their men from the farther side of the house and getting ready for a dreadful battle, for they fear Señor Gloster as if he were ten fighting men!"

"Do you see, Tom?" demanded David eagerly. "Something might still come out of it. Suppose what he says is true, and that really the men have been gathered to this side—we might slip in from the other side to the house!"

"And if it is not true?" asked Tom.

"Aye, that is the trouble! Or suppose they've left a good number still on the other side of the house?"

"You can stay here with Ramon, then, David. I shall

go first and see if the land is clear on the far side of the house. Is that a good plan?"

"You'll go alone, Tom?"

"It's better to do that."

"And I'll stay here and watch Ramon. That will be the only way we can work. Oh, Tom, go softly as a cat! Everything hangs on you, now!"

"Send your good wishes with me," said Tom, in his gentle voice.

"Do you think that wishes will help you, Tom?" asked the boy in his sharp way.

"I believe in them," said Tom. "Heaven gives a sort of strength to kind thoughts, I think."

29. *Alicia, Jerry And The Moon*

UNTIL THE rising moon stood behind his back, Tom Gloster circled eastward of the house. The landscape rapidly grew brighter and the moon climbed higher, and presently he could pick his way forward to the side of the big hedge that marked the outer boundary of the garden on this side. Beyond the hedge rose the great trees; and beyond the trees he had a glimpse of the long face of the house, turning white in the moonshine.

There was no difficulty about entering. It was an old hedge, and had grown up from the ground to such an extent that one could creep through it at many points. Tom crouched and looked through, to see a stretch of lawn, half lost in black shadow, half turned to silver by the moon. He was about to venture through, therefore, when he heard the slightest of brushing sounds, and he looked back in time to see the black silhouette of a man rising out of the very ground, as it were, and not twenty steps behind him.

Half turning, he gripped his revolver and waited breathlessly, as the man loomed bigger above him, the moon hanging like a great round ball of gold on his broad shoulder. But he went straight past Tom Gloster, and stooping, he worked through a gap in the hedge and crossed the lawn beyond.

He moved with the utmost caution, all this time, taking a good many minutes to pass from point to point, and often pausing to listen and look with the utmost intentness. He disappeared presently into a thick clump of brush which rustled about him for a moment, and then left the garden to silence and the moon. Almost immediately after this, two armed men appeared at the farther end of the strip of lawn. They walked slowly across it, their rifles lying in the crooks of their arms; and from their bearing it was plain that they were sentinels on watch. These, too, passed out of sight, and Gloster at once crossed to the bushes through which the other stranger had gone. He was filled with wonder, for it was apparent that the man had moved in much fear, and, therefore, as one who dreaded the very guards against whom Gloster was on the watch.

Cautiously stepping through this arbor of bushes, Tom came out to the edge of a small clearing with lawn about it, and in the center of this was a little summerhouse, all open at the sides, except for light wooden pillars which supported the roof, and vines which twisted to the top and showered down again over the roof's edges. He had almost stepped from the trees, when he heard voices close by; and then he made out in the shadow beneath the summerhouse a man and a woman talking. They left the shadow and came slowly across the lawn.

"I tried twice," said the man. "I tried twice, and each time I nearly stumbled onto some men carrying guns. What's going on about here, Alicia?"

"Shall I tell you, Jerry?"

"Yes, if you can!"

"You'll think that it's only a legend, of course. It doesn't sound real."

"They have the place guarded like a fort!"

"It's David, it seems."

"You mean the brat of a boy?"

"Why, you never liked poor David?"

"I don't see why you pity him. He's a hawk, that boy. He always made me uneasy."

"Of course he makes people uneasy. He grew up too young, that's all. He had to grow up. Poor David!"

"But what of him? I thought that he'd been shuffled out of the picture."

"He was. Shuffled completely out of the picture. I don't know exactly what's happened. You know that Beatrice doesn't confide her schemes to me. But it's plain that David didn't arrive at the ranch in America to which he was sent. We've had a wire to that effect, I think. I don't know. But one hears whispers and rumors. There are so many men around the house, and all of them appear to know something."

"What do they say?"

"A fairy tale."

"About David? I could believe anything about him!"

"Well, try to believe this: That while he and his poor guard were going through the Western range country, they were tackled by a whole crowd of Beatrice's hired gun fighters—"

"How can you say a thing so blandly about your own cousin, Alicia?"

"I'm not saying it. I'm telling you what rumor reports."

"Then were they both bagged and killed?"

"That's the point. The Gaucho was killed. David got away. They rode in a mob after him, and when they were about to ride him down, a hero rode out of the woods and turned them back."

"Well, it's possible that he might have had that luck."

"But listen to this: The hero then grows tremendously interested in David and actually takes him off the range and starts to bring him back home."

"Do you mean that?"

"I'm telling you the story. Of course, I don't know what to believe. The story is that when Beatrice heard that her little murder plot had failed, she sent for the wildest, most intelligent, most terrible, most relentless

151

monster of a man that ever walked outside of a detective story. I mean Christophoro Negro, of course."

"I thought his real name was Black?"

"Perhaps. They call him Negro, down here."

"And that fiend was sent after the boy? Then David's dead and at rest at last!"

"Hold on, Jerry! You haven't come to the real point of the story, which appears to be that the strange young hero from the Western woods—Thomas Gloster is his name, I think—in spite of Negro, and all Negro's hired men, and Negro's wicked wits—well, in spite of all those things, Thomas Gloster, if you please, brought David to San Francisco, and then on a ship straight down to Valparaiso! And Negro on that same ship, mind you, all the time!"

Jerry seemed incapable of speech.

"And then," went on the girl, "this legend has it that Negro tried to stop them in the mountains and bribed their guide—and failed! And that then, by bad luck, they actually rode into Negro's own town—the place where he's king, I mean to say."

"Great Scott! What happened then?"

"They just rode out again, Jerry! No, it was better than that! They got that famous murderer and horse thief and good fellow, General Carlos Ducos, to give them a helping hand. And away they went for home!"

"You talk as if you actually believed all this myth!"

"Well, I know that Beatrice has been raging for days. I know that she's growing pale and thin. Everyone can see the anxious look in her eyes—everyone except David's father."

"He never could see anything, of course."

"Not when Beatrice wants to hypnotize him. But she's afraid, now."

"What will happen if David gets back?"

"He'll have such a yarn to tell of attempted murder that even his father will have to rub his eyes and wake up. That's what Beatrice must fear."

"Then her hopes for her own boy will be ruined?"

"Yes, of course."

"Is she such a monster? And yet you're fond of her!"

They were moving slowly across the lawn, still, coming closer and closer.

And now the girl paused and raised her head a little so that the moon gleamed on her features, and Gloster could see a lovely, eager face.

"I'm fond of her. She can always be pleasant. Besides, she's kind to me; how else would I live except for Beatrice?" "That's what I came to talk to you about tonight," said Jerry. "I wanted to know if you wouldn't consider a change of address—for a while, at least."

She turned her head toward Jerry and watched him for a moment.

"I thought that you'd say something tonight," said she. "You still want to marry me, kind, gentle, patient, generous Jerry."

"I still want to marry you, my beautiful, terrible, cruel Alicia!"

"Why am I terrible?"

"Because you don't care about men. Because there's nothing that men can do to please you."

"A thousand things."

"Will you name one of them?"

"Go and find David and bring him to the house!"

"Do you mean that?"

"No, I don't. I don't want them to shoot at you, Jerry, because they shoot much too straight."

"Why do you care so much about David?"

"Because he's only a child; because he's having a cruelly unfair deal; and because that strange fellow from the West has done so much to bring him home."

"I'll go this moment to find what I can find. But if I try to bring him in, Mr. Parry will have me thrown off the premises again."

"That's another thing that you'd have to chance."

"I'm gone now. I mean to say—there's no use seriously asking you to pay any attention to what I really want, Alicia—yourself, that is to say?"

"Oh, I don't know! I hope that you'll still be patient for a while. I'm pretty young; I may grow older almost any day and give up this idea of mine about the sweeping, crashing, tremendous, overpowering emotion that ought to be love."

"I think you will change your mind about that. Then?"

"Then, of course, it would be you, Jerry. If you were poor, then I'd trust myself to marry you even now, and make you a good wife; but you're rich, and wealth tempts me terribly."

"I'll chuck the money into a laguna."

"You'll do nothing of the sort. You'd better go home."

"I've worked very hard to get in here tonight, Alicia."

"I know you have, and I thank you for coming. But I have to get back to the house. Beatrice sees everything; and what she doesn't see, she can guess at!"

30. *Tom Waits In Moonshine And Danger*

TURNING, Jerry went rapidly back through the bushes. Alicia, for a moment, looked after him, and then with a shrug of her shoulders, she glanced up to where the moon, climbing through the last branches of a tree in the east, now sailed forth alone into the heavens.

Tom Gloster stepped out of the shadow before her.

He had expected to speak as soon as he moved, but very often words came with difficulty to his tongue, and this was such an occasion. He simply stepped silently before her, and the girl, with a frightened gasp, whirled and bolted for the house.

If he could not find words readily, he could do the thing which was obvious. He must stop her, and he did. Speech could not halt her now; so Tom overtook her with a bound, caught her with one arm, and with his other hand he shut back the scream which was about to come from her lips.

She struggled with wonderful strength. There was no

feminine weakness in Alicia; she had all the snaky slipperiness that comes of muscles made lean and rubbery from athletic exercise. Tom Gloster tried to hold her gently; but it was vastly necessary that she should be kept from making a sound. So his hand pressed more firmly over her lips; and the arm which held her crushed her writhing body closer.

Suddenly she went limp. She hung like a rag over his arm, and Gloster grew dizzy with fear.

It was only for an instant. As suddenly as she wilted, she recovered again, breathing brokenly.

He said in a low, earnest, voice: "I didn't want to hurt you. I'm sorry! But I had to stop you and get you to listen. There was no one else who could do so much for us. I'm Tom Gloster—"

She, shuddering and white of face, grew suddenly more composed, more herself. The life which had been partly crushed and partly stifled and shocked out of her seemed to leap back along her veins with a single thrill,

"You are Tom Gloster?"

"Have I hurt you badly?"

He let her go with reluctant care, as though she might fall to the earth with the support of his hands removed; but suddenly she laughed into his frightened, crimsoned face.

"I don't know, just yet," said the girl. "When a python has hugged one, it takes time to recover the wits, you know. But I think I'm all right. You are Tom Gloster! But you're not a giant at all!"

"No, no," said Tom. "Of course I'm not."

She looked down at his hands and shuddered a little.

"But when my ribs were crackling and overlapping, I thought you were a giant."

"You've already heard a great many things about me that are not true," said Tom.

"Were you listening?"

"I couldn't help it very well," said he. "I didn't want to hear what you said to him. But there I was. And I was afraid to move for fear of being heard."

"You don't need to apologize."

She looked at him with a glance that could not stay still. Whether she was noting the shoulders, the long,

155

powerful arms, or the fine face and the quietly open eye of Tom Gloster, constantly her attention was stirring from one point to another, as though an extraordinary book had been opened before her, and she had only an instant in which to read it.

"And you heard only good things and things about yourself; you heard that you were a brilliant and wonderful person, Thomas Gloster!"

"I'm not wonderful," he assured her. His face burned. "I'm not brilliant. Not even my mother would ever say that. I'm very simple. I'm the simplest person in my family."

She stared at him a little. There seemed to be a great deal in that speech that interested her. She did not answer at once, but finally she said: "You've come here, then. It isn't a legend!"

"Not about the actual getting here."

"With David?"

"Oh, yes."

"Will you step out into the moonlight, Thomas Gloster?"

He obeyed. "I've never been called Thomas," said he in his simple way.

The moon shone full in his face; she saw its lines of dignity and strength; and most of all, she looked into the fathomless gentleness and peace of his eyes.

"It's not a fable! You've brought him here! And everything is true!"

"No, it's not all true. That I got here, yes. But it wasn't wonderful work on my part. You know, it may look a good deal, but taking things one at a time, it wasn't wonderful at all!"

"Was Christophoro Negro after you?"

"Yes, he was."

"Even on the ship with you?"

"He was disguised," said Tom Gloster, "so that I didn't know him. He was disguised to look like an elderly man, you see. He even had mustaches, and all!"

He smiled a little, in admiration of the supernatural cleverness of the false Colonel Bridges. But the girl said, "If Negro was making trouble for you, then it has been a miracle that you've come through! Heaven forgive Beatrice Parry for the harm she's tried to do you!"

Then she added: "Now tell me what I can do to help you!"

"You are a friend of hers?" said he, with a peculiar accent upon the last word. Because, during so many weeks of strain, "she" or "her" had been a ruling topic in his talk and in his thoughts.

"I'm her guest in the house."

"I can't ask you to do much," said he. "I only wondered if you'd arrange so that I could get to see Mr. Parry?"

"Of course I can arrange it." She went on: "There'd be no good in getting you to speak to him in the house. They're watching him. They'd shoot you down, surely. But perhaps I can get him out for a walk."

"Have I the right to ask you to work against your friend?"

"Stuff!" said Alicia. "She knows what I think of her schemes. Good heavens, you are Thomas Gloster!"

The idea continually dazzled and amazed her, as it appeared.

Then: "And the others?" she asked. "The fellows who are supposed to be guarding the house, this evening?"

"They're on the other side of the place. They caught a man we sent in to look over the ground. They bribed him to betray us, and now they're patiently waiting for us to walk into the trap."

Alicia laughed softly, delighted.

"And while they angle for you there, you slip up behind their backs and—Oh, Christophoro Negro, what a great fool you'll look in the eyes of the world, after this!"

"He may take us at any time," said he. "He's dangerous. Only, we've had luck against him. But can you tell me why David's father lets his house be guarded by all these men?"

"He doesn't know that his house is being guarded. He's the blindest man in the world, and his wife knows just how to keep him in the dark, you see."

He nodded.

"But can you bring him out?"

"I suppose so. I hope so. I'm going to try—unless

157

Beatrice Parry begins to suspect what I'm trying to do."

"I'll wait here by the summerhouse," said he. "Is that right?"

"That's right, of course. I hope I won't be long!"

She started away from him, and then turned her head to say: "You won't be nervous, waiting here?"

She did not wait for his answer, but laughed softly, assured. Certainly she had no doubt that this man was above fear of any kind.

She left Tom Gloster as bewildered as one who has seen a star shower glaring and dissolving in the sky. He remained close among the trees, looking dumbly about him. For still it seemed to Tom that ghosts were walking —where he had first seen Jerry and the girl, and where they had moved across the lawn, and yonder where he himself had stepped too brutally into the picture.

He raised the hand which had stifled her outcry, and looked at it, dazed, unable to understand what he had done. All at once Tom Gloster began to tremble, and his heart turned sick as it never had done before during this long adventure.

But this affair seemed unreal. All was composed not of flesh and blood but of moonlight and of shadow, until he remembered how he had caught up Alicia into his arms, and how he had held her, and how she had fainted in the might of his grip, and with what courage she had rallied, suddenly, throwing off her fear. A thousand apologies would not be enough to undo the insult of his touch, he feared. And yet how little she had made of it!

He rested his hand against the rough bark of a tree and shook his head. And remembering her beauty and the kindness with which she had looked upon him, Tom Gloster grew giddy, and wild thoughts leaped into his mind, and a hope which he knew to be absurd, and which he beat down, and suppressed, and which re-arose and filled him with absurd sadness and with equally absurd delight.

In the meantime, the moon climbed higher. The shadows beneath the trees shortened; the moon was almost as strong as daylight, and quite strong enough to make straight shooting possible. Every moment sadly increased the danger which he ran by remaining in the garden, and yet he could not leave. Gradually it became impressed upon him that the girl had been gone for a long time.

This worried him. But still, he could not be seriously upset. For it seemed to Tom Gloster as though he had within himself, on this night, a fountain of irresistibly bubbling joy.

That joy was shaded across, for the instant, at least, by hearing a sound behind him in the woods. He looked back, but he saw nothing drifting through the shadows, or crossing the black lines of the tree trunks. And yet he knew, with a sudden prescience, that danger was walking up behind him through the woods.

31. A Precious Pair

WHEN ALICIA returned to the house, she found Beatrice Parry in the hall, taking off a light coat and removing a loose cap.

"How did I miss you, Beatrice?" said the girl.

"By walking in the opposite direction," said the other tartly. "Where have you been?"

"Rambling. There's a marvelous moon, you know."

"Is there?" said Beatrice Parry.

She went up the hall slowly, pausing at the first door.

"The game's in my hands at last!" said she.

"Are you sure?" asked Alicia.

"I'm sure, at last. I'll have them all."

"Suppose your husband hears shots, Beatrice. Have you thought of that, too?"

"I don't care what happens afterward, as long as the thing's done first. But he won't understand. I can close his eyes, I trust."

She disappeared through the doorway; instantly she came back again.

"I'm nervous, Alicia. I want to talk to you."

"I'm nervous, too. You'd better talk to anyone other than to me."

"What's the matter with you, child?"

"I don't know."

"Where did you walk?"

"Up the side of the laguna."

"Wasn't it muddy?"

"Not if you pick your steps."

Beatrice Parry glanced down at the shoes of her friend and started a little.

"Well—" she began, and then she seemed to change her mind about speaking, and turned hastily back into the room into which she had started before.

Her start; and her sudden movement had been noticed by Alicia, but the latter walked on down the hall to the library. Beatrice Parry crossed to a side door of the house, where she heard a knock. She opened the door; before her stood Chris Black, alias Negro. And her eyes sparkled at the sight of his ugly face.

"I wanted you!" said she.

"Have you learned anything?" he asked, coming in and standing unceremoniously before her, without taking off his hat.

"I've learned something! What have you learned?"

"I only know that I'm worried. They haven't come. I don't understand it. There's been plenty of time for them to come on toward the house."

"If they do, have you enough good men?"

"Enough good men to beat an army, I think. But I have queer doubts."

"How can they avoid coming? Will they distrust the Gaucho?"

"I don't know. I don't think so. But that half-witted fellow, Gloster, has a sort of second sight. I can't tell what thought will jump into his foolish head."

"Tonight, will be the end of him, surely, Christopher."

He took off his hat, wiped his forehead, and pulled the hat firmly down over his eyes again.

"Tonight will be the end of him or me," he assented grimly. "I know that!"

"Are you becoming a prophet, too?"

"One doesn't have to be a prophet to understand that

160

my reputation has been blown up and smashed like a paper bag by this fellow. People look at me and smile, today. They've heard too much about this Gloster, and the way he's made a fool of me!"

"He's had madman's luck!"

"He's had a brave man's luck," said Black quietly. "But tonight he and I are sure to meet and have it out together."

"A fair fight, Christopher?"

"I fight to win, not for pleasure," he told her, in the most cold-blooded manner. "I came back here because I was worked up a little, tonight."

"So are we all, of course!"

"And, incidentally, I want to know if you're sure that you'll be able to handle your husband?"

"Of course, I'm perfectly sure."

"I'm not."

"You're not his wife."

"He's a lethargic sort of fellow, but once he's waked up, he's not a fool!"

"Perhaps not. But I won't let him wake up."

"If he goes out to examine, and finds, say, the body of his dead son, madame?"

"If you leave that body around, you're a greater and more helpless idiot than I imagine!"

"Would he bring the responsibility home to you?"

"He? I don't know. I don't think so."

"Hasn't he heard anything?"

"Very little. I watch him day and night. I knock the messages out of the air. I don't think that anyone talks to him, except Alicia."

"And what of her?"

"She's my friend."

"Is she with you in this?"

"No. She has no son to work for in the case," explained Beatrice Parry.

Black nodded.

"That explains her, does it? She has nothing against your business, then? Best of all, she also doesn't know what's taking place here tonight?"

"She knows a great deal. She's like an owl. She can see in the dark. But I never suspected her of anything until five minutes ago."

161

"Will you tell me why?"

"It was nothing real as a clue. It was simply something that troubled me for a moment at the time."

"I'd like to know what it is."

"She told me that she'd been walking by the upper laguna."

"That's not strange, on a night like this."

"It's warm, yes, but when I looked at her shoes, expecting to find traces of dust and mud, I saw only some bits of grass—flecks and streaks around the soles. You must understand that only one lawn has been cut today, and that's the lawn near and around the little summerhouse. Do you know that way?"

"I know every way inside and outside of the house," he assured her. "I can tell you every article of furniture and describe it to you. I can practically tell you every tree on the place. Then you ask me if I can find the way to the summerhouse? Blindfolded, Madame."

Her eyes sparkled at his self-confidence.

"If anyone in this world can catch that fellow, you're the man, Christopher Black!"

"Thank you. But I haven't beaten him yet. Who knows if I really shall, in the end?"

"I put my trust in you."

"That's more than a man's trust, I think," said Black.

"I think it is. But do you see the point of the cut grass on the shoes?"

"I suppose I'm fairly able to get at that point. Since there's no grass except the summerhouse plot cut today, then she must have gone there."

"She must! Then why did she tell me that she went the other way!"

"A little trick of the tongue, most likely," said Black. "I've seen it happen many and many a time before. There's nothing new about it."

"Why do you say that? Why should she have lied about such a thing?"

"Because it was of no importance."

"Do you think so? You don't know her. She'd never tell an untruth unless there was some great necessity for the insult. I know her quite well."

"Are you sure?"

"Yes, yes!"

"Very well, then. She had been out walking by the summerhouse."

"That's clear."

"What can she have done there?"

"I don't know. I've been trying to guess."

"You mean that you're afraid that she might take a side against you in this work?"

"I know that she would, if she guessed what I hope will happen this evening."

"You know that she would!"

"Yes. She's always taken the side of David."

"Why didn't you send her away from the house, this evening?"

"I tried to. I invited her to do a dozen things. She didn't want to."

"Suppose she wrecks this whole scheme?"

"I don't think that she will."

"You don't think!" exclaimed Christopher Black, with bitter emphasis. "I tell you this: I've done on this job ten times as much work as I'll ever be paid for."

"You can trust to my generosity, Mr. Black."

He looked her straight in the eye and smiled a little.

"I think that we know each other pretty well," said he.

She blushed, but only a trifle.

"You'd better have a look down at the summerhouse," she said.

"You think that I'll find something there?"

"I don't know. With your eyes, you might."

"I'll try. Mind you, though, I'm beginning to doubt. I'm beginning to feel that there's bad luck in this whole job, for me! There's been enough miracles already attached to it!"

"In the last rub, everything will come out. Go search around the summerhouse. I'm going into the library to see my husband. If shots are heard, I'd better be beside him to give his thoughts the right turn."

"That's right. If it comes to shooting, we'll try to gather up the dead; there'll be no captures made, of course."

"Of course," she said simply.

And Christopher Black turned from her without any other farewell, and left the house.

32. *Husband And Wife*

SHE WENT to the window which overlooked the path just outside the house. There was a faint shaft of light that struck out from the fan-light above the door, and by that light she saw two men move out from the shadows and go off with Christophoro Negro into the deeper shadows of the night. She nodded. She was not very hopeful, but she felt that she had done well in bringing up every possible clue that her keen, quick eyes presented to her mind.

Then she went to the library to keep an eye upon her husband.

Alicia had found him deep in a leather chair and deep in a book. His back looked broken, and his head was bowed so that his hair fell forward in a shock. There was something brutal about the heavy strength of the shoulders, and the arch of the neck which supported the weight of that ponderous, fallen head.

He grunted. He grunted like a grampus and did not look up from his book.

"Uncle David," said Alicia.

He snapped his fingers.

She sat on the arm of a chair facing him and chanted again: "Uncle David."

"Leave me alone, Alicia," said he. "I'm busy."

"Uncle David," said the girl.

"Dash it!" cried Uncle David.

"Uncle David!" murmured Alicia.

He looked up with a glowering suddenness.

"You've spoiled the best chapter in the book for me. What do you want, Alicia?"

"A little attention."

"You've got it."

He threw the book moodily aside.

"What's the book?"

" 'Cornered,' or something like that," said he. "I don't know what the title is. What difference does the title make?"

"Why, not much."

"For that sort of a book you were going to say?"

"For that sort of silly book," said she.

"Don't irritate me, Alicia."

"Why not?" said she.

"Confound it! Are you going to sit there and simply rattle at me like this?"

"Not at all. I'm being amused."

"By my clever talk, eh?"

"By seeing you boil. There's that old proverb, somewhere—blood boils without a fire."

"You are a fire," he insisted.

"Well, I see you sit and steam."

"And that amuses you?"

"A lot."

"You are cool," said he.

"Are you through with the book, now?"

"You've stirred me out of it."

"That's what I wanted."

"Will it do you any good?"

"It will, of course, if I have my way."

"Great Scott!" cried he. "Did you ever fail to have that, in the wide world?"

"Well, a good many times."

"Tell me what you want. I'll do it, I suppose."

"Come out for a stroll."

Mrs. Parry, concealed behind the wing of the door which allowed her to see without being seen, started; and all at once her face took on the look of one who has been stabbed to the heart. She was a pretty woman; five years before, she had been beautiful, perhaps; but now the anguish of rage, and astonishment, and fear wrinkled the last of youth from her face and showed her as she would be in middle age. It was like the slipping of an ugly mask over her features.

She gripped both her hands hard; she dug the nails into the palms of her hands; and this present physical pain enabled her to conquer the leaping of her heart. In another moment, she was able to stroll carelessly into the room, smiling.

"Why the deuce should I go for a walk?" her husband was asking.

"Because you need fresh air."

"Stuff! I can get that by opening the window."

"Can you get the moon, too?"

"What do you mean by that?"

"There's a grand moon sailing through the trees."

"The deuce there is!"

"Yes. Like a big yellow bird."

He yawned. He was gradually gathering himself, raising himself. Now his shoulders lounged back against the leather of the chair. His head rolled lazily back, also, and he looked at her with half-closed eyes.

"Here's Beatrice."

"She'll go along with us," said Alicia.

Mrs. Parry looked at the girl with a sort of concentrated coldness of hate, a poisonous distillation of fury.

"Why should we go at all?" said she. "I'd rather stay in—unless you want to go very much, David."

He did not answer. He had an unmannerly way of letting remarks go unanswered; and yet it was not quite as bad as it seemed. His thoughtful air appeared to indicate that he was taking the last remark under consideration, and that he was merely postponing his reply.

He said: "What's the stuff that I've been hearing, Beatrice?"

"What stuff?"

"That's been floating around."

"I don't know what you mean."

"Will you come here?"

She went to him. It was a most uneasy moment for her. There might be the greatest of disasters hidden behind the next five minutes, but she maintained her self-control with perfect skill.

"What is it, David? What's troubling you?"

"Gossip, Beatrice. Gossip that's running about the house."

"There's always gossip."

"Not on this point. Usually, they talk about everything to me, but not about this."

"Do tell me what it is."

He leaned forward and fastened his eyes resolutely upon her.

"It's this, my beautiful Beatrice—that David, my son, didn't reach the ranch, after all."

"Absurd! Where should he be, then?"

"Here, they tell me."

"Heavens, dear! Are you hearing yourself?"

"I'm hearing myself."

"You have a strange way of speaking."

"Because I have some strange thoughts in my mind. They tell me that young David has come back—and not with the man who went off to guard him and escort him on the way."

She made a helpless little gesture.

"You make my brain spin. Who has been saying such things?"

"A person who's in the house. I won't tell you which one. You ought to know that everything becomes known in this country, my dear, almost as soon as it's known to anyone between the Andes and the sea."

"A very curious story, David. I don't know what to make of it!"

"I'll tell you what I heard as I heard it. That when you persuaded me to send my boy to the States it wasn't because, as you told me, you were sure that he was not my blood, but because you knew he was my son and heir, and you wanted to shuffle him out of the way. And that you really tried to do that, and made an attempt upon his life which succeeded in taking off his guard, and that the youngster escaped by a hairsbreadth, and that he was helped by some fighting fool of an American cowpuncher to escape, and to come back to this country, bringing the boy with him. And that, all the way, you've dodged him with bullets and poison, and what not!"

He paused. He had spoken rapidly, the accusation coming out in a flood. And she listened, quietly nodding her head.

"No, they'll never stop," she said.

"Stop what?"

"Stop their hateful lying about me. They never forgive me for ruling the house a little sharply, David. I mean the servants, of course. I suppose one of them has told you this odd yarn?"

"I'll not say who told me. But there was a queer tingling feeling in me—that perhaps the yarn was right!"

"That the boy had come back?"

"Yes."

"It doesn't seem probable, does it?"

"No, of course it does not. But suppose it should be true?"

"It's hard to imagine, but suppose it should be true?" she said with wonderful calm.

"That he's actually managed to beat his way back to San Francisco, and down the coast, and across the mountains, and then over the plains back to this house?"

"Why, suppose he's actually tapping at the door just now?" she said, smiling.

Alicia had moved a little so that she could watch the face of her hostess, and now her eyes widened in heartiest admiration of such acting.

"Suppose it's all true, or only a half-part true? I'll tell you what it would mean to me, Beatrice. It would mean that no matter what his complexion is, he's my son, my own proper son! Because if I were a boy, I'd have his spirit to do exactly what he's supposed to have undertaken. I'd come back, and in spite of every obstacle I'd go to my father's house, and open the door, and tell him that murder had been tried on me, and I'd demand his protection! And, by heaven, he shall have it! He shall have it!"

He started from his chair, with fire in his eyes. He took his wife by both shoulders, with his great hands.

"Beatrice, Beatrice," he said suddenly, with a childish simplicity, "is it true?"

33. A Cry Of Mortal Agony

SHE HAD turned pale and trembled a little as he suddenly towered above her; now she flushed crimson.

"I don't want to answer such a horrible question," she said. "I don't want to believe that you've really asked it of me. David, what sort of creature should I be if I couldn't answer 'No?' "

He sighed. There was a veritable groan of relief in his voice.

"Say that again—unqualified! The 'no' and not another word!"

"No!" she obeyed.

Then she turned with a bright, bitter smile toward Alicia.

"This could be used in court, even. I see that you've got a witness ready for me, David!"

"Why, my dear," said David, "such an old friend as Alicia. What can't we say before her?"

"Oh, of course," said Beatrice Parry. "Of course, anything can be said before her. But you've upset me a little, with this—this very wild talk!"

He shrugged his shoulders and looked uneasily about him. The only sort of unpleasantness which he knew how to face was something that could be grappled with and fought with his hands. He said suddenly: "We'll go out for a bit of a stroll. The night air is cool and fresh. Come along, Beatrice. It will brace you up."

Once more the keen glance of Beatrice wandered aside and probed at the face of Alicia. Then it returned to her husband, and grew wide and brimful of tears.

"I can't go, David," she said. "I'm quite unnerved by

169

what you've told me. Oh, not what you repeated, but the fact that you could have taken an instant's thought of it! Could even have dreamed of considering the shadow of such a story! It makes me sick at heart."

She sank into a chair and covered her face.

Her husband, with a groan, turned to Alicia.

"I've played the mischief now," said he. "She's crying. Second time in her life I've ever seen her cry!"

But Alicia answered calmly: "Poor Beatrice! Of course she's upset a little. I'd leave her alone to work out of this low spell. There's nothing you can do for her. Let's go out into the moonlight at once; she'll follow in a moment or two."

"Yes, yes!" he said, glad to shrug this burden from his shoulders, and he hurried with her out of the room.

"David!" wailed Beatrice, in a voice apparently choked with tears, but he pretended to hear nothing, closed the door in guilty haste behind him, and went panting down the hall with Alicia.

Beatrice, left alone, forgot her tears on the instant, and in the first surge of her anger, she rushed to the door and grasped the knob; but then she seemed to realize that the way was not so simple for her. Grief and shaken nerves she now could show as much as she pleased, but she couldn't give away to the slightest touch of anger.

She hesitated then, desperate, not knowing in which direction she could turn, and murmuring through stiff lips: "Traitress! Traitor!"

Then she hurried from the room and into the hall, and the door slammed heavily as she swung it behind her.

She ran down the hall, now, like a wild creature. A door opened before her, a shadow appeared, and in the dim light of the hall, she saw a tall youth, Pedro, the horse-tamer. He had been a wild Gaucho; even now he was only half-tamed. Him she caught by the arm.

"Pedro, you have sworn to be my true servant."

"Heaven forgive me if I should fail in my duty, señora!"

"Then go out the front door and follow your master through the garden. Come close up. He is with Señorita Alicia. You must hear what they speak together. Do you understand?"

"I do."

"Go quickly!"

He was down the hall, running, like a graceful, big cat, and her teeth flashed in her smile of satisfaction. Pedro was a man whose loyalty she could count upon. And at least she established some check upon the others through him. But she felt cornered and hunted, and with all her heart she wished that this night would end—if only there could be accomplished the thing that she wanted!

In the meantime, Alicia and David Parry, senior, walked slowly out through the moonlit garden. She felt that she was late in fulfilling her promise to Tom Gloster, but that it was better to go on slowly, now that she had Parry with her, at last. For the great thing was bringing him out of the house without his wife, and she had jumped that hurdle.

David Parry stopped in the center of an open avenue, and spread out his big hands, and raised his face.

"Here's peace!" said he. "Here's real peace, Alicia."

"Yes," said she.

"Why walk? Why not sit here on this bench and enjoy things in general?"

"Because you'll miss something."

"Miss what?"

"The different ways the moon has of jumping through the trees, David. That's one thing."

"You're an energetic child," said Parry.

"I'm not so frightfully young, at that," said she.

"Confound it," said he, "you're like Beatrice, tonight."

"And how?"

"You have something on your mind; you're talking around a corner at me, all the time. What are you thinking about, Alicia?"

"Why, nothing."

"There's something you want me to do—now—in this garden! What is it?"

"To walk along and talk pleasantly, and not be disagreeable, as you are now."

He laughed. "I'll take orders for once," said he. "I'm tired of resisting everybody."

"They're tired of being resisted, too," she assured him.

They went on down the garden path. It wound in leisurely fashion, here and there, for the ideal garden path is that which goes most slowly from one given point to the next.

She stopped suddenly, and touched his arm.

Before them, the down-arching limbs of a big tree only partly screened them from the view of a little clearing, grass floored, with a fountain springing in the center, and the water dissolving in the pale, bright moonshine.

"Aye," said Parry, "that's a pleasant little picture. I'd almost forgotten that there was so much beauty in this garden of mine. But there it is!"

"Hush!" said Alicia. "I think that something moved behind us, yonder!"

"Where?"

"Behind that brush—"

He turned and sprang suddenly over the barrier, a gun gleaming in his hand. He came out again, noisily scraping through the bushes.

"There's nothing there," he said.

"If there had been," she commented, "what would have happened to you?"

"You mean that I'd have been shot if there'd been a skulker inside the brush?"

"Exactly that."

He shook his head.

"You're a clever little girl, Alicia, and you know a lot about many things, and you can guess a great deal more. But this is rather a different question, I take it—this about fighting men. I'll tell you the sad truth. There's hardly a man in a hundred who will stand a sudden charge. When men have their nerves taut, they don't like to be rushed. They want a chance to make up their minds. And a quick jump spoils their aim and breaks down their morale, as one may say! Now, if there had been a fellow lurking in there, when I rushed him, nine chances out of ten he would have turned and bolted."

"On the other chance, you would have died."

"Probably not. Revolvers are rather inaccurate, my dear. Don't believe the wonderful yarns that you hear about men and their shooting. The dead shots usually die young—because they miss—and at short range!"

She listened with interest to the reasoning of this fearless man, but still she kept an eye continually turning behind her. In the meantime, she was drawing her companion gradually toward the summerhouse where she had left the patient Tom Gloster. Parry could not help notice the glances she threw to either side, and to the rear.

"There's no one following us, if that's what you mean," said he.

"There is, though," she answered very confidently.

"Have you seen anything?"

"Hardly the stir of a shadow."

"Have you heard anything?"

"Hardly anything more than a heartbeat."

"Don't be mysterious, Alicia."

"I don't want to be. But I have the weight of somebody in my mind. Somebody sneaking up on us."

"Well—a whale can feel a whale in its wake!"

And he laughed.

"We'll go on," said Parry. "There's no good being troubled by ghosts. If we were, we'd never get anywhere in this world of ours, Alicia. Come along. Let's step out a bit more briskly."

"Just as you please."

They went through a rose arbor, the roses climbing thickly over an arched iron framework. And roses and leaves turned black and silver under the strong moonlight.

He paused.

"There's a fine fragrance here, Alicia."

"Yes. Such a shower of roses!"

"I don't mean the flowers."

"What do you mean?"

"Well, you're a clever girl, Alicia. Guess, will you?"

"I can't. You don't mean that heavy, sweet smell of the lilies?"

"No, no."

"It's something a little more strange than that? I can't tell what you mean, David."

He threw up his big head and laughed softly.

"I mean the fine fragrance of danger, Alicia. I mean the delightful bouquet of mystery into which you've led me."

"I?"

"Come, come!" said he. "I'm a dull fellow, with my

173

stupid stories of adventure to read, and my talk about horses and farming, and crops, but at the same time, I have a little touch of intuition as well."

"And what does the intuition tell you?"

"I hardly know how to put it into words. But I should say that the air is filled with excitement tonight. That's why I was fool enough to jump into the brush, a while ago. Because I actually felt that there might be someone hidden there!"

He laughed again.

"Great guns, Alicia," said he, "how I should enjoy with all my heart a real thunderburst of trouble, a real climax of honest fighting! I've not had my hands filled with it for these many years, you know."

"I know!"

"And I wonder, Alicia, if there isn't some such thing brooding in the air for me."

She could hold back no longer. She cried to him: "Oh, David. I don't know what fighting and danger there'll be, but I know that I'm going to introduce you to the strangest adventure that any man ever had!"

Now, as she said that, as though this had been a signal, waited for, there was a sudden fusillade of gunshots, and at the end, the long, high-pitched cry of a man in mortal agony.

"The summerhouse," cried the girl. "Oh, Heaven! I've been too slow!"

34. Voices In The Night

ALL THIS time Tom Gloster had been waiting in the shadow of the big trees near the summerhouse; now he heard, at last, what seemed to him the noise of stealthily approaching steps. He looked about him anxiously. It might be the girl returning with Parry, as she had promised. Or it might be deadly enemies. He could not take chances. To remain might be fatal; to leave might be foolish. Tom Gloster did the childishly simple thing of climbing the tree at his back.

Not so many men could have managed the feat. The trunk was too large to be girdled by the arms. He had to climb, using the rough projections of the bark for toe and finger holds. In this manner, he got to the first branch, fully ten feet above the ground, and upon this big limb, large as a man's body, he stretched himself out and lay at ease.

He was highly pleased by this maneuver when, a moment later, he saw a form move behind a nearby tree. It could not be Parry or the girl. When a man hunts, every movement of his body suggests the act in which he is employed. It is as significant as the stalking movements of a cat, the stealing foot, the bent back, the head thrust forward, the hands suspended. One glance told Tom Gloster that this was a hunter, and, therefore, he must be the hunted—and if he were hunted in this place there seemed only one explanation; beautiful Alicia, for all her apparent friendliness, had betrayed him.

His heart was fairly sickened by that thought. But he gritted his teeth and waited. It was not another moment before a second shadowy form appeared. Then a third came out, glided through a keen fall of the moonlight, and joined the other two.

"The bird's flown," said the first comer in Spanish.

"He's gone," said the second.

The third man had dropped upon his knees and was carefully examining the grass.

"He's been here," said he.

And Tom Gloster recognized the unforgettable voice of Christopher Black.

"He's been here," said Black, standing up again. "There are the prints of his shoes. I think I ought to know the marks by heart, by this time. They're measured and written down in my mind, you can be sure! It's Gloster!"

"Do you follow the trail out from here?" asked the first man. "Gloster here! Gloster!"

175

"He wouldn't dare to come alone," said the second speaker.

"He'd dare anything," answered Black. "There's no fear in him. He's too much of a fool to know what fear is!"

He turned, still on his knees, toward the tree.

"He's gone this way, for one thing. Not so long ago, at that. You see how the grass is springing back and slowly uncurling, after it was pressed down, here? He's gone— well, here the trail goes out."

He was directly at the foot of the tree, and suddenly it occurred to Tom Gloster that his refuge had been badly chosen indeed, when there was such a cat-eyed person as Christopher Black upon his trail. Black now rounded the trunk of the tree and suddenly returned to the side of it on which his companions waited, wondering and attentive.

He said in a low voice: "The trail goes out. That's odd. Whatever else Gloster could do, he couldn't make himself vanish into thin air."

He raised his head. The heart of Gloster stopped.

"By George!" breathed Black in a scarcely audible whisper. "The fool has gone up the tree like a cat!"

And he snatched a gun from his belt as he spoke.

Tom Gloster imitated that motion and fired point-blank at Black. He missed, but he saw the man immediately behind Chris Black throw up his hands and go down. Gloster flung himself from the bough from which he had fired.

Bullets had crashed against the branch he had just left. Bullets again rushed past his body, as he struck the ground. He bounded like a scared coyote behind the broad trunk of the tree, then turned and bolted for the first big tree behind; turned again, and put a bullet beside the head of the first of his pursuers, as he rounded the big tree.

The man recoiled, and Black, also, who was charging around on the farther side. At that moment the wounded man, recovering his senses and the dreadful sense of pain, began to scream terribly, and Gloster rapidly shifted away among the great shadows of the wood.

He paused for a moment to breathe, to let his heart grow quieter, and to listen.

There was a pandemonium from the direction of the summerhouse. The wild voice of the hurt man still yelled

176

for help and screamed in sheer blind fear of death and pain.

Gloster moved on, at last, not striving to go in any definite direction, but merely to get away from those unpleasant sounds. Then, out of the distance, a loud voice shouted in English, and again in Spanish. Gloster merely hastened his going.

He came on through the trees, across several winding, graveled walks, and then he saw before him the blink of a light, barely struggling through the foliage of a tree. He went still closer; suddenly he was aware of the loom of the whole façade of the house.

He stopped at this, amazed and blinking. Then he went forward more slowly, stopping and kneeling in the black shadow of a small clump of brush.

The glimpse of the house which he had seen before was nothing. Now the great length of the place filled him with awe, and the nearness, and the extraordinary height of the single story. For, in fact, for the sake of heat there was a dummy, or half story, on top of the real rooms throughout the house.

The servants came hurrying across the lawn.

He heard one say to the other: "Where is the master?"

And the second man answered: "Perhaps he hasn't heard. What was it?"

They passed on; suddenly Tom Gloster was saying to himself that though he had reason to fear what might happen to him in that house, yet he also should be grateful that he was not standing before it. For inside it was the man to whom he must speak.

He waited, gathering his resolution, for at that moment you may be sure that the long façade and its row of huge, glimmering, dark windows, was more terrible to Gloster than any dragon to a fairy-tale prince.

He stood up suddenly, telling himself that it was better to have the test soon over. He went on until he was on the walk surrounding the building; he passed on until he came opposite a window through which a woman's voice floated out to him, singing softly:

"Sleep, baby, sleep—"

There broke in upon the singing of the pleasant lullaby

the tired, cross voice of a child, saying: "I'm tired of sleeping. I won't sleep any longer."

"There, there!" said the soothing voice of the nurse.

"I'm going to get up," said the child.

"If you get up, something terrible will happen!"

"To whom?"

"To you, Roger."

"I'm going to get up, though. Nothing will happen to me."

"How do you dare to say that?"

"Because it's the truth!"

"It can't be the truth."

"It is, though. If I get up, you don't dare to touch me."

"I shall. You're a naughty boy!"

"You touch me, and I'll scream!"

"If you scream, your mother will spank you!"

He laughed with a malicious exultation.

"If she spanks me, I'll scream till I have a fit! She will never dare to spank me again!"

The nurse was silent.

"I'm going to get up now."

"Roger, will you please go back to bed?"

"There! You see that you don't dare to touch me!"

"Roger!"

"Stand away from me! If you touch me, I'll shriek!"

"You're a bad boy. I've a notion to spank you on the spot."

"If you do, my mother will send you away, and she'll give you no pay, either!"

"The law will protect me."

"It won't! We can do as we please, here! Who are you to stop us?"

"Oh, dear," said the nurse. "What ever have I done that I should be put here for my sins? Roger, will you leave that window!"

A child's mocking, contented laughter followed, and in the window appeared a small white form. Gloster, shrinking back in the dark shadow of the trees, watched with interest; he knew that he was hearing the voice and seeing the person of the rival claimant of the property!

35. Roger Runs

IT SEEMED to big Tom Gloster very odd that he should be idling beneath a tree in the black of the night and listening to the foolish chattering of a child, while the humming of bullets still sounded freshly in his ear! The voices had died away in the dark and in the distance. All was peace; all was hush; and the wind spoke and sighed among the trees. But to Gloster it was the hush that precedes violent action. The battle was to begin that would decide the fate of poor little David Parry, that would perhaps mean life or death to Gloster himself. It might be a battle of knives, or of bullets, or of mere words; and certainly there was a point of interest in knowing that now he heard the voice of the child for whose sake Parry's wife had driven young David away.

Now there was the sound of a little scuffle inside the room, and presently the youngster appeared on the window sill, laughing loudly. A white form dashed at it from the rear; the boy jumped down into the garden, and turned, still laughing defiantly.

The nurse, her voice frightened almost to a whisper, began to implore him to return, but he danced with the pleasure of a guilty freedom and defied her.

"It's better out here," said the child. "I'm going to stay."

"Come back! Your mother will whip you."

"She won't! She'll be terribly cross with you because you let me out."

"Roger, do you hear? Like a dear boy, Roger?"

"I hear, but I won't come. No!"

A flurry of skirts, an exclamation, and the nurse suddenly descended through the window. Roger, turning with a squeal of fear to bolt, tripped on a root and fell headlong with a squawk. Instantly the nurse had him in her hands, but at this moment an excited woman's voice called in the room: "Emilia!"

"Yes, Madame," said Emilia, her voice stifled by fear and by her exertions.

"Where under heaven are you?"

At the window appeared another woman. To see her, Tom Gloster had only the faint sheen from the half-hidden lamp within. It cast a glow upon her cheek, upon her throat, and by this he had to half guess at the rest of her face and know that she was very beautiful.

It was Roger's mother, then. And through the very heart of Tom Gloster leaped a thrill of fear and of wonder. For he had been hearing about this woman for so long that she had begun to take on a certain mythical aspect. Here she was in the flesh, whose name had hunted him and David through so many thousands of miles. He held his breath and listened more sharply.

"Here, Madame."

"You? Emilia? What—what do you mean by being outside the house—on such a night as this?"

"On such a night, Madame?" asked Emilia. "I didn't know there was anything strange about this night."

"You didn't know—you simpleton!" said Mrs. Parry through her teeth.

There was such a rich venom in her tone that Gloster, hearing, shuddered and moistened his lips. It suddenly cast a high light upon all the deadly adventures which he had had for the sake of David. He could see, again, the men moving to fling themselves upon him in the unlighted street, so far away, and the rush of Christopher Black like a madman charging down the slope, and the tall, sedate form of "Colonel Bridges," and Guzman in the railroad train.

"You thought it was nothing!" cried Mrs. Parry. "You heard the guns, I suppose?"

"I heard them. Whatever are they, Madame? It isn't the first time that I've heard guns here. I only thought . . ."

"You only thought? You only thought!" gasped Beatrice Parry furiously. "An excellent time for you to be thinking—yes, now or ever after, you—you creature!"

"Madame . . ."

"Will you come back this instant? Lift up my darling to me?"

"Yes, Madame. It was only because I thought that it would make him sleep a little better that I took him out for a tiny walk in the cool . . ."

"You took him out! I tell you that there are people here in the woods who would be glad to drink the heart-blood of my dearest Roger! Give him to me!"

The joyous Roger, however, danced at a little distance.

"It's a lie!" cried he. "It's a great lie! She didn't bring me out at all. I got away from her and she couldn't keep me from climbing out! And she had to climb out after me!"

"Roger!" groaned the unlucky nurse.

"Emilia!" exclaimed the furious woman. "You may count upon me to punish such detestable lying and negligence!"

"Oh, Madame, I was only meaning to get him to . . ."

"Be still this instant, and give him to me!"

"Roger, will you come here?" sobbed the nurse, now openly sobbing in fear and grief.

"I won't come! I won't come!" cried the gay Roger, dancing out of reach of Emilia's hands.

"I can't catch him. He's as active as a little bat!" said the nurse.

"A fine comparison to come from your tongue about my child. A fine comparison, indeed! Roger, do you hear me?"

"I hear you, mimsy. You can't catch me!"

She leaned far out from the window, and into the white shaft of the falling moonlight. And Gloster saw that she was lovely indeed, beyond his imagining. Far more beautiful than even Alicia.

"Roger, for goodness sake!"

"It's lovely out here," shouted Roger.

"Will you be quiet, darling, precious? I tell you that there are people about here who would snatch you up as a hawk snatches up chickens! They would carry you far away from me, and I would never see you again. Roger, darling, will you please come back to me?"

181

"Who are they? Who would want to catch me?"

"Men, bad men they are! Do you hear me?"

"I don't believe you," said Roger. "You're just trying to scare me back!"

Even in his hiding, the heart of Tom Gloster was stirred with some wrath because of the spoiled nature of this very unpleasing boy. Roger came closer. He was a dancing, leaping, little form of silver, as beautiful as his mother already, and already as evil, it seemed to Tom. All pity for this youngster who might be displaced by the establishment of David in his father's house now left him.

"I'm not trying to scare you, Roger! Everything depends on your coming back! Everything! Emilia, you stupid, blind creature! Why do you stand there! Do you want him murdered before my very eyes? Do you hear me? Emilia, if you'll catch him, I'll forgive you for ever letting him get away—if you'll only give him back to my arms, here!"

"I'll try, Madame! Roger, for goodness' sake, stand still! Dear Roger, pretty boy . . ."

She sprang at him in vain. He avoided her with ease, like a sparrow darting away from the lunges of a greedy hawk.

Then came hurrying footfalls inside the house, and a knock sounded at the door of an inner room.

"Come in!" called the anxious mother, hardly turning her head. "Who is it?"

"It's I!" said the sonorous, ringing voice of Christopher Black.

"You? Christopher, Christopher, what are you doing here?"

"I've lost the boy, and your own servants have him! They have him and they have the Gaucho. That Ramon is twice wounded. He fought like a maniac with his knife, but he's still enough alive to talk! I don't know what may come of this, Madame!"

"I thank fortune for it!" said the woman. "At least you have David. At least he will be in my hands. And what did become of that monster, that Tom Gloster?"

"He's still abroad. I've had my hand on him again, and the bird has slipped away once more."

"Do you mean it?"

"I mean it, of course. Would I report it, otherwise?"

Certainly the tone of Black was free and easy with the lady.

He added: "That woman, Juanita, is down here from the hills."

"Why does she come here?"

"Why do you suppose?"

"She wants more money?"

"Yes, naturally."

"The witch! The fiend! I've already paid her ten times over!"

"You're pouring water through a sieve. She still whines and begs as ever!"

"Ah, well, at least you'll make sure of her?"

"By violence? I don't think that you want to make an enemy of Juanita, Madame!"

"Hush, Christopher! We're not alone. There's that stupid Emilia outside. There's my darling, my precious child—and the scoundrel Gloster is still in the woods, perhaps!"

"He surely is."

"It was at him that you were shooting?"

"Yes."

"What happened?"

"He shot down one of my men. I think he killed the fellow."

"Did you get the body away?"

"Your precious husband and the other lady broke in at the wrong time. They're bringing him back to the house."

"This night makes me or spoils me forever," said Beatrice. "Now, jump down out of the window like a good fellow, Chris, and get the rascal of a boy for me. He will play the fool, with his very life in danger!"

Christopher Black instantly dropped through the window to the ground, and the boy, seeing him come, unafraid, but with a shriek of delight to see that the game was being taken up vigorously, turned and bolted straight for the spot where Tom Gloster stood beneath the tree.

And in that instant Gloster knew what he must do!

36. Where Men Know Men

VERY OFTEN ideas came to Tom in this fashion, with a
dizzy leap, as though they were born of lightning and the
wind.

He must take the boy!

All that he had heard from Christopher Black seemed
terrible in the extreme. His total work was undone. Young
David Parry was in the hands of the woman's domestics.
Heaven alone could tell how many moments of life would
remain to him!

But he would take this boy who was flung toward
him. The very terror of the mother lest it should happen
was the thing that inspired him; he would know, later on,
how the boy could be made use of. The small darting
form sprang close— Gloster, with one scooping movement, gathered him up and held him crushed beneath his
left arm. There was a gasp and a shriek from the boy.

Then Gloster stepped forward beneath the moon.

It seemed that surely he could finish the long and
wicked career of Christopher Black. The man was charging straight in upon him; but at the sight of Gloster, he
sprang to the side, like a football player dodging a
tackle. Still in mid air in his leap, as it were, he fired, and
the sound of his revolver joined with that in the hand of
Gloster. A wasp fled past the face of Gloster at a pro-
digious speed; Christopher clapped his hand to his
head, turned about, and slowly fell to his knees, then
forward, and collapsed upon the ground, face down.

And Gloster stepped back into the shadow.

The shrieking of Beatrice Parry ran into his brain like

a poisoned needle, stabbing him again and again in the very seat of life. The boy stirred and writhed.

"Be still!" ordered Gloster emphatically, and he raised his hand, the gun still in it.

He saw the beautiful face turn white; and the child was instantly quiet.

Gloster began to run, but he ran not six steps before he halted, to ask himself in what direction he should go.

He saw, for the first time, that he was stripped of everything in the way of power. Before, he had had the cunning wits of the Gaucho, Ramon; he had had the clever brain of the boy, too, to help him to devise ways and means. They both had known the country intimately well. Would it not be different now?

He was alone in a strange country. He was alone in a country as bare as the palm of his hand; and he could be sure that on the very next day literally scores of swift riders would scour far and wide to find him.

How could he hide himself, and how could he escape?

He would have no horses, now. There was no lucky meeting with any General Ducos now to be even prayed for. But it seemed to him that it was safer to remain among the shadow of the woods around the house than to go out into the naked plains.

Feeling this, he turned back.

The terrible screaming of Beatrice Parry had ended; suddenly other voices were just before him. And as he stepped into thick brush, which screened him from top to toe, he saw big David Parry, senior, come out into the open carrying the weight of a prostrate man, with Alicia behind him, helping to bear some of the burden.

There was a sudden groan from the wounded man. Parry paused and allowed the burden to settle to the grass.

"We'll have to change grips on him," said Parry in a calm and cheerful voice. "The poor fellow is suffering a lot. This is getting to be like a melodrama. Screams off stage on both sides of us at once. We pick up a murdered man in one place. Barely manage that, when we hear a woman yelling in the opposite direction, and a pair of guns there!"

"It was one gun, I thought," said Alicia. Her manner was as quiet as that of Parry. And the heart of Gloster was infinitely soothed, looking out upon her. She had not betrayed him, after all, and that knowledge was a salve to his very soul.

"It was not one gun," said David Parry the elder. "It was two guns, fired at about the same instant. Two revolvers, Alicia."

"Could you tell that?"

"It's not the first time that I've heard Colts barking at the same time."

He chuckled. "I'm beginning to enjoy the show a little, Alicia."

"Ah, David," said the girl, suddenly laying a hand upon his shoulder, "you should have been a soldier, not a landholder!"

"Should I?"

He was on his knees on one side of the wounded man, and she upon the other; and Gloster looked out upon the face of the man he had shot down from the tree with a peculiar sickness of the heart. It seemed to him a good face; strong it was not, but filled with an amiable weakness—the sort of a man who is willing to be laughed at for the sake of a good jest.

He groaned again.

"I think I must hold him further beneath the shoulders, Alicia."

"Let me run ahead to the house and get more help to carry him. If there isn't a stretcher, we can unhinge a door and carry him on that, I suppose."

"Do you think I'd let you take one step in these woods on such a night, my dear? My own nerves are jumping, I tell you."

"They are not. You're loving it, and so am I!"

"You are, Alicia? For the sheer danger of it all?"

"No, but because I've an idea that this night will go a long distance toward settling everything."

"Everything?"

"I don't want to talk any more about it."

"Very well, you don't have to. I think he's coming to. I hope he won't begin howling again."

The wounded man opened his eyes and looked wildly about him. Then he clasped his hand to his breast.

"Dios, Dios!" said he. "Still the music; but pardon, my dear friends, if I do not dance!"

He laughed a little; agony cut short the laughter and turned him a sickly pallor at once.

"Who's done this thing to you?" asked David Parry.

"A great man," said the other. "I have that consolation. When we are struck by lightning, we know that the hand of Heaven has thrown the shaft, eh? So I have been struck—by the hand of that famous man—that Thomas Gloster!"

"Gloster, Gloster!" cried David Parry.

"Tom Gloster!" breathed the girl.

"Why do you bring out Tom Gloster as if he were a long-lost brother?" asked Parry.

"I was bringing you out to try to get you to see him, tonight."

"You! Gloster! By gad, Alicia, you'll have my poor thick head staggered very shortly! I don't put any of this madness together, I assure you!"

"I can't put it together, either. I'm wool-gathering, very largely. But what made him shoot you?" she asked of the hurt man.

"To keep me from shooting him, señorita," said the other, and gasped in pain. "I don't think you need to carry me any farther, my very kind friends. It will be enough for me to lie down here and quietly die. I don't need the hands of any other man but a priest, just now. And I suppose I won't make a great pocketful for a holy man!"

He laughed again, ending in a snarl and gritting teeth. The fellow could not stop his mirth, even as he regarded his own death.

"I don't think you'll die," said Alicia briskly. "You have too much life left in you."

"Every insect wiggles when it's toasted," answered the other. "It's a consolation to have been cooked at such a celebrated fire, though. People will remember me. They will write me down on the list of Tomaso Gloster's dead men, will they not?"

"You couldn't have yelled so loud and so long," said Alicia, "if you were going to die. It doesn't happen that way, very often. Just keep your heart up."

"I'm trying only to keep it together," said the jester. "Because I'm sure that it is shot in two."

"We'd better start on again," said David Parry. "Will you tell me who brought you here?"

"Another great rascal. Christopher Black!"

"And what were you doing here?"

"Out hunting, ready to snipe or bag the boy, if we could."

"What boy?"

"Your boy—said to be your boy—your David Parry."

"Who sent Black on this job?"

"The evil one, I suppose," said the sufferer. "I don't know, I'm sure. But the wages were good, I know."

"You were hunting little David Parry?"

"Yes."

"Here at this house? He's thousands of miles from here!"

"Perhaps. Then we've been chasing his ghost across the Andes and the pampas."

"By gad," cried Parry, "then the rumor is true! They have been hunting the boy as was said. And he's come here!"

"He has."

"Thank Heaven that you were able to do him no harm."

"Thank Tomaso Gloster, or the ten thousand tricks that live in the wits of Tomaso Gloster. He is all that kept us away. What? One mangy goat of a Gaucho, and a little boy? Could they have kept Christophoro Negro away from his prey? That is a thing not to be asked where men really know men, señor!"

"I believe it! I believe it!" said Parry earnestly. "I want to meet this fellow. How shall I know him?"

"He is," said the fallen man, "about twenty kilos bigger than you and about ten centimeters taller."

"Hello! That's a giant, though."

"He's a giant, indeed. But as hard to hit as a giant's shadow."

"He's wrong," smiled Alicia. "Tom Gloster is no bigger than you. He's smaller than you David. But stronger, perhaps."

"Ah?" said the other doubtfully. "Well, perhaps! Let's

188

get on with our wounded fellow, then. Who knows what we shall walk into on the way!"

37. *The Answer Is*—

THE LIBRARY of the Parry house showed intimately the mind of the master of the place. It was big, it was spacious, it had good lines, but it was a hopeless jumble. Upon the walls he had hung horns and animal masks of all kinds. Upon the floor were stretched the wooly fleece of a mountain sheep, a royal Bengal tiger, and a fine specimen of grizzly bear. These skins, utterly out of harmony with one another, were placed regularly, side by side, three spots of totally incongruous color. The tiger skin had been badly cured, and the result was that it had shed a great deal of hair and had a sadly mottled, mangy look. It wore its mask as well, and looked like a very tired and ancient tiger indeed, for one of its great fangs had been broken, and now hung as by a hinge.

Upon the walls of this room, interspersed among the hunting trophies, there were all manner of crude weapons, from bell-mouthed blunderbusses such as might have helped Cortez enslave the Montezuma, down to Malay creeses and native spears with heads of broad bright steel, modeled after palm leaves.

Everything was huddled together—a bundle of poison arrows were tied to the haft of a rusty old Danish axe which might well have battered in Norman helmets at Senlac, and a Cromwellian morion appeared above a priceless coat of ancient chain mail! The room was furnished in the same random and magnificent fashion. There were excellent old Spanish chairs with leather backs— quaintly, curiously carved leather, over which collectors

189

licked their chops. There were old Italian chairs, stiff and royal; and among them overstuffed, comfortable, modern things; a classic divan stood rigidly against one wall, and facing it was a huge davenport.

The master of the house thought all these details congruous. He loved hunting trophies, and their age mattered nothing to him; the older the recollection, the more mellow, for him! And since he liked both comfort and beautiful lines, he insisted upon having both in the room with him.

Into this room he came, now, carrying the wounded man in his arms like a child, and laid him on the davenport, regardless of the red that instantly spilled down across the upholstery and onto the soiled white of the sheepskin.

A cluster of excited servants had followed him into the room, vainly proffering their services. But, in the meantime, a whirling madness seemed to have enveloped the house.

"Why's everybody screaming?" the big man asked of Alicia. "Have they all gone crazy, do you think?"

"We'll learn in a moment."

She touched the shoulder of a woman; the mozo threw up her hands and burst into tears.

"They are crazy," said David Parry. "Now, what the deuce is all this about, I wonder? Alicia, stand by and help me, will you? I'm going to finish dressing this man's wound's, no matter if he dies while I'm working and the very house falls about my ears. Lunacy seems to be blowing about in the wind tonight!"

As he said this, he stripped away his coat and turned up his sleeves. He caught a gibbering servant by the hair and shook him until his jaws knocked loudly together. Having restored the fellow's wits and self-control in this manner, he sent him scampering after hot water and a large basin, another had to run for scissors, a third must fetch the first-aid kit of the master. He had the room instantly in a turmoil, and the greater the confusion grew, the more perfectly was he at home.

Alicia, standing by and helping when she could, assisted Parry to strip the wounded man, until they could

190

see the purple-rimmed wound in his breast, welling red with a sullen steadiness.

At this moment the door was cast open and Beatrice Parry ran in. She paused at the door, clutching at the swaying edge of it to support herself.

"David! David!" she cried to him.

He had in his hand a sponge filled with warm water to cleanse the wound.

"Well?" he asked.

"Do you know? Haven't you heard?"

"Heard what? That this is getting to be a madhouse? I can see that for myself. What else?"

"Roger is gone! My Roger is gone!"

The big man started erect; his jaw thrust out dangerously.

"Roger?"

"It's that chief monster in the world, Gloster! Gloster has taken my boy! Do you hear me, David? He's stolen my boy—my darling Roger—he's gone away with him! Oh, Heaven, what shall I do? What will you do?"

"Roger gone?" said her husband. Then he added: "I'm going to finish dressing this wound."

"Finish?" she cried. She ran up to him and caught his arm.

"You think that I'm joking, David. You don't mean to stand here and do nothing? You only think in some strange way that I'm not serious! But I tell you, I saw him with my own eyes shoot down a man in cold blood and carry my darling away. I've sent half a dozen men to find you. Where have you been? And what are we going to do?"

"Roger is gone—Gloster did it. This Gloster seems a fairly successful young man in whatever he takes up. For my part, dear, I'm going to finish off this job before I lift my hand to anything else. But get the rest of the men out of the house and have them search everywhere through the park. Let 'em comb the garden! And have a patrol ride well out into the pampas, to see that he doesn't get off."

She could not answer for a moment. Her face turned livid, and such a look came into it as her husband never had seen before.

"It's true, then," she said. "You're going to stay here—

with your hands caring for this fellow—while my child is carried off and murdered!"

Parry had bent back to the work of examining the wound, and he answered, his head still lowered: "If Gloster has carried him off, he won't murder him. You don't carry people off if you want to murder 'em, do you, Beatrice?"

Beatrice Parry whirled upon Alicia.

"You—you!" she loudly stammered. "You've been working at his mind! Ah, I can see your handiwork in all this, you ingrate!"

Alicia looked at her as from a great distance, curiously peering to make out the loom of unknown land. Then she turned her back and bent all her attention to the task of assisting Parry.

"By heavens," cried Beatrice Parry, rage and grief half choking her, "it's true that you don't care a whit for any of us! Your horrible guns, your foolish tiger skins— they're what you love! Oh, that ever I should have married such a creature!"

And she fled from the room, calling orders to the servants as she ran. At that moment, the hurt man winced and ground his teeth.

"Have I handled you too rough?" asked Parry gently.

"You? Not a bit. If there's any water in my eye, remember the old saying, that a smoking fire, an onion, and a shrew bring tears."

Parry suspended his work with the bandage for a moment and looked at his patient.

"I don't mean to offend you, señor," said the other. "But you'll see how it is. It's better for you to leave me here and do what your señora wishes. A leaking roof and a running tongue always drive a man out of doors."

"Be quiet!" said Parry. "Be still, and I'll soon have this job finished, and save you for more mischief hereafter."

"Señor," said the other, "if I live after the great Tomaso had his way with me, I shall be a twice-famous man. If he could not kill me, no one can. When this is known, if I ever walk again, I shall go out as the cock of the walk!"

He laughed feebly.

"When you laugh, you hurt your wound again," said

Parry, wondering at the mingled effontery, assurance, courage, and whimsicality of this man.

"If I did not laugh, I should be screaming," said the Gaucho. "But I'll tell you what—you Englishmen and Americans never take thought that a good yell takes poison out of the heart and makes one breathe deep."

"I'll think of that hereafter," said David Parry. "Will you talk to me?"

He was working rapidly and yet with strength and gentleness to wrap the big bandage around the wounded Gaucho.

"I shall talk, señor, if my tongue will move. Whatever I know is in your purse, after tonight."

"Then tell me again: Why were you here tonight—in the garden, I mean?"

"All the reasons that brought the other here I cannot tell. I came here for money; the money was paid to me by Christophoro Negro, and what he wanted to do was to get rid of Gloster, I believe; and that was his main wish—and to get hold of your son."

"My son?" exclaimed the rancher, with a touch of ironic emotion.

"Why, I know that there's doubt," said the Gaucho. "But talk is a queer beast and it can run on both sides of the fence."

Parry said to him: "We are going to talk again, you and I."

"Gladly, señor—on earth or in heaven—or perhaps after a more unlucky journey!"

"Are you comfortable?"

"Almost."

The bandaging was finished. Parry stepped back.

"You could make all this perfect," said the patient.

"In what way?"

"With one taste of your fiery brandy, señor."

"You shall have it."

Parry gave orders accordingly. Then he added: "Is there any further hint you can give to me without betraying your captain?"

"You are my captain, señor," said the Gaucho. "You made yourself my chief this night, by your great kindness. Heaven forgive me if ever I look on you as anything else!"

He raised himself a little on one elbow.

"The old woman in the blue dress—you'll find the answer to the riddle in her girdle, and the answer in plain words is simply . . ."

Here, as he stretched forth his arm, his eyes blazing with what he was about to speak, a gun roared thunderously in the room, and the Gaucho dropped back, shot through the brain.

38. A Young Fox

WHEN TOM GLOSTER had seen the wounded man carried away, he looked down into the face of the child he was carrying and found the eyes as bright as those of a young fox.

"You've got an aching arm, by this time," said the child.

It was exactly the sort of remark that might have been made by the younger David Parry, and the similarity was so great that Gloster felt he could be sure of the paternity of this lad.

"My arm is aching," he admitted.

"Well, I weigh as much as a pretty big-sized bucket of water," announced Roger.

"You do," agreed Gloster. Then he nodded at the boy, and lowered him to the ground. "You won't try to run away?" he asked.

The boy laughed softly.

"I'm not that great a fool. I know you!"

"Who am I?"

"Why I heard! You're Tomaso el Grande."

"Tomaso el Grande?"

"Thomas the Great, of course! That's what the Gauchos all call Tom Gloster. I hear them talking all the time."

"And you won't run away?"

"Of course I know that you'd catch me, dead easy."

"Tell me—you're not afraid, Roger?"

"No, no, señor! Why should I be afraid?"

"Didn't we hear your mother say you would be murdered?"

"Well, she knows what I don't know. I know that I'm worth something to you, alive. What good am I dead?

"What good are you to me alive, please tell me?"

"Well, of course, everyone can see how I'm useful."

"Let me hear it from you, however!"

"I'll tell you, then. It's simply that my mother would do a lot to get me back."

"Perhaps she would. What of it?"

He felt as though he were following a light held in the hand of an enemy. He himself had not seen the way.

"Why, she has David, hasn't she?"

"Yes."

"You'll want to help him, I suppose. At least, that's the way you get famous—helping David to get here."

"Ah?" said Tom Gloster.

"But wouldn't mother trade him for me, and give him safely to you?"

"I would have a grand chance to talk to her about it!"

"You wouldn't talk, of course, but you'd send a message."

"So that she could send out twenty men to kill me, Roger? Is that good sense?"

The boy chuckled.

"You want to see if we're such fools. But we're not. She knows that if she sends out a lot of men, you'll simply make an end of me and then probably slip through their hands with no trouble at all!"

It was a revelation to Gloster. He had quite failed to think out all the advantages which he might draw from the possession of this little child; it had simply been the fear of the mother which inspired him, and now a sudden light was cast forward, and he saw a scanty chance of escape.

"If I made the exchange, do you think that I would be able to walk safely away across the pampas, Roger?"

"If she gave you David, wouldn't she throw in a pair of horses, and be glad to? Oh, and she'd throw in money, too!"

"Would she?" smiled Tom Gloster.

The youngster laughed once more.

"I know!" said he. "You don't work for money. All the Gauchos say so. Only to do good to people. I don't see why!"

Now when he heard these repeated references to himself as Tomaso el Grande, or Thomas the Great, and all the qualifications which went with that title, Gloster was not even flattered; for he felt as though the world had looked at him and his actions with a great magnifying glass, and had then made him out a giant indeed.

"Very well," said Gloster. "I think I'll start back toward the house."

"Good!" said the boy. "I knew you would!"

"You're not afraid?"

"Not a bit."

Gloster took him by the hand, and they walked on together through the shadows of the wood, or gliding rapidly across moonlit stretches. They made a strange pair, this abductor and his charge, and the child seemed to enjoy everything hugely, his eyes as bright as the eyes of a bird, as he peered from side to side. Tom Gloster wondered at him and at his dauntless courage. More and more he felt a kinship between this child and the youthful David with whom he had wandered so far.

They had to exercise the greatest caution, for the whole park about the Parry house was now alive with noise and with men. They constantly heard the hoofbeats of horses that swept back and forth, and shouts, and high commands, and answering cries out of the distance. Then, coming to the edge of a little copse, through which a thin stream trickled, they saw three riders storm furiously across a stretch of grass before them, men riding with their guns in their hands, and with working spurs.

"Look, look!" chuckled the boy, whom all strange and violent things seemed to delight. "They're riding right across the lawn that father has worked so long and sworn so much about. That shows how badly they want to find us, señor!"

196

"It does," agreed Tom Gloster. "They seem to have enough men here tonight to make an army."

"Well," said the youngster, "they haven't enough to take Tom Gloster, I know!"

"How do you know that?" murmured Gloster.

"Oh, when a bit of luck is coming, what can stop it? If I have a lucky day, I can do anything, and never be found out. But on a bad luck day, everything goes wrong!"

This bit of philosophy stirred Tom a great deal. And he felt that after all there might be much in it. At any rate, now this place and its great establishment of servants seemed to be in utter uproar and confusion. And if ever he had a chance to do something in spite of odds, this surely would be the time.

He and the boy turned a sharp corner of the path and a man fairly fell against them, as he ran in the opposite direction. Tom put the muzzle of his revolver beneath the chin of the stranger, who cursed violently.

"Let me go!" said he. "I have no money. You cannot rob me!"

"Simpleton!" shrilled the boy. "This is Tomaso el Grande."

"*Madre de Dios!*" groaned the man, and turned limp. "San Pietro give me guard!"

"Go back to the house," said Gloster, "and there you will find the señora . . ."

"Tell her that if she wants me back, she must send David down here, safe and sound. And a pair of fine horses, too. And if there's one stir and one sign of danger while we wait here, Señor Gloster has promised to put the point of a knife through my heart and go on his way."

"It's the little señor!" exclaimed the servant. "Oh, what a night this shall be to remember!"

"Do you hear?"

"All shall be done as you say."

"Will you know this place again?" asked Tom.

"Surely, señor. Is it likely that I shall forget the place where I have met Señor Gloster and his gun. Ha, señor, I dare say that there are not two other men in the world who have seen you draw your gun on them and have lived to talk about it afterward!"

He laughed cheerfully. The spirits of all these gloomy-

197

faced Argentinians, thought Tom Gloster, were like mercury; the slightest touch had the power to move them up or down.

The man left them, running back toward the house as fast as he could go.

"She'll never play fair," said Tom Gloster.

"Not if she has a chance to do anything else," admitted the child. "Oh, I know all about her. She's cruel, too. Every one has heard how cruel she is. But she'll pay high prices for me, because, you see, I'm the only living thing that's a part of her. That's what she tells me, all the time. You watch, now, and pretty soon, you'll see that men will come to get me!"

They waited in a thick patch of shade. They could look out through the clustered branches upon either side, and so doing, they waited in an utter silence. In that quiet time, standing without a movement, the big man and the small child, they heard all the sounds from the house more clearly; and whether it was the distant slamming of doors, or the far-off shouting, or the beating of hoofs, like hurried heartstrokes in the darkness, they read each sound and tried to attach to each a significance of some kind.

At length, they heard sounds that came straight toward them, and at last a voice that called stealthily: "Señor Gloster!"

"Here!" piped up the boy's shrill voice.

"Señor Gloster?"

"Here," said Tom, his gun ready to meet a rush.

"Señor, the message you sent has been heard. The señora feels that you are an honorable man with whom she can exchange confidence. She is glad to give you young David, but only if you will swear that, when you have him, you will take him away and never let him return to this house."

There was a slight scuffle, and then a sharp voice, the voice of David himself, calling: "Don't promise, Tom! Oh, Tom Gloster, don't promise that!"

"The young boy is foolish," said the voice of the messenger. "He has very few brains, or he would not speak in such a manner, of course. The señora asks you to make a quick decision, señor."

"I am sorry," said Tom Gloster. "We have done a great

deal, and suffered for a long time to come down here. Now you want us to go away again. No, we can't do that."

Muttered curses followed. Then, suddenly the voice exclaimed: "Take him, then, and give us the little one!"

39. In The Attic

SO MANY things were happening in the house at this moment, that it is necessary, to go back to David Parry the elder, as he stood in his library above the dead body of the Gaucho.

The hand of Alicia was pointing straight toward the door; he following the same direction, saw that the door slowly was closing, and a few thin wisps of powder hung like a blue-brown ghost in the air.

He went at the door like a tiger, dashed it open, and in the distance he had a bare glimpse of a form darting around a corner of the hallway.

He had been a champion sprinter, in his younger day, but never did he race so fast as he did down this hall. He had no gun in his hand; he needed no gun; he was ready to fight and to kill with his unassisted fingers.

The corner was a small passage which passed through a doorway, and the door at that moment was slamming shut; on the heels of that crash he heard the *cling* of the key turned in the lock, and the bolt jarring home.

Parry gave that door the weight of his shoulder, knotting the big shoulder up into a rubberlike pad to break the shock. A crack appeared from top to bottom of the door. He flung himself at it again, and then went stumbling through.

But before him he saw only the empty hall. There was no sound of footfall before him; there was nothing to call him in any one of the half-dozen directions in which the murderer might have fled.

Suddenly he turned about and went back toward the library. When he entered it, he saw Alicia standing before the hearth with a double-barreled shotgun in her hands; at the sight of him she winced and jerked the gun butt toward her shoulder, but instantly she recognized him.

He nodded grimly at her.

"They have you ready to believe in ghosts, Alicia, haven't they?"

She shrugged her shoulders.

"You look as white as a ghost, Alicia," said he. "Heaven knows that enough has happened here tonight to make even a man quake in his boots, but you're such a steady-nerved one that I haven't thought of such a thing as your being frightened."

She pointed toward the floor in front of her.

"Is that enough to give you the shakes, David?"

A dark little puddle was formed on the floor. It looked like ink. But at that moment a drop fell into it, and the splash of the drop was distinctly red!

"What!" murmured Parry.

He looked up to the ceiling and could see a mere streak there.

"It's not possible, you see," said the girl faintly. "That's what's turning my brain dizzy. Blood doesn't run out of the ceiling of a room, unless there's someone in another room above it, and there is no room above this."

"By heavens, there is another room!" cried Parry. "I mean, there's a dummy room with a five or six-foot ceiling over every one of these lower rooms!"

"How can we get at it?"

"Stay here. I know the way."

"Thank you, David, but I think I'll go with you, where-ever that is."

"Are you afraid here?"

"Afraid of being left alone, yes!"

"I'll send a trustworthy man to take care of you and to—"

"Have you a single trustworthy man in the house?" she asked him quietly.

He started. Then he answered: "No, I haven't one!

Now that I think of it soberly, I see that Beatrice has hired every one of them. They're her men, and they look to her for orders. I've been several sorts of a simpleton, in this proceeding. I should have paid attention to affairs long before. Alicia, if you want to, you may go with me up to that dark attic of ours. It isn't pleasant, though, and I warn you of it before you start!"

"I'll take this along to put sweetness and light into it."

She tapped the shotgun and David Parry smiled with his former grimness.

"These little indoor sports of the Parrys'," said he, "such as kidnaping and murder—you'll soon get used to 'em. They brace the nerves and give one a complete change."

He opened a closet at the end of the room and took out a pair of bright new revolvers. One he dropped in the pocket of his coat. The other he kept in his hand.

"Are those guns loaded?" Alicia asked him.

"Of course," said he.

"Are the cartridges honest?" she insisted.

He looked oddly at her and flushed.

"Do you think it's such an entire trap as that?" he asked.

He broke open the gun, took out a cartridge, and suddenly flung it across the room with an oath.

"A dummy! And so are these. All dummies!"

He whirled on her.

"How could you happen to guess at such elaborate trickery as that, Alicia?"

"Because I think that there's an elaborate trickster behind all this," she answered.

"Who, then?"

"I can't say."

"In the name of Jupiter," cried the hot-tempered man, "am I the only man in the world who doesn't understand all about this? The very servants gossip about it, and I learn what little I know by the echoes of the third-hand information that they have. That common Gaucho tells me there's a key to the secret—a woman in blue—look at her girdle! Why, hang it, Alicia, that's something out of the 'Arabian Nights,' and it can't be true. I feel as if the whole affair were an elaborate hoax!"

"They don't do that in hoaxes," said Alicia.

She pointed across the room at the dead man. Her host followed that glance and then hastily stooped, opened a box of cartridges, and rapidly loaded both the revolvers. As he straightened up he said: "You're looking pretty straight at me, Alicia. You-don't think much of me in this affair!"

"I think you're the safest man in the world to be with in this affair," she answered. "But the great trouble was before."

"You mean that I've brought all this on? Come, come! Don't tell me that in any seriousness!"

"I don't want to accuse you, David. Besides, we're on the trail together, just now. Shall we go?"

He looked keenly at her, and then in silence, he led the way out of the room.

There was less noise and disturbance in the house, at the moment. What sounds they heard were chiefly far away, confused, broken; so they came down the hallway to a door upon the right, which opened upon a very narrow and winding stairs. Up these they went, he leading the way with a gun thrust up before him, and stepping as softly as he dared to step. The girl, silent as a ghost, came behind, and they rose up into the pitchy blackness of the space above. They had to stand stooped, even Alicia; while her companion was bent over.

Parry fumbled in a pocket and brought out a small electric torch, but as he tried in vain to make the switch work, they heard the sudden opening of a door, though they could see nothing, and then a voice that called: half hushed and half straining to loudness: "It is Tomaso el Grande, Tomaso el Diablo!"

"*Dios! Madre de Dios!*" exclaimed a voice just before them, and something shifted to the side in the darkness.

Alicia jerked up her shotgun in readiness to fire, but big David Parry was instantly in the attack. He sprang forward with a roar and gave himself light by firing the Colt in his hand. The first flash showed him a darting form that sped across the darkness; the second showed him nothing at all. The man's form had disappeared through some doorway or hole in the wall.

202

At last, turning back, Parry called softly. Alicia fumbled her way to his side.

"You're a brave—madman!" she gasped. "Who was that?"

"I don't know."

And from the side a voice called: "Señor? Señor Gloster? Is it you? Is it you, Señor? I, for my wretched sins, would die here like a hurt rat. I have been only a rat. But having received these hurts in the way of duty, I thought that I might die and be forgiven. But you, señor, whose heart is a bottomless well of mercy—you have found your way by miracle to me. Señor Gloster, if it is you, speak to me!"

Said David Parry: "This fellow Gloster is at the bottom of everything. The puppy seems to have preempted all right to every decent action to which a man may aspire! Here, friend!" he called aloud. "This is not Tom Gloster, but David Parry."

"Heaven be praised!" said the voice in the darkness. "Heaven and St. Christopher, to whom I shall make all my prayers forever after. Señor Parry, give me your help, or soon I shall be a dead man. They have put me here to bleed to death, I think."

By the wandering, confused, blinding ray of the electric torch, they were guided to a far corner of the attic room, and there they found a long, gaunt figure whose clothes were streaked and clotted with blood. He had a face like the face of a goat, with big, round eyes, and a goat's beard beneath his chin.

But he smiled complacently at Parry and said to him: "You have reason to be good to me, señor. I am one of those who have helped to bring your boy home from the sea. The great Señor Gloster rode with me—Heaven defend and strengthen him!—and together we brought him home, until the cowards attacked us from behind while Señor Tomaso was away, and so they struck me down!"

In his powerful arms David Parry raised the stricken form.

"Cut the cords that tie my hands and feet," said the other. "I can walk as well as any man, if it's not too far! I've already worked the gag from my mouth, but I kept my tongue still, and waited for a better time."

Liberated, he rose to his feet and leaned upon the arm of Parry, shuddering with weakness. The girl took the torch before them to show them the way. And so they went down to the level of the ground floor.

"Unless this man is stopped with another gag of lead, Alicia," said Parry, "now we are about to learn some truth!"

40. *Beatrice Shows Her Skill*

THE POOR Gaucho who had been murdered in the library had been removed; upon the same couch where he had lain Ramon was now stretched out, his leathery skin looking wan and yellow from the terrible loss of blood which he had endured. He lay for a moment with his eyes closed. Then Parry offered him a glass of brandy. He drank it off without opening his eyes, but afterward he lay at ease, smiling a little.

"Every good trail," said the Gaucho faintly, "leads to a full stomach."

And he laid his hand comfortably upon the trail's end; after that he looked up to them.

"Friend," said David Parry, "you have spoken about Gloster."

"I spoke to him," said Ramon, "because when I heard that the rascals scattered, I thought that only one man could have done it, because I have seen that same man do so many other things."

"What have you seen him do?" asked Alicia.

"We'd better get him down to the immediate point of how he was placed there, wounded, in my house," suggested Parry.

But Ramon had heard the first question, and he laughed a little, weakly.

"Well—I have seen him hang by his hands from an edge of rock with three hundred meters of empty wind between his heels and the next ground. I have seen him hang like that, señor, with the rock crumbling under his hands, while I, known to him only as a traitor, climbed up over his body and so got to the trail above and to my life!"

He looked upon the two, with a faint, ironic smile.

"A traitor?" echoed the girl.

"Yes. Exactly that."

She sat down beside him.

"Are you in pain, Ramon?"

"No, señorita."

"You can talk?"

"Easily, señorita, if it will do good to Tomaso el Grande, Tomaso el Diablo, as the others call him."

"Thomas the Devil? Do they call him that?"

"Of course! But he's no evil one. He has a heart as soft as a woman's palm."

"Are you sure?"

"Señorita, I have ridden beside him, fought beside him, eaten beside him. He would listen to a child; his soul is as pure as the soul of a child. He is like a colt that has never known the bit or the whip; and yet he has been on the spur, but the wounds heal over and leave him unharmed. He is always made new. He is like a man who never has grown mature or seen evil in other people. He is a man without a sin. He is a saint, señorita!"

"And what are you, friend?" asked the rancher.

"I? I am one of the men of Christophoro Negro. That is to say, I used to be one of his men."

"Ah, do you see?" said David Parry. "What a lot of foolish lies we've been hearing! That Chris Black was the mortal enemy of this Gloster, this Tomaso el Grande, this Tomaso el Diablo. And now we find out the truth—which is that the man works for them both."

"I'll tell you, señor," said the wounded man, "what I did last. I took money from Christophoro Negro, I took a hundred pesos from him, and for that money, as advance payment, and more money later on, I was to lead Gloster

205

and the boy into a trap in the mountains. And the boy discovered the plot but Gloster, nevertheless, went on with me as a guide; he saved my life that very day. So I became his man. That is understood, señor?"

"I understand, of course. And he was kind to you, then?"

"Kinder to me than to himself. That man does no wrong!"

"And they call him Tomaso el Diablo? Now, Ramon, does it stand to reason that a man is called Thomas the Devil for nothing whatever?"

"For nothing? Is it nothing, señor, to have no fear, and to shoot swiftly, and not to miss? He fights, señor, like a man who has no understanding of death. That is why they call him a devil. And it is true, also, that he and the boy sat in a railroad compartment, and into that compartment there came four men. Every one of the four was a leader in the band of Negro. Every one was a man who killed by profession, but when Tomaso el Diablo looked at them with his quiet eyes, they could not quite make their hands fight. The revolvers refused to come out, and the knives turned to lead and stuck in the sheaths. And each man said to himself: "If I make an attack, I shall be the first one to die under his flaming guns!" That is why he is called El Diablo. In the little time of our ride from the sea to this place, he has grown famous. Every Gaucho knows him, and every man who ever has lived by the gun."

Parry insisted: "And the boy? Who is he?"

"Señor, he calls himself your son."

The rancher made a little gesture of concentrated fury.

"Do you see and hear this, Alicia?" he cried. "It's the same rumor, a little reënforced. I don't——"

The door of the library opened; Beatrice Parry walked straight in to meet the rising storm.

Her eyes were big and staring, and her face was white.

"There's no word. They've taken Roger forever!" she exclaimed fiercely.

Her husband overlooked her emotion. He went to her and took her by the shoulders, and then turned her so that the light fell with a cruel directness against her face.

"I've been hearing strange stories about you, Beatrice," he said.

"From whom?"

"From that man."

"Who is that man?" she asked.

"You don't know?"

"Certainly not!"

"He's one of the two who've been trying to bring David back to me—in spite of you!"

She regarded him without apparent fear or confusion.

"Will you tell me what's happened to him, David?" she inquired.

"What happened to you?" asked Parry of Ramon.

The latter looked upon the beautiful Beatrice with a smile, and there was veritable malice in the smile.

He said: "Do I see you at the last, señora? You have been in our camp talk all these nights! How am I wounded? By knife strokes, señora, delivered by your men when they surprised me and the señor's son tonight."

"My son!" cried Parry.

"Yes," said the Gaucho.

"What became of the boy?"

"She can tell you, señor. They carried me in one direction and they carried him in another."

Parry turned sternly to his wife. She looked at Ramon without bitterness.

"Has this poor lying wretch really imposed on you, David, dear?" she asked. "Have you actually been listening to what such a creature may have to say?"

He hesitated. Then he cried: "There's not a tone in the man's voice that doesn't seem honest to my ears!"

She smiled at him.

"Of course not! You're a simple soul when it comes to distrusting other people. How did he come to you?"

"I came to him. His blood ran down through the ceiling. There! That's the red mark of it above your head."

She shrank away, at that, as graceful as a cat as she tipped back her head to look.

Then she exclaimed: "If my men did this thing, David, why under heaven would they have brought this fellow here to the house to die, and to leak red over our perfectly good ceilings?"

"I hadn't thought of that," pondered Parry.

"It is easily answered," Ramon assured him.

"Answer it, then, if you can!" said Beatrice Parry.

"Who am I?" said Ramon. "I am dirt under foot. I am a nameless name. I am a breath of wind. But Tomaso Gloster is the man they dread more than fire! They took me alive, because they hoped that I could tell them where they would be able to find him. She, señor, she stood above me and questioned me!"

Suddenly he pointed a long arm at the woman; his hand trembled with violence. David Parry caught his breath.

"Is that a likely thing?" asked Beatrice. "Are you actually believing what the creature says, David?"

Ramon lifted the long, dank hair which streamed low and unkempt upon his forehead. And lifting it, he showed a red furrow in the flesh, rimmed with purple.

"What does that mean, in pity's name?" asked Parry.

"They twisted a cord around my forehead," said Ramon. "They twisted it into my flesh, and she stood by and watched and told me to speak, and then my pain would be ended. But I remembered my good saint; and I thought of how my life had twice lain in the hand of Don Tomaso, and of how he twice had spared me; and by the virtue of my prayer, the good St. Christopher listened and gave me strength to lock my teeth and to answer not a word."

He sighed, and closed his eyes.

Then Beatrice cried out, as though from the depths of thought: "Do you see what it is, David? The incarnate fiends have sent on this fellow—who's been in the hands of pampas Indians, no doubt—to tell this cock-and-bull story, and so keep your attention while they make off with Roger! Isn't that it? What else would explain everything? Tell me, David!"

Parry hesitated. The goatlike face of Ramon seemed to betoken a man who was ready for everything.

"They disguised me very well," said the guide, "when they painted the blood on my skin!"

"Listen!" said Beatrice Parry. "We all know that the

wretched Gauchos are never done with their quarreling, don't we?"

"I suppose we know that," admitted her husband.

"Why, then, the fellow was slashed in a fight with one of his companions, and when they saw that they could not move him, and would have to leave him behind after their raid, he simply said: 'Send me into the house. There I shall hold them with my words as if they were hawks under a hood!' And that, David, is exactly what he has done, while Gloster and the others ride off with my poor Roger. But what is that to you, David?"

She did not raise her voice; her quietness made the appeal all the more effective, and David Parry went suddenly to her. "I can't think it out," he said. "I'm not going to try. I feel that you must be right. I'm tired of doubting. But now I'm going to find my boy, and Heaven help those who have taken him!"

"Oh, my darling!" said Beatrice, and clung to him.

But her eyes looked over his shoulder fiercely, malignantly, toward Alicia, as though promising that her triumph was beginning, but that her vengeance was still to follow.

41. Before The Curtain Falls

VERY GLOOMY gray would the mind of Tom Gloster have been if he had known what was taking place in the house of Parry, and the acceptance of the wife by her husband again. But he had before him, at almost the same time, a great enough triumph to make his blood leap and sing. For young David Parry was brought back to him and stood there with his strangely grim, set face lighted with joy. David said to Roger:

"Do you know me, Roger?"

"Oh, I know you," said Roger. "Of course! And I suppose you're the one who'll put me off the place, as mother always has told me. Oh, but she hates you, David!"

"And you?" said David.

"I'm more fearing than hating you, because now I see that you'll win."

"Win what?"

"Oh, everything, now that you've got him to help you!"

Roger was amazingly old. In spite of his young years, he seemed far older than that prematurely experienced young man, David junior, and older even than Tom Gloster, with a peculiar instinct for penetrating to the heart of things.

He looked up to Tom Gloster, and smiled without malice.

"I've had a lot of fun with you," said he. "After I got over thinking that you'd break me in your big hands by mistake. Then I had a lot of fun. Good-bye, Thomas the Devil!"

He went off, laughing. He was part baby and part old man. Gloster never had dreamed of such a creature in the whole world. There were two horses in front of him. They glimmered in the light as though they were made of metal, with bright eyes of glass, transparent and unmoving. At the heads of these horses stood a man with a bandage around his head, a hastily put on bandage which lopped to one side and gave a peculiarly rakish, piratical air to the fellow.

"You're Christopher Black, again," said Tom Gloster.

"I'm Black," said the other. "I've waited just a moment and brought in the horses myself, because I wanted to make sure that you'd do the sensible thing."

"What is that?" asked Tom.

"You're to take the two horses, here, and ride off with the boy, undisturbed."

"Ah," said Tom.

The hand of young David fell upon his arm and gripped hard at the rubbery muscles.

"We want to make everything easy for you, Gloster. For one thing, we admire the way that you've fought us. You've really won your battle, because you've actually got to the Parry house, in spite of everything that we did to stop you—and Heaven knows, we did enough! But now that you see that you can't get inside, we'll trust to your word of honor that you won't try to sneak in again, but will turn straight back across the pampas, the way that you came. There's no danger for you, the instant that you take that direction. You understand, Gloster? No danger at all. And I have more than a thousand dollars here, for you. You'll have another thousand paid to you when you arrive in San Francisco."

"As if you could trust them, Tom!" muttered the boy.

"Oh, you can trust us, because it's worth that much to have you off this trail. We know that we could beat you, here. But it would cost lives. You never will be taken except at a cost of life, and we're tired of that. We've had enough of it."

"Is Ramon living?" asked Tom.

"He is."

"Bring him here and put him on another good horse, and I'll give you my promise to go."

"Ramon? Why, he's hurt a little. He couldn't sit on the back of a horse."

"Then I'll give you no promise," said Tom.

"Because of a rat of a Gaucho? Would you make all the trouble because of that?"

"Oh, he's a man," said Tom.

"Who sold you twice!"

"And then fought for us," said Tom. "You see that balances, pretty well."

"You've given up the fight, except for him? Then I swear that we'll send him after you, safe and sound."

"I can't take your promises," said Tom. "You've been a liar and a murderer, you see. You've tricked and twisted and tried to cut our throats so many times. If I could have Ramon, then I'd call it quits, because I really don't think that we ever could get to the house, tonight. But if he can't be with us, then we'll try our best again."

"Thank Heaven!" cried the boy. "Oh, Tom, I thought that you were giving up, for a little while!"

Black made a quick little half step forward, like one about to execute wrath upon the rest. Then he recovered himself. Slowly he drew himself up straight.

"That's all, then," he said. "I suppose that a fool can't

211

be parted from his folly. Go on, then, Gloster. I was stupid to think that you could learn better sense. Go on and run your head into the noose that's waiting for you!"

Tom and the boy mounted the horses. Instead of taking the open way across the lawn, however, they headed back through the trees which they had just left; behind them they saw Black rush Roger into cover, and then the sharp ring of his voice as he commanded his men to spread right and left and go forward for a shot, if they could.

However, to one part of his contract he had lived up. He had given them a good pair of horses, and now they launched those spirited animals straight forward across the park, heedless of what lay before them in the way of garden beds or lawns. Not even a random shot was fired behind them, and they came on safely through the width of the place before Tom drew rein and said to the boy, who had been riding boldly and well: "Now, David, what do you think?"

"I think," said the boy, "that unless I go to that house tonight, I'll never have a chance to put a claim upon this place. It'll be lost to me forever. But if we do get back—I smell scarlet!"

"What do you mean by that?"

"There'll be a death," said the boy, curiously quiet.

The moon was high and strong; by its light his face looked deathly pale, and since his face was thin, Tom looked upon him almost as a man already dead. He shuddered.

Then he said: "What will you do, David?"

"Ah, but there's no doubt of that! I've got to go back, of course, or else I'm denying my own name. But you, Tom, there's no sense in your going."

"Am I to leave you in the lurch?"

"It's not leaving me in the lurch. You've brought me the long distance. And after I got into their hands, you've taken me away from them again, and given me another chance to go free. You've given me my life, that's more than men can give to each other, most usually. No, no! There's nothing more that I should ask from you!" He added: "I've been pretty hard and mean, Tom. Oh, I've been as hard as a wolf's tooth. I'm sorry for that. Nobody ever had a better friend than you've been to me!"

It was the most emotional outburst that Tom ever had heard from the boy. And it was so unnatural for him to give way that even now, although the words said a great deal, he kept his voice quietly under control, as though he had thought out this viewpoint, without actually feeling it.

Tom Gloster said: "I think we'll go straight on together, David. This time we'll get to see your father if we have to shoot our way into the house. Which way does it lie from here?"

It was characteristic of the boy that, having taken the right attitude of gratitude and generosity, he did not insist upon it, but turned the head of his horse and pointed directly through the trees.

"That's the way. But we'd better go on foot, if we don't want to be heard."

They dismounted straightway and passed through a lofty grove, silently among the shadows. There was no longer any wind. There was no sound of hoofs, guns, voices. All the estate slept, or seemed to sleep, and this silence appeared more dangerous to them than the thunder of a thousand voices.

Then they saw the gleam of windows before them, and came out upon the side of the house. They consulted in a whisper together.

"There's the side door," said the boy, eagerly pointing. "There's one small bit of luck for us! They've left that open in their hurrying back and forth! Once inside, it won't be long before we find my father. He's likely to be in the library!"

They paused once more, to sweep the grounds back and forth with their piercing glances.

"Well, suppose it's only a trap?" suggested Tom. "Suppose that purposely they've left the door open to tempt us in?"

"Well, that might be," admitted the boy. "But I don't really think so! It's the long chance for us, Tom!"

They went suddenly forward, as though by a silent mutual agreement that they would argue and hesitate no longer but bring the matter to a conclusion.

They reached the door, stepping as softly as they could, and Tom Gloster thrust the boy behind him with his strong hand, and walked on in with two guns naked and ready for action.

It seemed to him that a sheet of flame sprang up from the floor toward the ceiling to greet him. A strong light flashed on, and the door jerked to behind him with a crash, while, at the same bewildering instant, a thunderclap pealed in his very brain and he sank down.

Before him, he saw Christopher Black, with a gun spouting fire from either hand, and behind Christopher Black there were others.

He himself was dropping into a pit of crimson fire, for the floor had turned to red flame, as it seemed to him. Down his face ran something hot, and wet, and thick; he knew that it was his own blood, and it occurred to him as strange, in the lightning cross and exchange of thoughts, that he should have the time and the faculty to know that that was blood.

Yet it did not occur to him that he was wounded in the head—fatally, perhaps.

Other things obsessed his mind. One was the pity, the dark, deep pity of this fate which had led him with David Parry to the door of his father's house and there had blasted all their work.

And another thing was a hope which grew up with his fear, that perhaps David had been right, but that only one death was necessary. That death would be his, and at this price the boy would be reëstablished in his right.

Or was the right really his?

And in that great instant of pain, and shock, and horror, and bewilderment, the tangle of his thoughts still moved forward.

He did not love young David. The boy was hard, and unsimple, and complex. He was brave, and strong, and true. Aye, but there seemed little softness in him; he had been starched, and the starch had turned to steel.

However, Tom was willing to lay down his life to accomplish this thing. And it seemed to him, moreover, that if he had remained at his home, he never should have done one thing of importance in all his life.

He had read a translation of Homer. It was one of the few books which had entered his life, and it had impressed him deeply. And he thought, in this moment, that perhaps his fate would be like that of Achilles, to have done great things, and then to die very young.

Not that he had done any really great things. No, at this he smiled, and this smile seemed, to those who watched, the most marvelous of all his deeds, for it was as though he smiled at them, and mocked at the crimson which ran down his head, and was sure of his own fate, and sure, also, of theirs, his enemies!

Of course, it was only an instant in which all this occurred.

The door opened; the guns flared; the lights turned on; the door itself was jerked shut by a cord prepared, and there were both David and the boy as helpless prisoners, and David was sinking down upon one knee upon the floor, and whipping up his own guns to return the deadly fire.

It seemed also to Tom, compared with the mad flight of time past his own senses, that the movement of his hands was not a jerk, but a slow drag. Everything was delayed, and slowed. The cry of David's fear and surprise he thought would never end or cease running in his ears, like the flapping of a red flag in a strong wind; or like the pouring of a river of lightning through the blackest night. And he saw the guns in the hands of Chris Black jerk and tip up at the muzzles as he fired.

"Ah, well," thought Tom Gloster, "if only I can raise the guns in time, I shall not miss with them."

And still smiling at this thought of his that he ever should compare himself with Achilles, he did manage to raise his Colt. And his first bullet shot sent Chris Black to the floor, prostrate and cursing bitterly; and his second shot turned the face of a man behind into a red blur.

Young David was holding a Colt in both hands, and shooting blindly above the head of his protector. At that, also Tom smiled, for he could see the bullets rake long furrows through the plaster of the walls. And long splinters heaved up from the floor.

David was shouting: "We'll kill them! I'll kill them all! I'll kill them for you. Tom, I'll finish them!"

He was like a young hawk, screeching above the battle before it knew how to use its talons.

Then another heavy blow struck Tom, this time in the

shoulder. His right arm went limp. The heavy blow cast him crookedly against the wall.

One revolver was gone. He had only his left hand remaining. That was Chris Black, who had fired from the floor; Chris Black, with a pale face contorted with the most desperate effort.

And three men stood in a row, packed across the hall. How strange it was that so many bullets could be fired and so little damage done!

Another bullet struck him somewhere, and then another. He heard the thud of them; he felt the weight of the nearly half-inch slugs of lead that plunged into him; but he felt nothing of pain. He concentrated upon Christopher Black, for that man was the chief scoundrel.

With his left hand, Tom steadied his revolver down to the mark and fired.

He saw Christopher Black jerk to his knees, and then to his feet; and then, with one leg trailing and with one hand clutching at the wall to give himself steadiness and strength, Black charged in on him, with a knife in his hand.

Tom raised the revolver again to fire. It refused to come up straight in his hand, for his left wrist seemed slashed across and powerless. And then Tom Gloster was sure of his death. He had at that moment only one great wish: That he could rise, and meet his death standing. And he smiled again, to think that even this simple wish should be denied him.

Then a lithe young form sprang before him.

David going to meet the knife and the bearer of it! David with his empty Colt clubbed in both hands!

At that moment the voice of a bull, not a man, roared down the hallway.

Then Tom's eyes grew dim. A curtain had dropped over them. He tried to raise a hand to push back the curtain, but he found that he could not lift his hands.

42. When Dreams Vanish

It was not a complete unconsciousness that overcame him, but forms became thick and confused.

There were many shots. The air of the hall became rank with burned powder, and then hands fell upon him.

"Oh," cried a voice he did not know, "this man is shot to pieces! Who is this?"

And he heard a girl's voice that he knew make the answer: "This is the one man that's worth saving in the lot. This man is worth all of you, all of you—and he's thrown away! That's Thomas Gloster!"

"Well, well," sighed Gloster, deep in his heart, "how kind of her to say such a thing—and shall I ever be able to see her face again?"

A time of confusion followed. He seemed to be borne forward; sudden and dreadful agonies began to assail him. He burned with torture; and he could feel his blood running, running, like the full current of a river, draining out his life.

"This way—gently, now! Poor fellow! Easily through that doorway. Steady, steady, for he feels every stir of your hands! To think he held them all back! He alone—"

They spoke like this.

One part of Tom Gloster's soul heard them and wondered at their reverent kindness. Another part of his soul floated in another region where even to breathe was unendurable torture.

"How are you! Do you recognize me? Can you speak?"

That was her voice. They had laid him down.

"That is you, Alicia," he said. "I can't see you. After a while, perhaps I want to see you before I die."

She started to answer him, and her voice broke. Then said the voice of the roaring bull, subdued now to a mutter: "Alicia, you're an hysterical little goose. Get out of the way! We've got to work on him!"

Then they worked on him. They cut his clothes away, and they washed his wounds. Every touch was like the touch of a flaming sword, thrust deep in him, and thrust through and through. He smiled a little, to think that such fire could enter flesh and not consume it to ashes.

They poured stinging brandy down his throat.

At that, his eyes grew clear; almost all the pain seemed to be swept away.

"Why," said Tom Gloster, "this is very good. You are all very kind to me."

He saw the owner of the bull's voice and knew that it was big David Parry, and that it had been he whose coming had scattered away the fighters from before him. Then he saw all the others—young David, with a lean face that looked as though it had been hewn out of gray-green stone—and Alicia—and Ramon, who leaned against the wall beside him with his Gaucho's cloak pulled over his head. The voice of Ramon was continually heard in a faint whisper. He was praying to his St. Christopher.

Tom Gloster felt like a man in armor, for here and there his body was gripped and stiffened by broad bandages. But the brandy burned deeper, closer to his heart; he began to feel at rest, and calmly happy, for life or for death.

Then he saw Beatrice Parry come to his side.

She said: "Poor fellow, poor fellow! Oh, David, I can forgive him for the harm he tried to do when I see his pain!"

"The harm he tried to do?" said her husband gravely. "We shall have to talk about this, my dear. Perhaps we'd better talk now. For all the rumors seem to be true— here's my eldest boy come back to me. And what will you make of that, Beatrice?"

"Your oldest boy?"

He was silent.

"I see that you still have the old fable in your heart," said she. "And we might as well have the thing out at once. I thank Heaven that I've been able to find, at last, his real mother. I have her in this very house. You shall see her now! She swears that she is his mother. She was his nurse, too!"

She called quickly to a servant.

Then people moved back a little from the couch where Tom Gloster lay, as though recognizing that there was another object of great interest. Big David stood by the hearth, his legs spread, his head lowered, more like a bull than ever; young David stood at Tom's feet, tense, his head thrown back, and his body rigid as steel. Only here was Alicia, sitting beside Tom and regardless of other people; and Ramon, leaning against the wall because he was weak from his wounds, still prayed.

Presently there came into the room a middle-aged woman with a shawl about her shoulders, dressed in a blue, cheap dress. At the first glance at her, Tom's heart sank, for she had the same sort of swarthy harshness that he was used to in the face of David the younger. She did not seem to know how to smile or to bow, but she stood erect near the doorway and she looked over the people in the room.

David the elder went to her with a slow, heavy stride.

"Who are you?" he said.

"Juanita Alvarez."

"Why are you here?"

"I came to see my boy."

"Where is your boy?"

"There!"

"Have you any proof?"

At that, she smiled indeed. It was a quick, sharp, keen smile.

"Why should I be offering proofs? He's in a good house. A better house than mine ever will be."

"Why do you claim him at all, then?"

"Because the señora tells me that I must tell the truth. So I have told it."

"The woman's face I can remember," said David Parry. "She nursed the boy. Is that correct?"

"Yes, señor."

"Do you know that for this sort of a fraud you can be put into prison?"

"Yes, señor."

"I've half a mind to put you there."

"Yes, señor."

"Don't say that again! Be still! David, stand beside that woman!"

The boy went to her slowly. He stood beside her and faced David the elder. And the big man suddenly turned aside with a groan, the likeness was so real. He said, his head averted: "Yet I wish to Heaven that my blood was in you! Whatever blood is in you, it's a true fighting strain!"

Then Alicia broke in: "Do you remember what we were told by the man who died in this room tonight? The woman in blue, David! And there she is!"

The big man started violently. He went to that grim-faced mountaineer and suddenly wrenched from her that big sash or girdle that went about her.

She uttered a great cry and sprang after it, but he fended her off with one outstretched hand; from the girdle came the sound of metal, clinking together.

She recovered herself at once; she shrank back against the wall and folded her arms. A great, breathless silence was on the room. They felt a crisis impended, but no one could guess what would be in it.

David the elder opened the girdle. He poured out a great handful of golden coins.

"There's nothing here but this," said he.

"But where did you get that?" asked Alicia of the woman. "Where did you get so much gold, Juanita?"

"Dear señorita," she answered, her voice suddenly musical, "if poor people work very hard, they will not be separated from their money. I have worked all my life—that is the honey I have found in the flowers of many days!"

"How does it come, then," said David the elder, with a sudden roar, "that every coin of it seems to bear only one date—one date, woman, do you hear?"

She did not wince, but here eyes flared suddenly aside at Beatrice Parry, and her nostrils widened as if with fear.

"Do you hear me, you?" demanded the big man. "I want to know where you stole this money!"

At this she shrilled at him: "I did not steal it!"

"We'll see what the laws says to that. There're a hundred of these coins, in the girdle of a woman like you. We'll let the law soak the truth out of you!"

Suddenly she turned her back on him. She faced Beatrice Parry with a sort of angry despair.

"I told you what would happen! I told you that they would get at the truth! But, oh, who would think that dumb metal would talk against me!"

Beautiful Beatrice bit her lips.

"I don't understand," she said. "I don't understand, David. What does it all mean?"

"It means," said he, in a deliberate voice, "that she got this money from you. Will you tell me why you paid it to her?"

"I? Not a peso did she get from me!"

"You lie!" screamed Juanita. "You paid it to me coin by coin. You swore that if I would say the boy was my own son—"

"You creature!" said Beatrice Parry through tight lips.

She said it quietly, but in such a way that all talk ended. She looked about her, at the pity and disgust in the face of Alicia, at the savage joy of David the younger; at the horror and dismay of her husband. Then she turned toward the door, but her nerve failed her, and suddenly she fled with a gasp of shame and fear.

It was like the vanishing of a dream, all the tall, proud fabric of her lies and of her crimes falling to dust in one instant.

But David Parry cried to Juanita: "It was you who nursed the boy! And can you swear who was his mother?"

"Man, madman!" she broke out savagely. "You were the husband of the poor lady! Would a saint like her have lied to you? No, not for a mountain of diamonds!"

David Parry turned in a lumbering, curious fashion and looked at his son. Young David was shuddering and sick of face. And the father grinned suddenly.

"Well," he said, "Thomas the Grand has brought you home, my son!"

43. A Whole Kingdom

THEY LET their horses idle up the road, and the fine animals, taking no advantage of the slackened reins, went
quietly along, sometimes touching noses for an instant,
and most of the time looking out keenly to either side,
for it was dusk, and all of man's world and all the world
of the beasts feels fear when the day is dying and wild
things come out to hunt and to be hunted.

"This is the place," said Tom Gloster. "This is the
place. It was about this time of the day. It was about this
time, a year ago. Do you smell the tarweed? And he
seemed to fly down the road like a bird out of my hand."

They went on again, the horses close together, and she
reached out her hand to him and let it lie in his.

"I'm half afraid," said Tom Gloster. "I'm half afraid
that I'm riding back into my old life, and that I may lose
you there, Alicia."

"Not in the thickest brambles," said she. "I could not
be scratched away from you, Tom."

They came to a bend of the road; below them lay the
dark of a little valley.

"That's where I cleared the brush away and made the
good farm land."

"Well, they never can forget what you've done for
them, Tom."

"They? Oh, they can forget! They know how to forget."

"And doesn't it make you bitter?"

"Oh, no. How could I ever be bitter, when Fate has
given me such a woman as you, Alicia! There is no joke
about that, is there? You are yourself. You're not some
other person?"

"That's a queer way to talk. What do you mean?"

"Only that it's like something out of a book—out of a fairy-tale. You know that the hero of a fairy-tale gets strange, enormous rewards—half a kingdom, and such things."

"Yes," said she. "Those should be the rewards—for heroes!"

He hushed her, when she said this. He had a guilty attitude toward her and toward life. He felt that he had to look up, into the heart of a mystery, to understand how he could have come to such miraculous happiness.

They came to the little house, and the great trees.

"That's the elm tree and that's the fig tree," said she at once.

"Yes, those are the trees."

"There are a good many voices in front of the house. Isn't that a guitar?"

"That's my younger sister. She plays a guitar. We'll go around through the field and come in the back way, past the wood shed."

This they did, circling softly through the darkness, with the stubble whispering around the hoofs of their horses; they dismounted and came into the back yard of the house.

All was quiet here; the wind blew the sound of the singing away; the air was full of the cool scent of the wet alfalfa; the only noise was the *whir* of the windmill, and the hurried, excited clanking of its gears.

They went softly up the rear steps of the house and at the door they paused and looked in through the screen.

His mother was wringing out the dishrag and hanging it to dry on two nails, behind the stove. It looked a grimy gray.

In her wet hands, she picked up a broom and began to sweep.

"Now you see what I've come from," said Tom Gloster in a whisper.

And the girl said in a voice that trembled through sobs: "Oh, the darling! The poor sweet old darling!"

She opened the door and went hurrying inside.

"THE KING OF THE WESTERN NOVEL"
is MAX BRAND

_____ **DRIFTER'S REVENGE** (84-783, $1.75)
_____ **PLEASANT JIM** (86-286, $1.25)
_____ **GUNMAN'S GOLD** (88-337, $1.50)
_____ **FIRE BRAIN** (88-629, $1.50)
_____ **INVISIBLE OUTLAW** (88-705, $1.50)
_____ **TRAILIN'** (88-717, $1.50)
_____ **MIGHTY LOBO** (88-829, $1.50)
_____ **BORDER GUNS** (88-892, $1.50)
_____ **WAR PARTY** (88-933, $1.50)
_____ **SILVERTIP** (88-685, $1.50)
_____ **MAN FROM SAVAGE CREEK** (88-883, $1.50)
_____ **CHEYENNE GOLD** (88-966, $1.50)
_____ **FRONTIER FEUD** (98-002, $1.50)
_____ **RIDER OF THE HIGH HILL** (88-884, $1.50)
_____ **FLAMING IRONS** (98-019, $1.50)
_____ **SILVERTIP'S CHASE** (98-048, $1.50)
_____ **SILVERTIP'S STRIKE** (98-096, $1.50)

WARNER BOOKS
P.O. Box 690
New York, N.Y. 10019

Please send me the books I have selected.

Enclose check or money order only, no cash
please. Plus 50¢ per order and 10¢ per copy
to cover postage and handling. N.Y. State and
California residents add applicable sales tax.

Please allow 4 weeks for delivery.

_____ Please send me your free
mail order catalog

Name_____

Address_____

City_____

State_____ Zip_____